ROTTEN

by

David R Ewens

Grosvenor House
Publishing Limited

This book is published by
Grosvenor House Publishing Ltd
28-30 High Street, Guildford, Surrey, GU1 3EL.
www.grosvenorhousepublishing.co.uk

A CIP record for this book
is available from the British Library

ISBN 978-1-78148-338-1

Disclaimer

This is a work of fiction. Names, characters, institutions, places, events and incidents are either the products of the author's imagination or used in a fictitious manner. Any resemblance to actual persons, living or dead, or actual events is purely coincidental.

About the Author

David R Ewens worked for many years in the further and adult education sector. He lives and writes in Kent.

Also by David R Ewens
in the 'Frank Sterling' series

The Flanders Case
Under the Radar
Fifth Column

Prologue

'What will you have?' said the woman.

'Scotch,' said the man who'd just arrived at the small table in the corner of the bar.

She set the drink next to her gin and tonic and looked around the busy pub. 'I want out. It's only a question of time before the wheels come off this whole thing. Ever since Eddie went, it's got totally out of hand. The woman is a megalomaniac. Quite apart from anything else, I can't stand the meetings – the table thumping, going from one cost centre to the next with all the criticisms, picking on a different person every time. And that creepy boy. It's all because she didn't get the top job – yet again. That's got to be it. Anyway, I've had enough. Tell me what I need to do to put this nightmare behind me.'

The man sipped his drink. He looked tired and ill. 'Wanting and getting are miles apart. Now she's got her hooks into you – and the rest of us for that matter – she's never going to let you go. We should just count our blessings on the meetings issue. There'll be no more for a while, with the new woman in. Now it's all going to be cloak and dagger.'

'She doesn't need the money. She's not interested in the events or the products. It's all just a big game, and we're the ones who take all the risks.'

'That's another reason why you can't quit. If it all goes tits up, nothing's going to lead back to her. You want out. Dream on. So do I. So do most of the rest of them, I imagine. There is no way out.'

The man and woman stared into their drinks.

'It was bearable before that little sod came,' said the woman. 'Where did she get him from? Are they related? They've got the same nasty genes.'

The man shrugged. 'Who cares? The result would be no different, link or no link.' He drained his glass. 'I've got to get back. If you do find a way out of this whole crappy mess, other than by doing time or in a body bag, let me know. God knows why you thought I'd have any answers.'

The woman watched him as he shambled away. Then she went up to the bar for another drink – this time she made it a double.

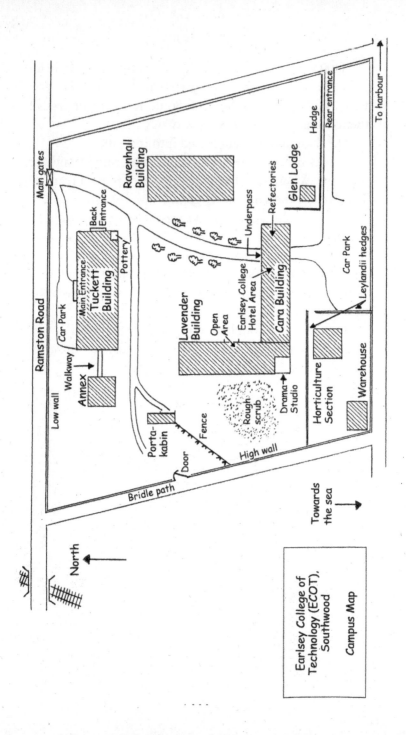

Earlsey College of Technology (ECOT), Southwood

Campus Map

North

Towards the sea

To harbour

Ramston Road

Main gates

Back Entrance

Pottery

Main Entrance

Tuckett Building

Car Park

Walkway

Annex

Low wall

Porta-kabin

Fence

Door

Bridle path

High wall

Rough scrub

Ravenhall Building

Lavender Building

Open Area

Earlsey College Hotel Area

Drama Studio

Underpass

Refectories

Cara Building

Glen Lodge

Hedge

Rear entrance

Car Park

Leylandii hedges

Horticulture Section

Warehouse

Chapter 1

Tuesday 6 October - The Tech

Rounding the corner at the end of the walk through the terraced back streets from Southwood station, on the Isle of Earlsey, Frank Sterling, private investigator, felt unease, bordering on dread. He emerged from the cocoon of neat, well-established Victorian terraces, Edwardian villas and 1960s apartment blocks and almost in front of him, across Ramston Road, was the Grade II listed façade of Earlsey College of Technology – the Tech, as it was universally known, or occasionally ECOT. Sterling disliked institutions of learning, whether they were primary schools, secondaries, colleges or even universities. It wasn't that he objected to learning – far from it – as long as no one tried to make him do it formally. He didn't want to be put in a classroom. Much better was all his quirky father had taught him, lone parent-style, and more recently knowledge gained through his own close friendship with Angela Wilson, Sandley's brilliantly talented librarian, who lived in the same row of modern townhouses beyond the Guildhall as he did. His learning wasn't systematic, and certainly not rigorous, as Angela often reminded him – but at least it was continuing.

The Tech brought up all the wrong memories, even if he'd never yet been inside. He pulled up his collar and hunched his shoulders – nothing to do with any autumn chill. 'Here goes,' he muttered as he crossed the road to the main gates and peered beyond them to the steps up to the college entrance. At reception in the lobby, there was a short wait before a secretary approached.

'Mr Sterling? The principal will see you now.'

He shuffled through to the large, light office at the side of the external steps he'd just come up. At first there appeared to be no one in the room, but then he noticed a small head with tight curls cut close to the skull behind a huge desk. When the principal stood up and walked round to greet him, he loomed over her small figure. Her skin was as dark as her hair.

'Mr Sterling, I'm Margaret Kingston,' said the tiny woman. 'Let's go over to the sofa. Adele,' she said to the secretary who had shown Sterling in, 'I wonder if we could have – well, what would you like, Mr Sterling? Tea? Coffee?'

'Coffee, please.' He wondered if anyone would ever be at his beck and call. The odds seemed giddily long.

'Thank you for coming over. I've got about half an hour till the SMT. That should be enough.'

Sterling had the sense that control of the agenda and the interview had already slipped away from him. There was a kind of dynamic, restless energy in the woman next to him. He felt her strong will and thought of steamrollers. Never mind. If it meant a commission, he'd bear it. He struggled with his unease, which was even worse now than in the reception area. He'd been in the offices of plenty of head honchos – head teachers, superintendents, even an assistant chief constable – and almost never for pats on the back. Jim Selsey, the grizzled old Police Federation rep in the Kent force, reckoned 20% of his caseload was defending 'Frank bloody Sterling'. Sterling hadn't been corrupt. He hadn't been a thug (although he knew how to look after himself). But his hot-headedness had led to what his loyal friend Andy Nolan, the one he'd shared squad cars with for all those early years in the force, called 'escapades'.

He dragged his attention back to the principal's office at ECOT. 'SMT?' he said.

'Strategic Management Team. Sorry, I get caught up in the jargon. My senior colleagues and I usually meet every Monday morning in term time, but we missed it for various reasons this week. That's why it's today. If I keep lapsing into technical terms, I'm sure you'll pick me up on it.' She looked very directly at Sterling. 'Your reputation precedes you. And that's why I wanted to meet you.'

Sterling spread his hands, palms up, on his lap. Angela had told him that Margaret Kingston, an acquaintance from London, had been in contact. 'How can I help, Ms Kingston?'

The principal nodded to herself, as if Sterling had passed a short invisible test. It's calling her "Ms", he thought. Angela, as much mentor as friend, had been teaching him well. Stuff you couldn't learn in a school or tech.

'I'd better start with some background.' She paused as the secretary knocked and came in with a tray. 'Thank you, Adele.' She waited again till the secretary withdrew. 'I moved down here in mid-September.

I had various posts in London colleges, and one for a short while back in my family's country, Jamaica. I started out as a Sociology lecturer and worked my way up. I was a deputy principal in Bexley and then this opportunity came along. Apart from Jamaica, it's the first time I've lived outside London, and it's still wonderful to be living by the seaside. For one reason or another, the last principal left suddenly. He retired early, and I had to get special permission to shorten my notice period at my last college. I arrived here just after enrolments and the beginning of the new academic year. The timing isn't brilliant. But moving on ... What do you know about further education colleges, Mr Sterling?'

'Not very much. I didn't go down that route myself. I went straight into the police.' He didn't mention his aversion to education establishments, whatever their ilk, and that included the police training centre when he was a cadet.

'Well, perhaps that's an advantage. Anyway, it's a vital time of the year. Successful enrolment and re-enrolment, and a successful and smooth launch of the new term, secures and stabilises funding and is a springboard for development.'

'Interesting,' lied Sterling. 'So why, if we can sort of cut to the chase, am I here?'

Margaret Kingston was not used to being interrupted. The steamroller was in danger of stalling, and she seemed about to make a sharp riposte. Then she smiled. 'Angela told me it might be a bit like this.' She handed Sterling his coffee and took a sip of her own. 'Cutting to the chase, as you put it ... I've been here for five weeks and something's amiss. Enrolments are satisfactory. Everything seems to be running relatively smoothly. Within the usual parameters, everyone's doing their jobs, as far as I can tell over this short period of time. But I've been around colleges for years, and something is definitely not right.'

Sterling waited. Margaret Kingston took another sip of her coffee. Even in the quiet grandeur of her office, Sterling could hear sounds from outside – footsteps coming up into reception, the creak of the door, a loud eruption of noise from a corridor, perhaps a class changing. A small shadow passed in front of one of the windows.

'I just don't know much more than that, Mr Sterling.'

'Well, not to beat about the bush, Ms Kingston, it's pretty vague. Maybe we should take a different tack. If you don't know what's wrong, from your experience of colleges, what kinds of thing do go wrong?'

The principal brightened. 'That's not a bad approach. Wow, though. The stories I could tell.' She nodded again. Her decision to call in PI Frank Sterling might be vindicated. 'Firstly, there are accounting scams, especially in connection with enrolments. As well as fees from students, in some cases, we get public funding for enrolling and keeping learners. The longer we keep them, the more we get, and if they are successful in getting the qualifications they've signed up for, we get money for that too.'

'Like a taxi meter and the fare, and a tip at the end.'

'Well, I suppose so. Anyway, there have been instances in colleges where claims are made for ghosts – forms are submitted where no learners exist, especially if work is franchised by colleges to partners or subsidiaries, and lots of variations on that theme.'

Sterling thought of arrest and conviction statistics in his former profession. It was the same everywhere. There was a system. And then the system was abused.

'Another scam is defalcation, which I guess is a fancy word for embezzlement. I was in one college where the student union co-ordinator skimmed a large amount of various income streams into his own pocket. Somewhere else there was wholesale theft of materials from the various sections of the construction department – paints from painting and decorating, wood from carpentry and joinery, and so on. One lecturer's home was called the Hackney Annex. After that there's what I'd call the non-criminal stuff – affairs between staff and such like, occasionally relationships between staff and students – not exactly desirable, against the disciplinary code but not out-and-out illegal. It's not just ordinary employees either.' The principal smiled. 'It was before my time, but there was a principal in the West Midlands who went off long-term sick. A union official caught up with him running a pub outside Manchester with the vice-principal he'd run off with, who'd gone off sick just before him. I can tell you, the fallout from that was spectacular.'

'But nothing like any of that here, except maybe the personal shenanigans. Nothing concrete.'

'Nothing concrete, as you say. But something's up. I know it. I haven't got to where I am without having an instinct.'

'So principals have gut feelings, just like coppers,' said Sterling. 'Well, Angela will probably have told you that I'm pretty much a one-man band. What do you want me to do?'

'Shake things up, Mr Sterling. Get to the bottom of it. Liberate me from the shifty glances in the corridors, the knowing looks in meetings, the mystery illnesses and absences in my staff, the air of secrecy, and even fear, about the place. I'm too busy running everything and planning the future. The college is still in the 20th century, so it really needs bringing up to the standards of the rest of the sector, and modernising. For goodness sake, the hairdressing area is in attic space at the top of three flights of stairs in this old building. We still actually run a kind of mini-hotel in the building down the slope. Why can't those hotel and catering students go out to real hotels on practical placements? The different blocks are named after British educationalists. Even the college name is old fashioned. What college has 'Technology' in the title these days? Earlsey College has a nice ring, don't you think?'

'ECOT to ECo' murmured Sterling. 'A nice green ring to it.'

'Are you taking the mickey?'

Sterling smiled a Mona Lisa smile.

The principal smiled too. 'You're right. I get on my high horse and then I start ranting. But you get the drift I expect. Anyway, back to you. From what I hear, you've got an excellent record for getting results.'

'I've had my moments. But what I've been asked to do has normally been more specific. Find a missing person. Track down money. Verify an insurance claim. I'm not that comfortable with what you're suggesting – kind of agent provocateur stuff.'

'So ....?'

Sterling considered, as he found himself doing at this stage before every case, his utilities bills, his credit card, which had taken some hits over the last month, and all his other outgoings. He'd always be a beggar, never a chooser. 'OK, I'll do it.'

'Excellent.' From being close to stalling, the steamroller picked up and began its relentless roll again. 'I've had a think, and it would be best if we took you on as a consultant. We can get you an identity pass and I'll arrange a further authorisation giving you permission to go pretty much anywhere on the campus. What I'm asking you to do is unusual, of course, but it's not unusual for us to have consultants around the place, observing lessons, looking at the books, helping us prepare for inspection.'

'So it would be like doing a mock inspection.'

'Oh no, Mr Sterling. Absolutely not. I'd never contemplate a mock inspection. It would be a recipe for things going wrong, for the "inspectors" and those inspected. There's a world of difference between preparing for inspection and undergoing a mock inspection.'

Sterling had got into trouble before about slack use of language. He'd had a deaf client whose daughter was a wheelchair user. They'd had plenty of tilts at him over disabled stuff – all those arguments about being disabled but not having a disability, society disabling you and not your impairment. Now he was moving into another unfamiliar social world. 'Right,' he said. 'I'm helping you prepare for inspection rather than doing a mock inspection.'

'Correct. I think we'd better widen the scope as well – a multi-pronged approach.' She hummed under her breath. Then she said, 'You're preparing us for inspection, and part of your remit is also to look at procedures and processes, and possible reorganisation. That's if anyone asks. With my authorisation, you don't have to explain yourself.'

'Good. That might be tricky, particularly early on. I know little about colleges. Before we go any further, we haven't discussed my terms.' Sterling told her his daily rate. 'The minimum period of engagement is three days. It's Tuesday morning now and I might as well start straight away. I suggest I come and see you next Monday morning with a report, and you can decide then what you want to do next, if anything. I'll contact you earlier if something important comes up. To be honest, I'm not that optimistic.'

'I have every confidence in you, Mr Sterling, or I wouldn't be doing this. The college isn't that flush with cash, and the corporation had to be persuaded, but whatever is wrong needs sorting out. Goodness, is that the time? I'm going to be late for the SMT meeting. I'll tell Adele to make the arrangements, and while I think about it, she can support you while you're on this job. She's my PA, but she's very competent and will be able to accommodate the extra work. You can wait here when I've gone.'

'Right. Before you go, though,' said Sterling, 'can you arrange for me to have a list of staff and car registration numbers? I imagine your premises manager will have some such thing for parking permits.'

'Why do you need that?'

'Fancy cars sometimes indicate dodgy goings on. It would give me a starting point.'

'Well, there may be data protection issues....'

'Your authorisation will cover that. It'll save me hanging round waiting for owners to claim cars and get suspicious.'

'Alright. No need to bother the premises manager. All college data comes to me, so I've got a copy here.' The principal handed over some sheets from her filing cabinet. 'One last thing. I wonder, now that you're on board, as it were, if I can call you Frank.'

'Of course,' said Sterling, 'Margaret.'

Chapter 2

Tuesday 6 October - Mooching

'Follow me, Mr Sterling,' said Adele the secretary. She led him to the reception desk in the lobby where he filled in his details and received an identity card in a transparent plastic holder which he slipped round his neck with the lanyard in the college's green and purple colours. 'Frank Sterling, Consultant' was visible in large letters.

'Car registration?' said the secretary.

'I haven't got a car. It's train, bus and Shank's pony for me.'

'Right.' She gave him a curious look. Surely consultants always had cars. 'OK,' she said, processing and accepting the information. 'Now to the secretaries' office.'

In the office, which she shared with other administrative staff dotted at computer stations around the room, she went behind her desk and plucked a sheet of paper from her 'Pending' tray. 'Your authorisation.'

'That was quick,' said Sterling. 'She's only just gone to her meeting.'

Adele smiled a small smile. She was a willowy, pale woman with wispy blonde hair. Her grey eyes were rimmed with red, as if she had been crying. 'Ms Kingston dictated it to me on Friday. We've not known her long here, but we're finding out that she usually gets what she wants. If anyone wants to know more while you are on campus, refer them to the principal's office. She'll have told you that she's allocated me to support you while you're here and she's arranged this as well.' She handed Sterling another sheet on which was a list of afternoon appointments. 'Those are interviews with the rest of the Senior Management Team.'

Sterling looked first at the principal's authorisation. 'Mr Frank Sterling is a consultant who has been engaged directly by me to examine all aspects of the college's work, procedures and processes, in readiness for our next Ofsted inspection and other quality initiatives, and in preparation for possible reorganisation. Please extend every courtesy to him as he goes about his work, and co-operate fully with any requests or questions that he has.' It was signed in a bold hand and had the college's stamp with the current date. Although it had looked as though the principal had spontaneously decided his brief, it was all pre-planned. That aside, what did 'Ofsted' stand for? He'd better find out before he was caught out. He already felt enough of a fraud. He looked at the interviews. It was time to halt the steamroller.

'Can you cancel all these, please?' He'd do things his way. 'I'll let you know if I want to meet them at any stage.'

'The principal will be surprised,' murmured Adele.

Sterling shrugged. 'I can't be doing with being told what to do.'

'You get used to it eventually,' said the secretary.

'Not me,' said Sterling. Whoa, he thought. Not too cocky. He changed tack. 'I wonder if you have a little map of the campus, so I can have a walk about.'

Armed with the map and the parking list, Sterling set off round the main block, learning along the way that it was the Tuckett Building. As he left the front lobby, he sensed a presence behind him and turned. A man was leaning nonchalantly on one of the frames adorned with panes of stained glass that divided the lobby and various offices, including reception and the principal's office, from the rest of the floor. He looked as if he was in his fifties. A grey, old-fashioned double-breasted suit hung comfortably from his narrow frame, loose but at the same time a good fit. The red and white striped tie looked as if it represented a club. Michael Caine glasses emphasised the old-fashioned look. The face, smooth with a hint of lines across the forehead and high cheekbones; the eyes, small, dark and hooded; and the hair, longish, dark, full on the scalp and swept back behind the ears, gave the impression of long periods in a wind tunnel. Or a wolf. What was the technical word? It came to Sterling. Lupine. The man nodded, and then faded back beyond the frame and out of sight.

The ground floor contained little of note – just the lobby, offices, classrooms, a staffroom, a boardroom, toilets and at one end what seemed to be the college's library, except that it went by the title 'Learning Resource Centre'. But just next to the LRC was a door that looked more interesting. Sterling found himself in a kind of elevated interior walkway, with windows on either side, a kind of poor person's Bridge of Sighs. He looked down towards a Portakabin that could have been a temporary classroom. Behind that was a high boundary wall, built with grey cobblestone, and set in it, virtually out of sight for anyone but a seasoned observer, an old and dilapidated wooden door.

A door in a wall: it triggered the memory of Penny Morrissey, a fellow police cadet all those years ago in Ashton Police Training Centre – sexy, pretty, clever. Everything she did, Sterling soon discovered, she did to get on. That's why their little fling hadn't lasted. How could another rookie cop be of any use? She'd moved on to one of the sergeant-instructors, and later on to a chief inspector, from what Sterling had heard. But it wasn't just about people with her. If there was a short cut or an advantage to be gained from some course of action, she was on to it; the dodgier the better. The door in the wall at Earlsey Tech was just like the one in at the Centre. She'd got hold of a key, and came and went as she pleased, as if coming straightforwardly through the front door like everyone else was somehow beneath her. The lesson about ambition had passed him by, but he'd learnt a good one about deviousness from that girl. He'd have a look at that door later.

For the moment, he turned his attention to the warren of offices at the far end of the walkway, in an annex that had clearly been attached to the main building later on. Down here were the marketing manager, the programme manager for Social and Health Care, the premises manager and an assortment of other managers and officers.

The door of the marketing manager's office was ajar, so Sterling knocked. He might as well start staff engagement here as anywhere else.

'Come in,' said a rich, confident voice.

Sterling pushed the door and entered. The room was small, with an old-fashioned multi-paned window whose paint was peeling. The overall effect would have been poky but for the fact that the walls were a brilliant white and virtually unadorned except for strategically hung framed ECOT logos (a herring gull on top of an open book in different versions), posters advertising its courses and benefits, and Gold Star educational marketing awards. A small shelf on Sterling's left contained books on marketing – *Strategic Marketing*, *The Marketing Plan* and others. An immaculately dressed man in a navy-blue pinstriped suit with a red carnation in the buttonhole half rose from a high-backed black chair from behind a matching minimalist black desk and top-of-the-range laptop, also jet black. Sterling could see no paper anywhere.

'Good morning,' he said.

'Good morning. Joe Speltman, college marketing manager,' said the man in his brightest networking manner, half-rising from his chair. 'And you are....?'

'Yes, it said that on the door. I'm Frank Sterling, erm, consultant.' The marketing manager's hair was fascinating him – not the light brown colour but the bouffant effect, swept back and upwards in glossy profusion to match the man's tanned skin.

'What can I do for you, Mr Sterling?'

'I'm doing some work for the principal connected with inspection and maybe reorganisation. Tell me what you do.'

Sterling's vagueness didn't trouble the man in charge of marketing. He launched into a passionate discourse about its benefits and key purpose in helping the college thrive. It wasn't just advertising and promotion, posters and prospectuses – far from it, he said in a voice almost edged with contempt. Knowing the catchment area, knowing the market segments, knowing the economy, knowing the population profile, knowing the strengths and weaknesses of the college and shaping its offer, pricing, global marketing – he covered them all, and more, in a breathless patter. Research was particularly crucial, he'd said finally. Sterling was invited to look at the laptop and was quickly bewildered by the graphs and charts that sped across the screen before him – detailed analysis from internal college information systems to local, national and international census and social data.

'You know,' said Speltman, 'from this desk I can find out absolutely anything there is to know about anyone and anything.'

Sterling reeled back into the smaller black visitor's chair. 'Well, I think I get it,' he said. He suspected that the egotist in front of him barely required an audience, and certainly not an excuse to promote his talents. There was a sinister aspect to the talk about research.

Then a new, petulant edge entered the other man's voice. 'I'm a fish out of water here,' he whined. 'I shouldn't just be a *manager*. I should be at the top table. I should be a director – *Director of Marketing*.' He savoured the words, as if saying them might turn dream to reality. 'They need my skills for strategy. They need my knowledge. After all, Mr...' – he peered at Sterling's credentials as he had already forgotten his name – '... Sterling, knowledge is power. So, maybe a reorganisation, eh? Maybe some restructuring.

Promotions. Well, I hope you'll be able to take that message back.'

Sterling puffed out his cheeks, bulged out his eyes and shook his head, as if recovering from the brilliance of the tour de force he'd just witnessed. 'I certainly will,' he fibbed for the second time that morning.

Back at the reception area in the main lobby, having extricated himself from the grip of Speltman's verbiage, he sat in one of the visitor's chairs. So, that was the ground floor of the Tuckett Building, including the marketing man's droning. He plodded up the stairs to the first floor. The layout was pretty much the same as on the ground floor, except that there was no reception area. Immediately above the principal's office was the director of curriculum for Arts, Social Science and Social Care. The next set of stairs upwards was much narrower, and led off into the relative darkness of the hairdressing section, as the sign above them indicated.

Sterling went back down the stairs the way he'd come and continued downwards past reception to what the map termed the lower ground floor. It was shabbier down here, as if the college had given up on the need to impress anyone. By the stairs was a kind of caretaker's office-cum-depot. Sterling glanced inside. There was a makeshift desk with a few papers scattered around, a stack or two of chairs and tables, some dark curtains and all the other discarded detritus of a large organisation. Behind the desk was a more solid inner door with at least three heavy locks and bolts.

He had a sudden idea that he needed to execute before too much thinking ruined his nerve. He rummaged quickly in his pocket for his keys, sorting through them with hands that had started to tremble. Sandley Library door key would do – Angela had a spare. He slipped it off the ring and stepped quickly into the cubbyhole, where a pegboard was propped carelessly on the desk and against the wall. He glanced over it. 'Back wall door key' looked the most promising, but it didn't look much like the Sandley Library one. He slipped it into his pocket, shuffled another, similar one from the bottom left hand corner into its place and put the Sandley Library key in that corner. Perspiration trickled down the side of his face and his pulse throbbed in his ears. Even Margaret Kingston's authorisation wouldn't cover key-pilfering.

Opposite was a room that looked like a hospital ward. To give himself the appearance of focus and purpose and to calm himself down, Sterling stationed himself at a glass panel at the top of the door and watched a demonstration of lifting and carrying using a hoist. The student in the harness was giggling as the transporters strapped her in and went about their business. The lecturer, a tall, middle-aged woman with sallow skin, looked on with a benevolent smile. From somewhere nearby Sterling could hear the regular nearby clack-clack of a photocopier. A moment later, the caretaker stumped down the corridor and into his room, preoccupied, tutting and shaking his head. He didn't even notice Sterling a metre or two away as he slammed the door. Who dares, wins, thought Sterling. He noted more robust locks on the outer door – a deadlock, a padlock and a Yale. This was a room that was rarely left unattended.

His recovery almost complete, Sterling ambled further down the corridor towards a set of scuffed and battered doors that constituted the back entrance of the building, with various vending machines standing like sentinels as he approached. He thought about the scams Margaret Kingston had mentioned. He looked at the machines, which sold the usual array of drinks, crisps and chocolate bars. It wouldn't be hard to fiddle things if supervision was loose. There was the usual arrangement, a series of letters and numbers in front of each item, A1 down to L5. You put in the required amount of money and pressed the appropriate buttons and the item chosen corkscrewed and dropped into the tray below, with change going to a separate dispenser. He looked more closely at one machine. Although there were the options of L1 to L5 on the front panel, there was a metal plate bolted across the bottom of the glass panel, covering up the L products, if there were any. He put in a pound coin and pressed L2. The coin simply returned to him in the dispenser every time he tried it.

If it had been any other circumstance, Sterling might not even have noticed. But his perceptions had been heightened by Margaret Kingston's briefing, including his sixth sense. There was no hurry, as he was still getting familiar with the college, and other things, like the door in the wall, were more currently alluring. But that metal plate, and what might be behind it, was something else he'd come back to.

As he moved to the doors, there was a low sound that increased in intensity, like the beginning of a tidal wave. Up till now, he had wandered about in virtual silence, seeing hardly another soul. Now from every door and every direction came a noisy cacophony, the rumble of feet and a swell of voices. Then came the students themselves, laughing, talking and shouting as they jostled round him in the corridor and in front of the vending machines. Morning break. He struggled through the crowds into a covered area of a bicycle park and smoking shelter adjoining the back entrance. He caught the tang of cigarettes lighting up. A boy with bleached blonde hair, well apart from the others, lit up and took a greedy drag, tilting his head and expelling a thin stream of smoke through nose and pursed lips. He gave Sterling an appraising glance and turned away. Sterling moved round to the back of the Tuckett Building. Now he had a better idea of the layout. It was constructed on a slope, so the main entrance was on one floor, and the back entrance came out further down on the lower ground floor.

'Can I help you?'

Sterling recognised the question and the tone, which meant 'What the hell are you up to?' He turned to the voice, which came from a door at the corner of the building. It belonged to a young blonde woman standing arms akimbo with long legs encased in close-fitting blue denim jeans under an artist's smock. He knew what it was because of the smears of colour, paint and clay and other materials less easy to identify.

'Not really. At least, I don't think so. I'm a consultant. Working for the principal. Here.' He offered the letter of authorisation.

The young woman scanned it, reached out for his identification card and pulled it towards her. 'Frank Sterling, consultant,' she said. 'Another bloody consultant. What is it this time? 100% student-centred learning? The ten commandments of the Common Inspection Framework? How to sweet-talk Ofsted?'

Sterling smiled. 'Shouldn't you be offering every courtesy as I go about my business? And co-operation?'

She turned round and headed back through the door. 'Hmph,' she said from the back of her head. 'I'm making myself coffee before the next round. Want one?'

Sterling followed her in, and found that he was in a pottery classroom. It had a warm and friendly if Spartan atmosphere. There were a number of benches and tables in the middle of the room, and at the back towards the end, two kilns. Potters' wheels were dotted around, and on shelves at the sides were examples of students' work. He spotted a garden gnome, seated by itself with a fishing rod, looked down at him cross-eyed from a higher ledge.

The young woman saw his upward glance. 'Big Ears helps me maintain discipline. I tell my students that he sees everything. It works too. They can be so naïve. Sit there,' she said, indicating a nearby bench and table. 'I'm Elinor Laski. You might as well call me Ellie. Everyone else does.'

'Well, you know who I am.'

The young woman put a mug of coffee in front of Sterling. 'No sugar, I'm afraid. I don't take it myself and I rarely entertain down here.' She plonked herself down opposite.

'So,' said Sterling. 'You teach pottery.'

'No. This is just a front. I'm an astronaut. I'm building a rocket out back. To escape the teeming millions on this doomed planet.'

'Got room for any passengers? I'm fit. I'm young. Everything's in working order. I'd be an asset, seeing as I agree about the planet.' Sterling sipped his coffee and winced. It tasted awful and came too soon after the cup he'd had with Margaret Kingston.

'Food for thought,' said the potter. She eyed him appraisingly. 'Yes, I teach pottery, mostly on the 'A' level programme, and some bits and pieces on other courses. I've only been here a few weeks. I came down from Birmingham. I'm used to schools, and younger kids. This is very different. More laissez-faire. More bunking off and the like. Fewer rules. The staff are more mixed too – the high-powered contingent on the higher education and business courses and the crafts people on the vocational programmes. Still, it's a job and a change. It's nice by the seaside.'

'The principal said that. You must have started at the same time.'

'Ms Kingston. Down from London with all these modern, progressive, metropolitan ideas. In this back-water. Not that I disagree with her. Far from it. A place like this needs a kick up the bum. It's too white, provincial and complacent. But I'm telling you, she's got a job on. There's a big constituency here who have got things just the way they want them, and they'll fight to keep it that way.' She brushed her hair back behind an ear. 'So, Frank Sterling, consultant, what's your role in all this? Are you one of these fancy change agents taken on to facilitate our radical, game-changing journey? Are you going to be our pathfinder, our trailblazer, moving forward?'

'Something like that,' said Sterling. It seemed as good a description as any, and although it was clear that Ellie Laski was using the jargon ironically – the stuff about change agents and pathfinding – it might come in useful. 'You seem well up with it all. I wouldn't have thought teachers would be that fussed. It's more managerial, as it were.'

'Yeah, well.' She wafted her hand about vaguely. 'It's like osmosis if you're around it. Before you know it, you're parroting the words yourself. And my Birmingham job was more senior than this, so I've had some practice.' She switched quickly, not inclined to talk about herself. 'Well, what's your schedule?'

'How do you mean, my schedule?'

'Well, what are you actually doing and when are you doing it? Are you going around observing lessons? Are you meeting with programme managers and directors of curriculum? Are you going through the college paperwork – the self-assessment reports, the data – enrolment and results and so on? Visiting Student Services to see what they get up to, going over to the Students' Union to see what they do? The schedule. What's the schedule?'

'I'm mooching about at the moment.' Sterling shifted in his seat. This was an unexpected and highly informed inquisition. Clearly she wasn't exaggerating about her last job. 'Having a butcher's. Observing the lie of the land. Getting the feel of the college. Then I'll go into things a bit more deeply. I've noticed one or two things already. Then I'll follow up the initial leads.'

'Jesus,' said Ellie Laski. 'For a consultant that's the most jargon-free statement I've ever heard. Actually, that's promising. Consultants aren't usually human beings.' She paused and looked up from her coffee directly into his eyes. 'To be honest, you talk more like a plod than someone to do with education.'

There was a hubbub at the door, and then it burst open and a few students spilled in, laughing and playing tag, led by a girl in a short green skirt and white fishnet tights and a boy in skinny jeans and a bomber jacket.

'Oi,' said Ellie. 'Wait outside a moment. I'm not ready yet.'

'Ooh, snarky, Miss,' said the girl.

The exchange was good-natured but, Sterling noticed, everybody did exactly as they were told, and with alacrity.

'OK,' said Ellie. 'Round two coming up. I'm kicking you out.'

'Thanks for the coffee. Before I go off mooching, anything or anyone I should watch out for?'

Ellie had started to get up from the table and then stopped, the coffee mugs in each hand. 'Yes,' she said. 'Jane Casterton, Curriculum Director for Arts and Social Sciences etc. Evil woman. A bully. Manipulative. And probably worse, if I can come to that conclusion after only a few weeks. You need to watch out for Hissing Sid Brown too. Looks a bit like a starving wolf. Don't ask me why, but he's dodgy, though having said that there's a human being as well in there somewhere. Don't ask me why 'Hissing'. I don't think anyone knows.'

'I think I may already have spotted him,' said Sterling. 'See you around.'

'I won't object. Come for coffee again if you want. You know when break is,' said Ellie.

Sterling eased through the jostling, colourful knot of students outside the pottery, ignoring their cheerful little 'whoos' and 'who is he, Miss?' questions. It was good to have met Ellie Laski, and useful, but the new period had arrived just in time. Saved by the bell, he thought.

Chapter 3

Tuesday 6 October - Stirring

After the fifteen-minute buzz of activity, the movement of students in little platoons, lecturers hauling large bags about and the mobbing of the vending machines and smoking shelter, the college subsided back into order and silence. Sterling took the path parallel to the back of the Tuckett Building and followed it around to the Portakabin and annex at the side. Above him, the glass-panelled walkway he had crossed earlier was empty. The Portakabin was a science laboratory and there was a blue glow of Bunsen burners. The path continued between the lab and the annex. For a moment, Sterling thought he'd lost his bearings since he could see the tall boundary wall but not the door. As he got closer, however, it appeared beyond the back corner of the lab. He realised that it was only visible from the walkway and some of the annex windows.

He tried not to glance around. Nothing could be more natural than a member of staff, or an authorised visitor, exiting from the site by the back door. The key fitted snugly and turned smoothly. Although the door itself was old, rotting at the bottom like jagged teeth and with paint peeling from it in vertical strips, the lock was certainly in good condition. So were the hinges.

The door swung noiselessly towards him and he slipped through, locking it behind him. The leafy bridle path on the other side of the wall disappeared into the distance down towards the sea, one side abutting the college wall and the other a mixture of dense high hedging and trees.

There was a dank, musty smell of rotting leaves mulching and combining with the packed, coarse earth to make a soft, squelchy surface underfoot. In the near distance, about 50 metres away, Sterling could see the occasional brief dull glimpse of cars as they passed on the Ramston Road. He sensed a railway cutting beyond the hedge and trees, the one he'd been through earlier on the train to Southwood station. There was a muffled quietness in the small lane, sound absorbed by the overgrown vegetation and reflected away on the college side by the thick wall. Sterling came out onto the road just above the college at the railway bridge. He had been right about the cutting. He strolled back down to the Tech's main (and official) gates. On the bridle path, his unease about being in a learning institution had faded. Now it was coming back, but it was time for some more mooching.

He wandered down a narrow, tree-lined roadway to what looked to be the business end of the college. To his left was the Ravenhall Building, housing Design, Technology and Construction, and to his right Lavender, with Business Studies, Higher Education, A Levels and Access. What did Access mean? he wondered. Down in front of him, joined at right angles to Lavender, was Cara, housing the Hotel and Catering Department, through which the road ran in a kind of underpass to the area beyond. All the buildings were modern, functional and workaday – you'd find them in every town in the country. More interesting was the attention of a gardener with bright red hair and pale skin at a rose bed in front of the Ravenhall Building. As his mate weeded on his hands and knees, he rested, hands clasped on the top of his rake, chin clamped on hands, and stared with no hint of friendliness in his freckled face.

Sterling carried on through the Cara Building, noting within the underpass the automatic plate glass sliding doors to Earlsey College Hotel on one side – the training hotel the principal had mentioned – and a more commonplace entrance on the other. Emerging from underneath Cara, to his left, beyond a scrubby low hedge, was a squat, two-storied building of red Kentish brick, by the looks of it built in the inter-war period and well before the rest of the college. Further on to the right was a new light-timbered construction, like a large chalet, all gables and glass, with offices and classrooms. It was attached to a large area of greenhouses and flowerbeds, with a dark green, windowless corrugated structure in the far corner which looked like a warehouse and loomed over the little enclave. 'Horticulture Section' said the sign over the chalet entrance.

The older building, labelled Glen Lodge on Sterling's map, exerted the bigger pull, because parked in the only available bay outside it was a BMW Z4 roadster of recent registration. Sterling consulted his list for the owner and then ducked under the entrance gable and into a dingy hallway. From the room next to him came the faint, urgent sounds of voices, and more than that, grunts and small cries, over a background of pulsating music, as if from a television. As he approached the door handle, the noise stopped abruptly and in the sudden silence he passed into a large room like that of a motor parts shop or wholesale electrical supplier.

There was a counter in front of him and behind that TV monitors at various points high on the three walls without windows. Perhaps it was those, now blank, from which the sound had come. In the corner was a glass cubicle in which a large server hummed. Sterling could just make out three desks and chairs amidst the clutter of the room, which consisted of cardboard boxes piled high and precariously, shelves on each wall with boxes full of the mysterious paraphernalia of electrical technology, and leads and equipment strewn everywhere. At the far end of the counter was a plastic goldfish bowl of subtle, complex design with a little mechanical fish meandering around, so good that Sterling momentarily mistook it for the real thing. A small black cable snaked from the bottom of the bowl and disappeared, presumably to a socket amidst the hotchpotch beyond the counter.

'Yeah? What?' said a voice from somewhere in the room.

Sterling struggled to identify a face to attach it to. 'Frank Sterling,' he said to the empty space in front of him. 'Doing some work for the principal.'

The face popped up above one of the piles, like a duck in a fairground shooting booth. It was younger than the voice had implied, small-featured and gloomy-looking, with a nose squashed sideways and never straightened, atop a scrawny neck and a torso that looked painfully thin. 'What work?'

That got your attention, thought Sterling, but the man had asked a good question. Snooping around and stirring things up was what Sterling was doing. 'A consultancy project on the college's structure and processes,' he said, 'with the other aim of helping the college prepare for the next Ofsted – in a trailblazer project.' Ellie the potter would be impressed with his quick grasp of the jargon.

'Trailblazer? That's a new one. They normally call them pathfinders. Anyway, what's that got to do with me?'

Sterling cursed silently to himself. He'd played too fast and loose with the jargon and it was catching up with him. 'Everything and everyone's in the mix in projects like this. Tell me what you do and how you fit in.'

'I haven't got time for this.'

Sterling shrugged. 'Well, how can I be positive about what you do?' he said, looking around at the chaos.

'Alright, alright.' The thin young man with the bent nose emerged from behind a stack of boxes and threw down a cloth. He looked at Sterling's ID and at the authorisation. 'We might as well get it over with. Then I can get on with some work. I'm Glen Havers,' confirming to Sterling that he owned the Z4 roadster, 'and this' – he swept his hand round the room – 'is Glen Lodge, which is an in-joke in the college, but just a coincidence. This shith... This place has been around a lot longer than me. I don't know what it was originally built for but now it's the command module of this crappy place, aka the Technical Support Centre, and I'm the Senior Technical Support Officer. Me and my two assistants keep the place going. The principal's computer crashes? We fix it. Some lecturer needs a telly to play a DVD? We set it up. A visiting speaker needs to use a laptop and projector? We fix it. A new sound system comes in? We make it work. We do pretty much everything electrical, and we help support the computer network. That's why the server is sitting over there. I report to the Technical Services Manager, and provide back-up for the technical helpline. Two curriculum areas need us more than most: music technology and performing arts.'

'Performing arts?' said Sterling.

'Plays. Bands. Musicals. Dance. Film projects. That kind of stuff. Without me and my little team this whole caboodle would grind to a halt.'

'Interesting. Very enlightening,' said Sterling. 'Isn't it a bit unusual for general technical support and IT to be so close together?'

Havers shrugged. 'Maybe. Everywhere's different. It's always been like this here, right from when I joined and computers were clumsy, chunky things. We showed early on we could manage it all, and we got senior support.'

'Yes? Who from?'

'Jane,' said the young man. 'Ms Casterton, I mean. One of the curriculum directors. If it ain't broke, don't fix it – that's what she said. We don't need a consultant to tell us that.'

'Right. Good,' said Sterling. 'Well, I think I've got enough for now, so I'll let you get on.'

'Wait a sec. Aren't you taking any notes? Isn't that what consultants do? Take notes. Carry clipboards.'

'I do all that later. First impressions are important. I mull it all over, and then I write it all up. What you've said is crystal clear.' Sterling turned to go. With his back to the technician, he looked casually at the door through which he'd entered. A duct on the wall ended at a small junction box over the top hinge, from which a small loop of cable entered the door. There seemed to be no signs of any electronics on the door itself, the security features – bolts and a keypad – having been built into the frame. What distinguished this door from the others he had seen was a large metal fingerplate above the handle. Sterling reckoned he was looking at a proximity detector for alerting when visitors arrived. 'Was there anything good on telly?' he said.

'What do you mean?' said Havers. He busied himself with a video camera on a tripod.

'There was something on when I was in the corridor. It sounded interesting.'

'We have the monitors on all the time. I never notice. Maybe *Jeremy Kyle*. *Real Housewives of Orange County*. I dunno. One of my team is mad on *Countdown* later on in the day. I never even notice the televisions anymore, but they help the time pass when it gets slow.'

'I expect they do,' said Sterling. 'See you around.'

Outside in the watery autumn sunshine in which the Z4 roadster glinted, he asked himself the obvious question. How could a technician afford such a beast? It was possible, but a stretch. He looked at his watch. It was 12 o'clock. He had time to stroll over to the Horticulture Section before lunch. Separating it from the Cara Building was a leylandii hedge. There was no one in the reception area, so he moved on to the greenhouses and flowerbeds. Everything looked immaculate, just as his OCD self liked it with his garden at home. Some autumn flowers he couldn't identify stretched out in rows beyond the greenhouse.

He gravitated towards the warehouse structure, which was not just in the very far corner of the Horticulture Section but the far corner of the college as a whole. It fitted against the tall flint boundary wall that stretched right up to Ramston Road at the top and the newer brick wall along the road to the harbour, marking the bottom boundary of the campus. On the heavy door were a padlock and a combination lock panel, and the structure appeared to have no windows. No one was taking any chances on forced entry.

Any moment now… But this time there was no indignant 'Can I help you?' Instead, a calm voice called out from behind him. 'Frank Sterling?'

Sterling turned round. 'Yes, that's me. How did you know?' he asked the woman in front of him.

'Your reputation has preceded you,' said the woman. Her well-proportioned outdoor face had a hint of freckles under the tanned skin. Her arms were similarly tanned and freckled, and muscular, noted Sterling. Her skin highlighted her blue eyes, above which one eyebrow twitched quizzically. 'Actually, news can travel pretty fast round here. How can I help you?'

'I'm just looking round really at the minute. I notice this is the Horticulture Section. What do you do here, Ms….?'

'Pat Manton.' She put out a callused hand. 'I'm the Section Manager. Most of our courses are part-time, so we're part of the Continuing Education and HE programme area. But because we're in this little corner, we get pretty much left to our own devices.'

'The hedge must help,' said Sterling, 'and I see that your bit backs on to the bottom wall and the side wall.

Cosy. Compact. What's this building here?' he said, gesturing towards the dark green corrugated warehouse structure.

The eyebrow twitched. Surely Pat Manton couldn't think of a career in poker. 'It's set up for experimental growing – hydroponic and in artificial light. But it was dependent on funding, and unfortunately our applications from a European project and a matched amount from our educational agencies haven't been successful this year. A shame, but that's why we've currently got this white elephant in the corner.'

'Can I have a look inside?'

'Oh dear, Mr Sterling, I'm afraid not. Things have gone bad to worse with that structure. Not only did we fail to get funding, but then after that we had an asbestos scare. So no one can go in until that's sorted out.' She grimaced. 'Health and safety. But take it from me, there's nothing to see.'

Sterling nodded, and then looked out over the rows of neatly tended plants and the greenhouses. 'You've got a nice little operation going here – all very neat and orderly.'

'Thanks,' said Pat Manton. 'Come on. I'll give you a quick tour.' She guided Sterling away from the dark building in the corner. As they walked round the plots and greenhouses, she talked. 'There are plenty of opportunities for gardeners in the stately homes and big gardens all round here, and then there are the local nurseries and salad companies. Some of our students will start out on their own and eventually run their own businesses. Horticulture is, or can be, a pretty good profession these days.'

'And how many students do you have?'

'Just over 40. We haven't been going long, so we're building up.'

'Very interesting,' said Sterling. His own garden was neat and tidy enough but lacked colour at particular times of the year. 'Do you do kind of leisure courses for non-professionals, maybe in the evenings, to help them improve their skills? You know, courses for amateur gardeners?'

'No, nothing like that at the moment. I think the principal's got plans like that for across the whole college, but nothing's come out yet. To be honest, my team and I have enough on our plates with what we've got. Evening and weekend stuff is out.'

'There might be a market at some stage. Anyway, thanks for the tour. It's about lunchtime. Where can I get a bite to eat?'

'The student refectory is on the second floor of the Cara block.' The horticulture section manager pointed to beyond the leylandii hedge. 'And the staff refectory is on the third. Seeing as you're a consultant, I reckon you can take your pick, and if you've got hours to spare there might be a place up in the training restaurant. The entrance is in the underpass, opposite the entrance to the hotel bit.'

'Right,' said Sterling. 'I think I saw it as I came through.'

He left the Horticulture Section to go to lunch. There was something about Pat Manton, and it wasn't her wholesome, outdoorsy attractiveness. She was standing with folded arms at the entrance, leaning on a post, and looking very much as if she was preventing him from sneaking back in.

Chapter 4

Tuesday 6 October - Oxymoron

When Sterling was sure that Pat Manton had given up her sentry duties and returned to her office, instead of going straight up to one of the refectories, he slipped out of the rear entrance behind Glen Lodge and turned right and right again into the road at the bottom of the college. It was as he predicted. The roof of the warehouse structure canted south to pick up the best of the sunshine, and was covered on every feasible part of its surface with solar panels in three columns. Between the columns, he found what he was hoping for: not just one skylight, but four. Now he could eat.

Going up to the student refectory, the one Sterling had chosen for lunch, was like approaching rapids. First it was still and quiet. Then there was a growing vibrancy and expectation on the bare stairs and in the stairwells, with clusters of young people going up or down or simply mooning around, but when Sterling opened the café doors, there were the rapids. A wall of noise hit him and he reeled at the contrast from his leisurely tour. Struggling to orient himself, he lurched over to the queue. Seeing that he did not know the drill, a friendly young girl with long black purple-streaked hair and a goth t-shirt, all skulls and daggers, got him a tray with a little smile and a look to the floor. The price for a cup of tea and a bacon butty was ludicrously low. He thought of the tired cardboard supermarket sandwiches near his Sandley office and the king's ransom they cost. This was good. He searched for a quiet spot amongst the throng. A man in his early forties, older than anyone else in the room except those behind the serving counter, was sitting in a corner hunched over his tray in the only place with a spare seat opposite.

Sterling went over. 'Is this seat free?'

The man looked up, distracted, a hunted look in his eye and a permanent-looking frown in his forehead. 'Eh? Yeah. Be my guest.' His navy blue suit had long lost its sheen of newness, and his tie was spotted with what looked like old food stains. He glanced at Sterling's identification tag. 'Consultant,' he said. 'Shouldn't you be on the third floor?'

'Fancied a quiet lunch by myself. I was wrong about quiet.' Sterling looked at the ID tag of the man opposite. 'Dan Edwards, Programme Manager, Continuing Education and HE,' he read out. Pat Manton's immediate boss. 'Pleased to meet you. Why aren't you on the third floor?'

'Same reason as you. So I could eat quietly and not be hassled over staffing or timetabling or a whole array of other rubbish I have to deal with all day long. So that I didn't have to talk to a consultant. So I could let the waters of Lethe wash over me and carry me away to oblivion.'

'That bad,' said Sterling. 'I'd better shut up.' He took a bite from his bacon butty.

Dan Edwards ate a chip of his own and gave Sterling a long look. 'If you're a consultant, you'll probably want to talk to me at some stage anyway, so it might as well be now. And you're not likely to bring problems.'

'That's true enough. I'm on a kind of fact-finding mission, I suppose. There's talk of trailblazing, but that's a bit of jargon too far. What does a programme manager in a tech do?'

'Don't you know? I suppose not, if you're asking.' He looked up at the ceiling, as if he was trying to keep his emotions in check, or about to recite, and then back to face Sterling. 'The grunt work. Lecturers think they do it. Technicians think they do it. But it's the programme manager who has to do the timetabling, find the staff to go in front of the classes before the beginning of the academic year, sort out the disputes, do the appraisals, cover sickness, deal with the disciplinary issues, listen to the grievances, take the flak for the results, or the student drop out, or whatever's on the menu for a particular week. We have to balance the programme area budget, or not, given the current squeeze, keep costs down and numbers up. We're the ones who get in at ten to eight in the morning and leave at seven at night – nine if we're on evening duty. We even have to do our quota of teaching. In a phrase, we shovel the shit.'

'Sounds like it. How long have you been doing the job?'

'Came here a couple of years ago. Haven't stopped since. At least, that's what it seems like.' He ate another chip. 'So, what's the consultancy about this time? People like you are always around.'

Sterling looked out of the window. He knew the sea was nearby but this floor was too low for him to see it. Instead, beyond the leylandii hedge, the green warehouse building in the Horticulture Section drew his attention.

He turned back to Dan Edwards's open, careworn face and made a decision.

'The principal has been here a few weeks and thinks something is up, something out of the ordinary. She's asked me to see if I can find out what, if anything. What do you think?'

'What, if something's up? God, I'm too busy keeping my own little show on the road to worry about the rest of the place. It's a college. There are loads of people here. There are bound to be issues – dealing, rip-offs of one kind or another, bullying – of staff as well as students.... Bullying,' Edwards repeated, running his hand through his hair.

'Let me guess,' said Sterling. 'Jane Casterton, Curriculum Director.'

'You've been busy,' said Edwards, 'though it's no secret. Her meetings ... she hectors, she raps the table; she makes the PMs' lives a misery.' He stared unseeing at the wall and then re-focused. 'It's a backwater too, of course, down here in Earlsey, so that's a factor in the atmosphere. It means you get eccentrics, much more than in other places. But whether all this constitutes enough for the principal to engage a consultant to investigate...' He shrugged. 'Good luck with it. Maybe I'm a bit naïve but I haven't seen or heard anything out of the ordinary.' He got up and picked up his tray. 'I've got to get back. I'm teaching on top of everything else this afternoon and I haven't done my photocopying.'

'Thanks for talking to me,' said Sterling. 'I wonder, could you keep our conversation to yourself? My official brief is about preparing for inspection and reporting on structure – whatever all that means.'

Edwards gave a grim little smile. 'What conversation? If you want a conversation, maybe we could have a pint sometime. I'll be free one evening in a couple of months. Possibly. One last thing, since we slipped into confidences. The bullying I mentioned, and the person who does it ... I wouldn't want that to come back to me....'

Sterling nodded and zipped his thumb and forefinger across his pursed lips. He watched the programme manager weave his way through the human traffic towards where the trays were emptied and stacked. Edwards moved as if there was a weight on his shoulders, a programme area monkey on his back. Sterling had known police managers like that – the permanently furrowed forehead, the obsession with keeping the lid on overtime, nit-picking over equipment. He was glad he was out of it.

He looked round the heaving room. A harassed member of the catering staff with blotchy red arms cleared the table next to him, sweeping detritus from a tray into a large transparent plastic sack and putting the tray onto a wheeled stainless steel rack. She blew out her cheeks and swept a wisp of hair from her face, rolling her eyes fractionally as she caught Sterling's glance. There was a faint, greasy smiley face on the side of the rack.

Something light caught Sterling's eye in the far corner. The boy with the bleached blonde hair was standing over a table with another group of students. Flanking him on either side were two others. Even from his place in the corner, Sterling could see them for what they really were. Bruisers. Bullies. Enforcers. One of them, over six foot and solidly built, was chewing gum, his jaws moving in a regular, leisurely, circular motion.

The other was smaller and wiry, with a hard stare. The students at the table, boys and girls, were different from the slouchers around the rest of the room. Their backs were stiff and straight. When Blonde Boy reached out to the one who was nearest, he flinched, submitting to the tousle with a frightened little smile and a slight backward jerk of the head. Blonde Boy and his mates moved on, like a politician and his aides working the room, and the table watched uneasily as they went on their way. Eventually, Blonde Boy noticed Sterling in his corner with the remnants of the bacon butty. He nodded and moved on. I know you, said his expression, and I know why you're here.

Sterling finished his lunch and emptied the tray at the waste station. Enough talking to people. He'd have a look round this Cara Building, including the hotel section, another quick mosey around the one attached at right angles to it – what was it? Lavender? – and then he'd call it a day. He still felt oppressed. The unease hung around like a miasma, and probably always would while he was here.

Beyond the hissing plate glass doors of the hotel, when Sterling had found it, the young receptionist in purple and green livery behind the counter in the atrium was going through her patter. She pointed up at the gallery on the first floor. 'The bedrooms are up there. The lifts are in front of you, next to the fish tank, I mean the aquarium.' She put her hand to her face to stifle a giggle.

'So how does it work?' said Sterling.

'How do you mean?' said the girl.

'Well, I'm a customer wanting a room. Can I book any day of any week? Can I get something to eat here if it's the weekend? Is there Wi-Fi in the rooms? Mini-bar? Bar? Staff on hand when the college is closed?'

The girl giggled again. She had some work to do if she was going to make it as a hotel receptionist. 'Sorry. Yes, it's a fully working hotel, called Earlsey College Hotel. We've got six bedrooms. There's the training restaurant and bar during term time, and we open them if we're fully booked at weekends and holidays. Otherwise guests can go into town to eat. Students in the Hotel Section do all the jobs, like night porter, housekeeper, and so on.' She turned her small mouth down. 'That's if you're on the roster. Mrs Jenkinson decides that. If it's work, like at the weekends, and not work experience, like I'm doing now, you get paid.'

'Who's Mrs Jenkinson?'

'She runs the Hotel Section. Either you're in with her, or you're not.'

'And you're....'

'Not. Not yet, anyway. Don't know why.'

Sterling had his own theory. 'Thank you for your help. I'll let you get on.'

He wandered through the rest of the Cara Building, back and forth along each floor from the reception area at the bottom and then upwards. The 'Earlsey College Hotel' area wasn't exactly cut off on each floor from the rest, but by locking various doors at the stairs, it could be, and presumably the lift, with doors on each side, could also be fixed so that only those on the hotel side opened. He wondered if there were currently any guests. He'd forgotten to ask. Apart from the hotel, the refectories and the training restaurant at the top, from where he could see the North Sea, the block housed a collection of classrooms, demonstration theatres, staffrooms, offices and large, commercial kitchens. At the corner where another set of stairs was housed, he slipped into the Lavender block. According to the signs, here were Business Studies, A Levels, Continuing Education and HE. Some of this would be Dan Edwards's territory.

Once through the Lavender Building, a duller area of classrooms and staffrooms where he learned little, he made his way back up to the main building, Tuckett. At two o'clock, the campus was eerily quiet again. He remembered occasions as school when he had been out of class, often when he was on the way to see the head teacher after another misdemeanour. He couldn't shake off the feeling that he was doing something naughty. Really, he'd had enough of the college and was looking forward to escape and the train journey back home to Sandley.

'Did you work for the previous incumbent, Adele?' he said to the secretary, when he'd managed to find her shared office.

'For three years,' she said.

'And are you still in touch? Do you have contact details? I'm hoping that he'll find time to meet me.'

'Time is what he's got plenty of. I can give him a ring if you like. When would you want to see him?'

'Maybe sometime tomorrow? Tomorrow morning?'

In her jaded manner, Adele pressed some buttons. 'Mr Prestwick? Adele here from the college. I've got a consultant here who hopes to have an appointment to see you.' She listened for a few moments. 'What about?' she said to Sterling, her hand over the receiver.

'I really need some background about the college, and who better to provide it than the previous principal? It will help me get a proper feel for the place. I can speak to him if he wants.'

The secretary put her hand up and turned back to the phone. 'He wants some background to the college, and he says you're the best person to supply it. OK. OK.' She turned back to Sterling. 'He can see you at 11 tomorrow morning. He lives over in Deeping. Alright?'

'Excellent. Please thank him. Presumably you have his address.'

She nodded and turned back to the receiver. 'Yes, I'm very well, thank you. Yes. Yes. Things are obviously a bit different.' When she'd said her goodbyes, she looked up at Sterling. 'I was pretty sure he'd agree. He gave 15 years to this place, and he's struggled to replace it.'

'Thank you for doing that and for the address,' he said, brandishing the sticky note the secretary had written on. 'I'm off now. Things to check at the office.'

Adele went back to her typing. As Sterling emerged from the office and into the entrance foyer, the man from the wind tunnel emerged through the door to the corridor. The timing was surely not a coincidence. 'Good afternoon, Mr Sterling.' His voice was hoarse and reedy.

Sterling put his hands in his pockets. 'You know, I've only been in this place since earlier today and whether it's up here or down at the far end, loads of people already seem to be familiar with my name, even before they see my ID.' He paused. Two could tango. 'Mr Brown.'

Hissing Sid's face gave nothing away, but he inclined his head forward in a little bow. 'You've made some progress, then. Perhaps you'll know that I'm one of the only ones to do any work around here. Real work, that is.'

'Can't say I found that out. So I've only got your word for it. Anyway, I'm off now so I expect I'll see you around.' Sterling turned towards the main doors.

'Before you go....' Hissing Sid looked beyond Sterling's face, 'I expect you'll be in tomorrow. You look as though you're due a haircut. Why don't you come up to the hairdressing salon on the second floor tomorrow late afternoon – about 5 o'clock? We can do you a free cut. I've got some good students, and you'll get a feel of the day-to-day things we do.'

'Alright,' said Sterling. Sid Brown might have an agenda of his own, but where was the harm?

His work all but finished for the day, Sterling went outside and looked around the car park at the front. There were no more Z4 roadsters like Glen Havers's, but one or two models at the luxury end might at some stage reward further investigation.

Back in Sandley, his friend Angela was already in the snug of their local, the Cinque Port Arms, the *Times* crossword set out next to her usual tipple, a gin and tonic. Sterling looked at her as she concentrated on a clue, unaware of his presence at the bar. It was a lucky friendship, forged when Angela had first moved down to Sandley, four doors along from Sterling's own house, and had been burgled within the first few days. Sterling had been the investigating officer on his last case in the force. He'd been intent on showing her that the burglary was an unfortunate fluke, and that the area she'd moved to was picturesque and attractive, with a good community spirit, and from there the friend-ship had blossomed. He was white, Kent-born and bred, and never inclined to leave. She was black and London-born, although her family were from Trinidad. Tonight, her fine wrists and neck were as usual adorned with delicate silver bracelets and necklace, and she wore a black trouser suit and white blouse from her day in the library.

Any hostility in the conservative community of Sandley at the arrival of a black woman from London as its new librarian had long since dissipated because of Angela's dedication and charm. With her library skills and a double first degree from City University in German and History, she'd also assisted Sterling in some of his cases. She had been instrumental in enabling Sterling to set up his small office at the top of the stairs from the library, smoothing his passage of negotiation with the county council and endorsing his application. The big mystery, which no one locally had been able to fathom, was why Angela had upped sticks from the metropolis for this dozy backwater.

Sterling had a good inkling of what he brought to the table. His small-town mentality didn't bother Angela, and she appreciated his quirkiness, his burning independence – which had caused him to break from the police and set up as a private investigator – and his humour. He was bright too, in a rough diamond kind of way, and willing to learn – hence the crossword in the pub most nights.

He turned back to the bar, patrolled by another friend he was lucky to have, Becky Strange. She and her husband Mike, who ran and owned the pub, were ex-members of a never-identified branch of the security services. Neat, tidy, efficient, highly skilled and devastatingly effective as a team, they had come to provide discreet ad hoc and bespoke rescue, protection and related shadowy services for Sterling. Angela had connected them all in one of his first cases and the mutually beneficial association had continued after that. Mike and Becky had left active service after an incident in the Middle East that had left Mike with a slight tremor, and, although the pub was comfortable and profitable, Sterling knew that their new, quiet, conventional life wasn't enough. That suited him very well.

'Thanks, Becky,' he said as he took a pull of the pint of Spitfire she had dispensed. 'Before I get started on the crossword with Angela....' he stood on the bar rail and leaned forward, checking left and right for eavesdroppers, 'I've got a little expedition in mind. Might you or Mike be available?'

'Ooh, intriguing. Well, Mike's away for a few days, so it'll be me. Why don't you catch up with me a bit later on and let me know what you have in mind?'

'Done.' Sterling took his pint back to the snug.

'How did you get on today?' said Angela.

'OK. I met your friend Margaret Kingston, and I got the gig.'

Angela looked back down at the crossword. 'She's not exactly my friend, Frank, whatever she says about it. But she did contact me about you after all the publicity from that last case. And you're building a reputation for getting results.'

'Yeah, handy,' nodded Sterling. 'What about Margaret? To give me a bit more background.'

'Four down. Five down,' said Angela. 'These are difficult.' She looked up at Sterling with her dark, clever eyes. 'If you don't mind, Frank, I don't really want to talk about her because I don't want to think about London. Surely the assignment's about the college, and she's only been there a few weeks.'

'OK, Angie. Objection noted. Move the paper over so I can have a good look.'

A pint later, with the crossword all but completed and the pub beginning to empty at the end of the evening, Sterling returned to the bar.

'So, Becky, this project. I've got a job at the Tech in Earlsey, but I can't get where I need to go by what you might call conventional means. I'm hoping that you can help me with the unorthodox approach.'

'Breaking and entering then.'

Sterling screwed up his face. 'I suppose so. But it should be quite straightforward.'

'Hmm. Straightforward and Frank Sterling together virtually constitute an oxymoron. You usually get an experience that's the exact opposite.'

'And that's an oxymoron?'

'Yes, and so is "silent scream", when I think of the trouble you could get me into.'

'Come on, Becky. It spices up a quiet life.'

She pushed over a pen and notepad from behind the bar. 'Go on then. Do a sketch for me, so I can picture it.'

'OK,' said Becky when he'd finished. 'What about CCTV?'

'None that I could see except over the door. In my admittedly limited experience of schools and colleges, there's only CCTV in places where there is expensive equipment like computers.'

'Patrols, dogs?'

'No – no signs. It's not like a university campus that's open 24/7. I checked and it closes after the last evening class at 9 pm.'

'Well, it looks relatively low risk and it will be a bit of light relief. And I guess you have some authorisation anyway.'

'Good news, Becks. Thanks.'

When they had finalised arrangements, Sterling walked Angela home. 'What were you talking to Becky about, Frank? It looked like a bit of plotting.'

'You know my policy, Ange. I love you to bits but we don't want to put Sandley's most talented librarian in a compromising position.'

'Its only librarian, the way things are going.' She gave him a quick hug outside her front door. 'Be careful. You know what you're like and the scrapes you get into. And crossword assistants are thin on the ground in this town.'

'See you soon. I may not be in the pub tomorrow. I'm getting my hair cut.' He walked over to his own house a few doors down. In store would be much more than a haircut.

Chapter 5

Wednesday 7 October - Eddie Prestwick

It was two buses to the ex-principal's house on the border between Deeping and Wallston, next to the green where the lifeboat house loomed over the shingle beach. That was no problem. Sterling was fond of Deeping – the tang of the sea; seagulls wheeling and squawking in the October breeze; blokes (almost exclusively blokes) fishing in the middle distance from the pier. You could cycle or walk from Sandthorpe Castle at the north end right down to Wallston Castle at the south and see every stage of England's history. There was a four of rowers on the choppy water heading north parallel with the shore. The cox was hunched up and looked frozen. Her high voice, calling the stroke, drifted over to land.

This was another place he'd spent some of his formative years in during his father's restless progress through the East Kent coastal towns. What had his father been looking for? A woman to replace the mother of his son? Or had he not been searching but running away? Sterling always knew when they were moving on. His father got restless and critical.

'This one-horse town,' he'd say, and then they'd be off to the next one. Sterling had first kissed a girl one dark night on the beach by one of the winding engines for the fishing boats. Stacey. She was pretty, a good kisser, and a kind girl. It didn't mean he'd made a success of hanging on to her. She might have been the first of the muck-ups. Maybe she was still here in town, married with kids.

The ex-principal's house was one of a line of Edwardian villas whose gardens stretched down to a cycle path and walkway between the town and the beach. Sterling vaguely remembered that there was a plaque to the surgeon Joseph Lister on one of the other houses around here. He'd been much too interested in Stacey's charms at the time. All of them had complicated veranda constructions on the first floor, and Edward Prestwick's was no exception. It was painted white and looked pristine. A small, faded woman answered the door, and with barely a word led him upstairs towards the veranda Sterling had just looked at.

A tall man, completely bald except for some residual dark hair behind his ears and tapering down to just above the nape of his neck, rose from his armchair, tossed the paper aside and put out his hand. 'Eddie Prestwick', he said. His skin was sallow and smooth, but Sterling could see the little veins like cracks in a pane of glass radiating from his nose. He was at leisure, and wearing a dark suit, though without a tie, and instead of shoes there were slippers on his feet. It looked as though he had been about to go somewhere official but the event had been cancelled.

'Frank Sterling,' said Sterling.

The ex-principal's slender hand was firm and slightly clammy. 'Let's go onto the veranda. It's still just about warm enough if you keep your jacket on. I think the sun's just going over the yard arm. Drink?' Sterling knew he wasn't being offered tea or coffee. Just in time he avoided a reflex glance at his watch. 'Sure,' he said. He was a PI and he'd come by bus. There was none of that, 'Sorry, but I'm on duty' nonsense, and of course, no car. And drinkers talked more easily if they were in drinking company.

'Scotch? Ice?'

'Both, please.'

Prestwick looked pleased in a melancholy way. He and Sterling sipped their drinks and looked out towards the Goodwin Sands. There were tankers and wind turbines on the horizon, and sailing dinghies near the shore, eager beavers working a triangle, obviously racing. Down below them on the cycle path, a young rollerblader in all the gear – matching fluorescent green helmet, kneepads and fingerless leather gloves – hissed by, his foot strokes – forward left and forward right – bold and expansive zigzags.

'This is excellent,' said Sterling, tipping his tumbler in a little toast. 'And it's a nice spot.'

The ex-principal shrugged. 'A single malt and the view lose their allure after a while. Like everything else. Especially when there's a surplus of time. So, Mr Sterling, state your business.'

'Right. Well, your successor at the college has asked me to look into one or two things for her, not necessarily linked to education. In fact I know little about education except as a reluctant recipient. That's why she got me in. Fresh eyes. New insights. She pointed me in one or two directions, but they weren't the way to go in my view, and anyway I'm no good at following directions. Much better to meet her predecessor. So here I am.'

'Well, that's not much to go on.' Prestwick had the manner of someone used to getting quickly to the nub. 'Never mind. It's not as if I've got anything else to do. What do you know about FE, Mr Sterling?'

'FE?'

'Not very much then. FE stands for further education, and it fills a niche, for a certain kind of student, generally following the vocational route, between school and HE – higher education – universities.'

Sterling nodded. He didn't feel any more knowledgeable. Time to roll with the punches. Listen; don't interrupt, he told himself. You'll get to it.

'FE. The most maligned sector of education, and the one most messed about because government ministers, from whatever party, don't understand it – their own kids went straight from sixth form to university.' Prestwick leaned forward, rolling his tumbler gently back and forth in his slender hands. 'I'll give you an example....'

Sterling sipped his drink, as if he was musing on what the man was saying as he ran sadly on through long-defunct agencies, initials and acronyms. He saw with complete clarity why the ex-principal, whose lip had curled into a sneer, had agreed to see him. 'Alphabet soup,' Sterling murmured at the end of the lecture.

'Exactly,' said Prestwick. He thought he'd found a sympathetic ear. 'It wasn't just all that policy and support stuff. When I started, we weren't just giving carpenters and brickies and so on a trade. We wanted them to be citizens. We wanted them to think about things. When NVQs came in, that all went out of the window. Oh, there was the 'underpinning knowledge and understanding' in all those silly units, but it was all about a facile reductionism. I found myself leading an organisation that was doing things I no longer believed in. And all those stupid, expensive top-down initiatives – where are they now?'

Sterling, more indifferent to than overwhelmed by the technicalities of education, waited till Prestwick had taken another long pull of his Scotch. It was a question of timing. He felt relaxed himself as the alcohol found its way into his bloodstream. 'But that's not why you left,' he said softly.

The ex-principal looked up from the golden amber swilling in his glass. 'No,' he said. 'That's not why I left.'

'So....?'

'They said I'd lost it. I didn't have a grip on things. Everything was falling away.' There was a small but unmistakeable whine in the ex-principal's voice. 'Bastards.'

'Who?' said Sterling.

'The chair of the corporation for one. Jane Casterton for another. She slipped the stiletto right between my shoulder blades.' He looked at Sterling, his eyes coming in to focus, as if he was seeing his visitor for the first time. 'You're good, Mr Sterling. Winkling this out of me. It's a lonely business being a principal, even if you've got the power. It made me used to keeping my own counsel. I haven't ever talked about this to anyone.'

'It won't go any further,' said Sterling. 'What about your wife? Didn't you discuss it with her?'

'Huh. You saw her when you arrived. She's had what she wanted from my career – this house, the lifestyle – but she's never been interested in the detail.'

'And were they right? The bastards.'

It was quiet in the room. From the shore came the faint slapping of waves breaking on the shingle. A clock ticked from somewhere nearby.

'There was no disaster. Enrolments were OK. We were hanging on to students and they were doing OK. But yes, I suppose things were slipping away. I couldn't be bothered anymore. I'd stopped being a leader. The college was treading water, and that wasn't enough. And there was another thing. A sense that something wasn't right – a feeling that grew stronger towards the end. It was as if there was something parallel going on. You'd get the feeling in meetings or in the corridor that there were things you didn't know about. That feeling made my apathy worse, and by the end, either I was paranoid or I'd really lost it.'

'Well, if it's any consolation, your successor has felt the same disquiet. That's why she's asked me to look into it.'

'And what have you found?'

'Not much at the moment – I've only been looking at it for a day or so. But there are some interesting lines of enquiry, as they say. If I find anything, I expect you'll hear about it one way or the other.'

The ex-principal blew out his lips. 'I'm not sure I care. I'm glad I'm out of it. They got rid of me, but they enhanced my pension and added extra years. We won't starve.' From self-pity, he'd made the transition to smugness. 'Top up?'

'Alright,' said Sterling. He could sober up on the train back to the Tech at Southwood, and he'd even have time for some lunch in Deeping in his favourite café opposite the pier. Maybe, too, he could get Eddie Prestwick on to specifics, if there were any.

Chapter 6

Wednesday 7 October – The Haircut - Thursday 8 October – The Raid

The stairs up to the hairdressing department were narrow and dingy, and made steeper through a combination of the slow train journey to Southwood from Deeping, the walk from the station to the Tech and the continuing effects of the single malt (which made the walk more of a totter). Sterling plodded on, resisting the temptation to rest two-thirds of the way up. He remembered vaguely that one of Margaret Kingston's grandiose plans was to relocate Hairdressing and Beauty Therapy to somewhere more accessible. He smiled ruefully. Even if you had all your faculties you needed the fitness levels of a triathlete to get up here. At the top he smelt the lingering scents of a hairdressing salon – the sharp, heady tang of the peroxide and other more mysterious odours.

At the reception desk opposite the stairs, the receptionist, young and heavily made up as if she was about to go on a TV talent show, stopped her gum-chewing and smiled. 'Good afternoon, Sir. How may I help?'

From nowhere, Hissing Sid appeared. 'I'll look after this, Lettie. Right, Mr Sterling. I'll get you one of my best girls.' He made a strange clicking noise with his tongue that carried across the salon. 'Hannah,' he said. 'Customer.'

A girl detached herself from the gaggle gossiping and giggling in the corner. She was of average height, a few inches over five foot, but her black satin leggings emphasised every curve of her slender lower half, and a soft, close-fitting long-sleeved black cashmere top, cut low, emphasised a generous cleavage. She tripped over in what looked like diamanté ballet flats, cheerful in every easy brisk movement. 'Yes, Mr Brown.' Sterling caught a barely discernible glance between the girl and the man who clearly ran the salon and called the shots. 'Come this way, Sir,' she said to Sterling, leading him to a barber's chair in a windowless corner of the room. Some halogen lighting bathed the area in a garish light.

After she had fussed around, arranging a gown and a kind of thin rubber pad around his neck and shoulders, she stationed herself behind the chair and addressed Sterling through the mirror in front of him. Her face was small and perfectly proportioned, and framed against immaculately cut straight black shiny hair growing out to just below her shoulder. Her complexion was flawless, and if she was wearing make-up it was artfully applied. Her brown eyes had a playful, friendly quality.

Sterling couldn't stop thinking about his barbershop in Sandley, where he'd had his haircut for the last five years. You went in and sat with other blokes on a kind of window seat by the door waiting for your turn. There was the *Daily Mail* to read, or old copies of *Autocar* and

GQ magazine. At least *Penthouse* and *Playboy* were no longer strewn around. Throughout the shop was that dense mixed-up smell of damp hair, masculinity, Lynx and obscure hairdressing preparations. He remembered it right from when he was a kid and his father took him for his monthly short back and sides in other identical barbershops in any of the coastal towns they happened to be living in, and it never changed. Brian, his current barber, was adept with scissors, comb and clipper, but his paunch and fat fingers were in sorry contrast to the vision standing behind Sterling.

'Right, Sir,' said the girl Hannah. She ran her fingers through Sterling's hair. 'Lovely. Dark and wavy,' she said, choosing not to mention the flecks of grey at the temples. 'My favourite in a man. How would you like it done?'

'Like this but shorter. So when I next have it cut in three weeks, it looks the same as now.'

'OK,' said the girl. 'I can give it a bit more shape if you want. Layer it a bit more.'

'Fine.' Sterling wasn't fussy about his hair, unlike some men he knew.

The girl set to work. She was good – confident and efficient. As she relaxed into her task, Sterling relaxed too. The spiel started, as it always did – talk of holidays, prospects for the weekend.... Sterling closed his eyes and his thoughts turned back to Brian, who supported Coventry City but more importantly, for him, the England national football team. If Brian was feeling genial enough after cutting Sterling's hair, he'd show him pictures on his mobile telephone of bars in the Ukraine or Moldova (wherever that was) and huge, ornate, intricately patterned, 'ethnic' pitchers or Toby jugs of beer the locals probably dusted down for herds of visiting George Cross fans, whose faces, including Brian's, invariably looked red and bleary.

But there was no talk of football and beer here and soon the girl changed tack again, more personal. 'What brings you up to our little place, Mr....?'

'Sterling. Frank Sterling. But 'Frank' will be fine. Hannah.' This girl was easy to talk to.

'Ooh, nice and friendly. So, Frank....?'

'I'm a consultant. Just doing some work around the college.' Keep it vague, he thought. Talk of inspections and trailblazing would only lead to embarrassment. 'Mr Brown introduced himself to me and invited me up. Always on the lookout for models, I expect.'

'You could say that,' said the girl. She smiled to herself and looked away. They were quiet for a while as she combed and snipped in a steady rhythm, taking clumps of Sterling's hair in her fingers and cutting across the ends.

'What about you, Hannah? How come you're up here?'

'Well, obviously, I want to be a hairdresser. This is my second year. Maybe I'll open a salon when I've got a few years under my belt. I could have gone into a hairdressers' and got my NVQs that way, on day release. But college is much more fun than a boring apprenticeship.' She giggled.

'Oh?' said Sterling.

'Well, for a start, you don't just get to do ladies. And another thing.' She looked at him in the mirror and stopped her snipping. 'You know. College. More choice, like.'

'Right,' said Sterling, nodding. He thought he knew what she meant. A girl like Hannah. He felt old for a moment.

'Are you local, Frank?'

'Sandley. You?'

'Whithampton. The other way up the coast. Easy ride down on the train.'

In the mirror, Sterling saw Hissing Sid, hovering in the background like a wraith.

At the end of 20 minutes, Sterling was a long way from the 'sir' he had been at the start, or even 'Frank'. 'Sweetheart' and other endearments had replaced them, and he was enjoying the girl's bubbly disarming enthusiasm.

She took a mirror to the back of his head. 'There.'

'Very good,' said Sterling. He recognised himself, but a more svelte, elegant, trim version.

'I enjoyed doing that. It's usually older folk up here, if they can get up the stairs. Nothing wrong with that, of course, but it's not often we get a good-looking bloke with young springy hair.'

Sterling felt his neck redden.

'Ooh, hang on a second, sweetheart. I've missed a bit.' The girl approached Sterling from the front and side, leaning in very close. Her chest pressed and rubbed against his upper arm. He felt her breath on his cheek, and caught the scent of Chloë perfume. She snipped fussily round his ear and then whispered. 'I can do much, much more for you than cut your hair, sweetpea. And it would be much more fun.' Then she stepped back with a small smile, not far from a smirk, peeled off the gown and brushed stray hairs from his neck and shoulders. Sterling sat where he was for a moment, waiting, hoping that the sudden agitation he felt would subside. As he squirmed out of the chair, the moment passed.

'Thank you very much, Hannah,' he croaked. He wasn't naïve, or rather, since his stupidity over a woman in an earlier case – an East Kent femme fatale, as someone had put it – he was more realistic. This come-on was too unsubtle to be other than some kind of set up, and soured his enjoyment of the chat during the haircut. But if the girl was part of something, perhaps he could turn it to his advantage and get information from her. 'Let's have coffee,' he said.

The girl shrugged, as if hors d'oeuvres were unnecessary when the main course was in prospect. 'OK.'

'Tomorrow? Lunchtime? You get lunch, don't you? 12:30 in Southwood Beach Parlour on the front?'

'Sure. I can do that.'

'How much do I owe you?'

'Oh, we don't charge, Frank. You're like a guinea pig. For us to practise on.' But she didn't object when he slipped a note into her hand.

Sterling went down the stairs back into the main part of the Tuckett Building. He shook his head, hoping for clarity. Nothing like that last bit ever happened when he went to Brian.

'So, Frank, what are we looking for?'

Sterling looked at Becky's profile in the ghostly glow of the dashboard, as her eyes focused on the road. He mused again on how lucky he was to have not just one but two former active agents as friends and still willing to undertake the odd unofficial mission on his behalf.

'Nefarious activities, as Angela would say,' said Sterling, 'or at least, evidence of them. The principal of that college is right. There's something going on, but the people doing it are clever. For the moment, I just want to get over the wall by that warehouse in the Horticulture Section and onto the roof, have a gander and then get out. It shouldn't be difficult.'

'Famous last words,' said Becky. 'Still, an in and out job, and a bit of excitement. You should be right – not too demanding, given that I've also got a pub to run.'

'Yeah, thanks for doing this. I know how busy you are.' Sterling rubbed his hands together. He'd had time for a quick bite to eat and a few hours' sleep before setting off with Becky in the pub's dark blue van, but he still felt leaden. Now they were close to the target, as Becky put it, at the bottom of the bridle path by the side of the college.

'Let's hope there are no dog walkers,' she said.

'At 3 a.m.?' said Sterling.

'You'd be surprised. The number of missions cocked up by Joe and Josephine Public.' She parked the van between two parked cars beyond the bosky, dark opening. Then she tied up her hair and slipped it under a dark woollen cap. 'Hoods up,' she said. 'In case there is CCTV somewhere around. Got your camera?'

Between them they slipped out a retractable ladder in a matt black colour.

'This is light,' said Sterling.

'Carbon fibre. Come on, let's get it into the path and out of sight.'

Sterling had noticed the autumn wind buffeting the van on the way over from Sandley. Even in the shelter of the wall and the hedge on the other side it puffed and squalled around them like a malfunctioning wind tunnel. He could smell rain in the air, and feel light spits stinging his face.

Becky was finding firm foundations for the ladder. 'There,' she said finally. 'That should be good to start with.' She shinned up the ladder, most of her slender dark figure disappearing in the turbulent gloom. Sterling could hear the muffled thuds and light clangs indicating that she was getting things in place. As he kept watch on the path, she appeared back down beside him, demonstrating her usual stealthy quality on expeditions.

'It's all ready. The ladder's in three sections. This first one goes up the wall and I've put the padding over the broken glass along the top. The second part is hinged over onto the roof. Because we're approaching the roof sideways on and it's canted in front of us, I've made sure that one of the legs on the last bit of the ladder is longer than the other so it's stable. How do you want to do this? I can go over if you want, and report back.'

'No, Becky. It's my gig, and if something happens at least I've got authorisation to be on the premises.'

'In the early hours?'

'I'm a consultant with a wide-ranging commission.'

'Well, take care up there. I've tested everything but you can never be 100% certain.' She stepped aside and made a bowing movement, with a small flourish, to introduce him to the ladder.

I might have been a bit rash, thought Sterling, as he looked up into the night. Becky is the competent one.

Too late now. He grasped the sides of the ladder and began his ascent. At the top, away from the relative shelter of the track, the squalling intensified. Darts of wind plucked at his black jeans and hoodie. It wasn't too cold, but he was grateful for his fingerless gloves and even more that he'd thought to put on his boots with their heavily ridged soles. He went over the padding under the ladder and on to the horizontal section over to the roof.

'Don't look down,' he muttered to himself. He looked down into the inky abyss. He and Becky had calculated that it was about seven and a half metres from roof to ground. He'd probably survive that if he fell, but not without a broken limb. A brief wave of panic enveloped him – the old Marchurch Dreamworld rollercoaster effect. Now he was too far from the wall and too far from the roof. He clung to the ladder and closed his eyes. Becky wouldn't judge him if he called for help, but it was pride that spurred him on – that and the knowledge that the end of the journey was only half a metre away. A moment later, he clambered on to the small space on the roof between the side and the first column of solar panels he'd seen in sunlight the day before, pausing to gather his wits.

He edged sideways like an alpinist to the nearest of the four skylights. Looking down, he quickly realised that there was nothing to see because it was entirely blacked out. What a waste of a journey. More out of duty than expectation he edged his way up to the next one, and the result was the same. He made his way over to the far end. He'd come this far, after all. The top skylight showed nothing either. Already Sterling was thinking how else he might find out what was in the building. But when he came to the fourth skylight, the one at the bottom far end, an eerie dull glow beckoned. Having got accustomed to the layout and how to negotiate it, he shuffled over. Clearly the intention had been to black out the fourth skylight in the same way as the others, but a small patch of the material had come loose. Sterling stared down into the warehouse structure, his eye right over the source of light. He didn't need long. 'Bloody hell,' he muttered, his words carried away into the windy night. He fumbled for the camera from the pouch strapped to the small of his back and started snapping.

Going back across the horizontal section of the ladder, adrenaline level still high and flushed with the success of the expedition, Sterling got careless. Half a metre from the wall, a gust coincided with careless co-ordination of hands and feet. He tipped from the ladder and found himself hanging one-handed desperately above the narrow space between the building and the wall. 'Becky,' he hissed. 'Becky. I've got a problem here. Becky,' he shouted more loudly.

Her face appeared over the wall, taking everything in immediately. 'You need to get your other hand on the rung and then swing your legs up and hook them into the rungs further along. All I can do is catch them and hook them if you can't get them high enough. Go on. Do it now before you get too weak.' Her presence and sense of authority were reassuring. A minute later, he was jackknifed over the top of the wall, wheezing for breath and shaking, and a minute after that, in a heap at the bottom of the ladder. 'I'm getting too old for this,' he said.

'You should have let me go,' said Becky as she finished retrieving the ladder and the padding. 'Did you find what you were looking for?'

'It's a dope farm. Cannabis,' he said.

Becky whistled. 'Well,' she said. 'Everything's gone our way so far. Let's get out of here ASAP.'

As the van pulled quietly from the kerb and off into the centre of Southwood, she glanced into the mirror and chuckled.

'What?' said Sterling.

'Dog walker,' she said. 'Just going up the path.'

Sterling leaned back and closed his eyes. His arms ached up at the sockets and he knew some bruises would come up later. Still, mission accomplished and home free.

Twenty minutes later, Becky pulled up outside his door. 'What are you going to do next, Frank?'

'Have a kip, Becky. I'm knackered. And then download the photos. What we found out tonight will go in my report when I see the principal next Monday. There's more going on, though, I'm sure of it. I had my haircut at the college yesterday and somehow I got played. I'm having coffee later on with the girl who did it and maybe I'll find out something from her. I needed to get her out of the college. Neutral ground as it were.'

Becky smiled a small smile. 'Always the charmer, eh, Frank?'

'No idea what you mean,' he said, as he opened the van door. 'Thanks for your help, Becky – it really made a difference. See you later.'

Chapter 7

Thursday 8 October - Deeper

Sterling sat in the café and stirred his coffee. After crawling into bed in the early hours and getting up in the late morning he felt rough and tired. The train journey to Southwood from Sandley was beginning to feel like a commute. Now he barely noticed, as he had the first time, the white clapboard windmill across the water meadows just beyond Sandley station, or a mile further on the Roman fort perched on the escarpment, or the pharmaceutical factory, laboratory and office complex from the other window, or the huge old wind turbine, like a silent, abandoned Martian war machine on the very edge of the Isle of Earlsey. There were too many other things to think about.

He looked around the café. It was clean and bright, but as far as he could make out, the décor hadn't changed for 20 years, and no amount of cleaning could disguise the general air of scruffiness. There were dents and scratches on the table, and scuff marks on the padded seat, which was moulded in some complicated arrangement to the seat next to it and bolted to the floor. On the wall, next to a gilded mirror, a little boy in lederhosen, with his back to the beach, licked a large cornet. There was more ice cream around his lips than in the cone. To Sterling's certain knowledge, the picture, like the rest of the décor, hadn't changed from when he came here after walks along the cliffs with his father. The kid would be a man. Somehow, the thought made him gloomy.

'Oh my God, Frank, what's happened to you?'

Sterling hadn't noticed Hannah's arrival, perhaps a small miracle given the interest elsewhere in the café. He realised that he didn't even know her surname. As he half rose to greet her, he took in her brown ankle boots, the sheen of black winter tights over her slender legs, the brown mini-skirt and the fleece-trimmed collar of a short suede jacket pulled up around her neck and ears. A small matching handbag, hardly larger than a purse, hung at her waist on a thin strap down from her shoulder

'Worked late, got up early,' he mumbled. She had the knack of putting him on the defensive.

'Right,' she said knowingly, and something else, too soft to hear exactly. Could it have been 'Hope she was worth it'?

Sterling's deaf former client was adept at producing phrases similar to what had been said but which he hadn't heard properly. Sterling tried it, letting spontaneity come up with something. 'Sorry? Open sea surfing?'

The girl laughed as she slid sinuously into the moulded seat opposite. 'No, not that. Never mind.'

'Well, what would you like, Hannah?'

'Latte, please, sweetpea. Perhaps we can share a sandwich. Got to watch my figure.' She patted her flat midriff. She was as brisk and bubbly as in the salon yesterday.

Sterling returned to the table with the order. 'Thanks for the haircut. I'm really pleased with it.'

'I enjoyed doing it. Like I said, it's a change from all the old codgers and biddies.' She stopped. 'I shouldn't really say that. Older people I mean.' She leaned forward. 'A sandwich and coffee is very nice, but did you have a think about the other thing, Frank? You know, a bit of fun....'

'I did, only....' said Sterling. His face and neck were warming up again, and the girl had flushed a little too, as if startled by her own boldness, or maybe something else. As well as the flush, the tip of her tongue was moistening her lips. 'Well, call me old-fashioned, but I'm not used to this. Here we are chatting again, and I don't even know your surname.'

'Williamson,' said the girl. 'Hannah Williamson. Nice to meet you, Mr Old-Fashioned.' She was teasing him again, but kindly.

They fell quiet, sipping their coffees, sharing the sandwich and staring out towards the sea beyond the railings.

Sterling shifted in his seat and changed tack. 'There's a boy around college I keep seeing. His hair is bleached blonde and he looks fierce.'

Hannah looked at him sharply. 'Johnny Fontana.' Her face fell and her eyes went from the window to the floor. 'Johnny Fontana,' she said again. 'I can't shake him off. I wouldn't mind, but...' Her eyes returned to Sterling's face. 'I'd steer clear of him if I were you.'

'OK,' he said. There were times to persist and times to desist. He tried another angle. 'We should go out one evening, just the two of us. Not just a quick lunchtime. What about tomorrow evening?' His conscience gnawed at him. He didn't want anything to do with this girl beyond getting the information she might have. There'd be no date. But why go about things so deviously? Why not ask outright?

'No can do,' said Hannah. 'I'm rehearsing.'

'Saturday?'

She looked at him in a way he couldn't quite interpret.

'No, that's the performance.'

'A play? Up in Whithampton? Or down here? Can I get a ticket?'

'Yeah, a play. Kind of. Not up there. In college.' She rummaged in her handbag. Sterling recognised the diversionary tactic. Then she finished rummaging. 'What is this, Frank? *Who Wants to be a Millionaire?* One minute we're fixing a date, and the next, it's all these questions.'

'Sorry, Hannah. It's the consultant in me.' (Or more accurately, the plod, he thought to himself).

Now the bubbliness was gone. 'There are no tickets. It's a private thing. Look, I've said way too much already.' There was that trademark little smile again. 'It must be your cheeky face. Anyway, I'd love a date, Frank. It would be nice to do things the old-fashioned way, and be with someone – no offence, sweetpea – a bit more mature. Just not this week. Forget all I said about Johnny Fontana. Forget about the play. I can't say any more. It's more than my life's worth. Literally.' She drained her cup. 'I've got to get back. Thanks for the lunch.' She searched again in her handbag, this time drawing out a small notepad and scrawling quickly on it. 'Here's my mobile number. Take me out next weekend, Frank.' She edged out from between the seat and the table, leaned into him and gave him a peck on the cheek. Her cheerful manner had returned. 'And catch up with your sleep beforehand. I like a man with a bit of go.'

When she'd gone, Sterling hunched forward and stared at the Formica tabletop. Amongst the scratches and indentations of decades past were some crumbs from the sandwich and a blob of drying milk from Sterling's cappuccino. It had been a fruitful lunch, even if Hannah had been vague. But liking her spirit worsened the guilt of using her. He consoled himself that she was probably doing the same to him, or at least allowing others to use him through her.

He'd finish his coffee, and then see if Dan Edwards was about in the afternoon. After that little lunch date, he had something new to check.

In the Lavender Building, Sterling eventually found the right door. Will Johnson, Programme Manager for AS and A Levels, and Dan Edwards, Programme Manager for Access and Continuing Education. He knocked and waited.

'Yes', a voice called out. Even from behind the door Sterling caught the tone, a curious mixture of hurry, harassment and resignation. He put his head around. Lucky. Only Dan Edwards was in the room.

'Ah,' said Edwards. 'The trailblazer. Where's the flame thrower?'

'Got frisked at reception. Had to give it up. Got a moment?'

Edwards looked at the twin piles of paper on his desk and at his computer screen. Behind him on a built in arrangement of ledge and cupboards were further piles of papers. At the far end of the office, the other pro-gramme manager's desk almost exactly replicated that of the hard-pressed Edwards. On the ledge, as if marking the boundary point between the territories of each manager, was a small balancing toy – a silver Zeppelin with two travellers in the basket below that rocked slightly on its axis from some obscure move-ment of air. The room had no other personal adornment of any kind.

'What the hell. I'm sinking so deep it makes no difference. What do you need?'

'A short tour, that's all. Have you got a little theatre or drama studio in this block?'

'Sure. Let's go.' Edwards slipped on his jacket and they were on their way.

After a short journey along the corridor, down some stairs and along another corridor, they surveyed the empty, stark workspace. It was bounded on three sides by heavy blackout curtains on an all-round rail. Spotlights were suspended from the ceiling on a network of tracks. At the end furthest from the door was a small stage with an apron jutting out at the front, and around the apron were clustered about 20 chairs in the green and purple livery of the college, in two banks, one raised above the other. Everything together conjured up an intimate air.

'I'm no expert,' said Edwards, 'but I think the stage is movable. You can put everything exactly where you want it for any given scenario. So you can put on drama, dance, stand-up, whatever you want, and of course everything can be cleared away when it's used for day-to-day teaching and demos.'

'Neat,' said Sterling. 'It's set up now. Is there a performance coming up?'

'I don't think so. Not that I'd know because it's not my department. But there are usually flyers circulating, and maybe an e-mail, and I've seen nothing. December and the end of the college year are the main times – when students are being assessed or finishing their courses.'

Sterling poked behind the curtains. There was plenty of room for people, props and all the other paraphernalia of performance, with even more space, when he investigated, behind the stage itself.

'What's your interest, Frank? Will you be presenting a strategy to make this into something even more zany and exotic? That's what consultants do, isn't it?'

'Not this one, Dan. I'm a nooks and crannies kind of man. You get answers in the shadows, in my experience. So I'm just checking something.'

Edwards shrugged. The euphoria of walking away from his responsibilities, however temporarily, was wearing off. He looked at his watch, curiosity overwhelmed by to-do lists. 'I'd better get back. Can I leave you to it?'

'Sure,' said Sterling. 'Thanks. Let's do that pint sometime. I'll catch up with you about when.'

After Edwards had gone, Sterling did a whole circuit of the room behind the curtains. There was only one window, in the wall behind the stage, next to the emergency exit, and it looked out onto the wall beside the bridle path. The casement was hinged at the top, and prevented from opening more than a few inches by a bar at the bottom. Sterling felt in his pocket and drew out his mini tool set. The stubby Phillips screwdriver eventually began to turn, and in a minute he had loosened the two screws holding the arm in place. He left the handle vertical and stepped back against the curtain to survey his work. Only a close look would show that anything was amiss.

Just after he left the drama studio, a surge of students swept past him in the opposite direction, parting either side, as if he was a rock in a river. He stopped in the corridor, letting them flow by. He'd not done badly over the last two and a half days. He had got himself around the college, having a gander here and there, talking to people, shaking things loose. He'd likely made a friend or two, which would be handy, and likely a few enemies, which might be handy in a different way. He'd got some decent leads, not least from Hannah Williamson, and from her too a decent haircut. Best and most successful of all, there had been that discreet bit of breaking and entering – leading to a real, tangible result.

But he had the same feelings as the day before. If Margaret Kingston hadn't called him in and told that something was up in the college ... if he'd just had an afternoon going round as an ordinary visitor ... if he hadn't had that lesson in deceit from Penny Morrissey in the Police Training Centre all those years ago ... he wouldn't have had any hunch that things were amiss. It was only when you looked, really looked, that things didn't add up.

He knew the next step. One name had kept cropping up on the lips of many of the people he'd spoken with, and for the challenge ahead *mañana* wouldn't do anymore. He left the Lavender Building by the main door, walked through the little square and trudged up to Tuckett.

Chapter 8

Thursday 8 October - Jane Casterton

'Jane Casterton,' said Sterling to Adele. 'Is she in? And can she see me?'

'I wondered when you'd get around to her,' said Adele in a low voice. 'But I haven't got her diary, Mr Sterling. Jean, over there, does most of Ms Casterton's work.'

Sterling walked over. 'I wonder if Ms Casterton can see me this afternoon. Frank Sterling, consultant, with a brief from the principal.'

The other secretary, a sour-faced young woman with a tiny mole on her neck, looked up at her computer screen without speaking and worked the mouse. Sterling could see the calendar flickering. Then she picked up the phone. 'Ms Casterton, the consultant Mr Sterling is asking to see you. Shall I send him up?' She listened for a moment. 'Twenty minutes,' she said, and returned to her typing.

'Thanks so much,' said Sterling to the top of her head. Adele caught his glance as he left the room. He was almost certain that she momentarily rolled her eyes. He'd had a sly glance at the computer screen from an angle, and Jane Casterton had no meetings or interviews. She just wanted to keep him waiting.

Half an hour later, he knocked on her office door on the first floor and entered without waiting. She was at her desk, a large affair facing into the rest of the room to the right of the door. She looked up, disoriented slightly, and glanced at her watch. 'A funny twenty minutes, Mr Sterling.'

It felt like the beginning of a playground lecture. He had had plenty of those, and reacted accordingly. 'Yes, well, I got caught up in something, and it took longer than expected.' He was careful not to apologise for looking out of a window over to the Ramston Road, watching the traffic and working out exactly what he wanted to get from the forthcoming encounter.

The curriculum director motioned him brusquely to a squat chair in front of her desk. There was no cordiality here. This was going to be an interview. Sterling looked at the woman in front of him. He'd sometimes heard the expression 'beady eyes', but he'd never before met anyone with eyes that qualified. Now he had. Jane Casterton's were such a dark blue they were almost black, and he could not distinguish pupils from irises. They fixed on him in a hard, shrewd, appraising stare from a small, pale face. Although she was partially hidden by the desk, she looked broad about the beam and not flattered by the beige twinset she was wearing, with an almost inevitable pearl necklace. It was hard to tell her age – anything, he thought, between early forties and early fifties. Sterling wondered whether there would be a handshake. Though he had never set much store by them, some people believed that from a handshake you could come to an accurate conclusion about a person's character. But it was quickly clear he wasn't getting an opportunity to judge.

'Right, Mr Sterling. I'm very busy and by rights you've got 10 minutes less than the original allocation. I understand from Margaret that your remit is to help us prepare for inspection, and at the same time look at our processes, structures and procedures with a view to possible reorganisation. Margaret was also open enough to say, in confidence to the SMT, that there is a strong subtext, which is for you to find out if there is anything else, less salubrious, shall we say, that she and the senior team should be giving our attention to. So tell me, what have you found out?'

'No, no, Ms Casterton,' said Sterling. He wasn't going to let things run away from him. 'This is not how it's working. I'm asking the questions. You're doing the answers.'

The frumpy woman smiled a tight smile. 'Touché, Mr Sterling.' She sat back and steepled her fingers. 'Well, go on then.' She said it lightly, but her eyes glittered. 'Ask away.'

'OK, let's get, as you put it, to the less salubrious stuff first. Is there anything amiss in the college, to your knowledge?'

'Mr Sterling, I've been in this place girl and woman, as it were. I know all its good points, bad points, little quirks and virtually everything else there is to know. I know all the staff and every year a good proportion of the students. It's the usual situation in any organisation – the good, the bad and the ugly – but the good far, far outweighs the other two. There are peccadilloes and problems. Even I'm not so idealistic as to deny that. The principal is going to be a breath of fresh air for this place – in fact she already is. She's young, energetic and bright, and she's got some interesting ideas. It's a real advantage that she's come from London and is from what you'd call a diverse background. She's going to make a real difference. But this bee in a bonnet about things not being right – in my view, it's misguided. Someone looking in from the outside might even detect a hint of paranoia. Of course I'll support her in any way I can, which is what I'm doing now of course, but I speak my mind too.'

'Very frank,' said Sterling. 'So what does need changing?'

'Where do I start? The former principal let things slide, despite the warnings of the SMT. We were coasting. Some of the programme areas need shaking up. There are some weaknesses in teaching and learning in some parts of the college. We haven't been energetic enough in pursuing new funding, and we could do with some building work. I'm right with the principal on many matters. A hairdressing department on the top floor of this building and no lift – what were our predecessors thinking? There are other examples here and there, as well – annexes in the other Isle of Earlsey towns that should have been closed years ago – that kind of thing. But some things have been working well for years. Some courses produce outstanding results time after time. "Don't throw the baby out with the bathwater" is what I often say, and I think Marg…. the principal is listening to me.'

'You seem to have a pretty strong grasp of things here, Ms Casterton, and a good idea of the best direction of travel. Did you apply for the top job – a person with your experience and knowledge?'

'Oh no.' The shift of focus onto her talents and ambitions produced a sudden coquettish air. 'I do have an ability to see the big picture, and you're right that I have the experience and background. But I'm very content with looking after my areas of responsibility. I love the arts and social sciences, and social care, so I'm completely in my element, and as you can see ...' – she motioned to a large, heavy looking figure of a golden 'tick' with tiny wings at its base – '...I have won the top honour from Investors in Quality for my curriculum directorate work. I think I'd have struggled if I had to get to grips with the vocational areas and go out to bat for the whole college. You could say that I've found my level.'

Sterling stuck out his bottom lip and nodded. 'Right, I think that's pretty much everything, unless you've got anything else you want to add.'

'So I'm allowed to ask a couple of questions myself now, am I?' At the beginning, Jane Casterton's hostility was tangible. Now she was almost simpering.

'You can ask. I might not be able to answer.'

'What next, Mr Sterling?'

'Next is a report for the principal, who I'll see on Monday afternoon. What happens after that is a matter for her of course.'

'And obviously there's no chance of a preview.'

'Obviously.'

'It's certainly not about "trailblazing", is it, Mr Sterling? Or pathfinding. Or inspection. Or reorganisation.'

Sterling smiled. So she'd received reports about his activities. 'You've got me there, Ms Casterton.'

The coyness was gone as the woman stood up to signal the end of the interview. 'And,' she said softly, 'you don't really know much at all, eh, Mr Sterling?'

He shrugged. 'Not really,' he lied. 'Not at the moment.'

Her almost-black eyes glittered as she finally held out her hand. The handshake was limp, clammy and with fingers only – the furthest possible from a proper hand clasp. I wonder what that means, thought Sterling.

Just before he reached the door, there was an urgent rap and he stepped aside, for a brief second out of sight, as it swung dramatically open.

'He's getting people jittery,' said the boy with bleached blonde hair, Johnny Fontana, from the doorway. He followed Jane Casterton's eyes and focused on Sterling standing behind the door.

'Johnny. Our star student. Come in, young man. Meet Frank Sterling, someone who's come in to do some independent work to help the college.'

The young man, who looked thinner close up and was wearing skinny blue jeans that emphasised his spare frame, came over and offered his hand. This one was firmer, and his gaze held Sterling's unblinkingly. 'I've clocked you,' said his blank expression, just as it had in the student refectory, but this time he seemed to be trying to memorise every detail of Sterling's face.

'What were you saying, Johnny?' said Jane Casterton.

'Mr Lund. Scaring the pants off everyone preparing for their practical assessments.'

'He knows what he's doing. It's all part of the challenge of being successful. But do get back to me if anyone needs further reassurance.'

'I'll leave you to it,' said Sterling. 'Thank you for the meeting, Ms Casterton.' He turned to the young man. He couldn't resist it. Mr Hothead. 'For a moment there, I thought you were talking about someone else.'

Sterling went down the stairs back to the reception area. That was sparring rather than the Margaret Kingston steamroller style. He needed to collect his thoughts again before trekking over to the station. He'd narrowed it down to three aims before the meeting. The first was to stir things up and force a slip or a disclosure. He'd done that, but in the most unexpected way. The second was to probe and provoke, and he reckoned he'd got under Jane Casterton's skin on the odd occasion. But the third was the most important. The odds were that she was central to what was going on and he'd needed to meet her. Now he knew how formidable she was.

He thought about the blonde-haired boy. The kid had improvised cleverly, but the Mr Lund thing would have fooled no one. The link between the boy and the curriculum director was interesting too. In Sterling's experience, the big cheeses never concerned themselves with mere foot soldiers.

He wondered what he'd given away. Not much information. Her networks had already been busy. She didn't seem to know about the breaking and entering. She'd been able to weigh him up and judge the threat – one step before neutralising it, if he gave her the chance. She'd already have known that he'd be reporting back to the principal. On balance, he'd come out of it all right. But there was one thing, amidst all the swirls, insinuations and undercurrents of this case, about which he had no doubt. He didn't trust Jane Casterton for a single second.

He looked at his watch, sprang up and made for the heavy door. If he walked briskly he'd be able to get on the 16:20 back to Sandley. As he crossed Ramston Road into the cut his unease sloughed off like a snake's dead skin.

Chapter 9

Friday 9 October - Task force - expansion and reprise

'Here we go again,' said Becky, stirring her Friday morning coffee at one of the tables in front of the bar. Sterling had strolled over directly from his house behind the Guildhall. That was the advantage of having publicans for friends. There was almost always someone about.

'I know,' he said. It was no good pretending he didn't understand what she meant. 'I wouldn't ask if I could think of any other way of doing it. I'd try and make it as, erm – what's that word? – oxymoronic as possible. A straightforward Frank Sterling operation.'

'Looking at what you've got in mind, Frank, I think we can forget the 'oxy'. This is going to be very dangerous if your hunch is right. Dangerous to the point of foolhardiness.'

'But it might well be a case-breaker.'

'Let me think about it, Frank. Mike will be back' – she looked at the sturdy, complicated-looking watch on her slender wrist – 'in a couple of hours. He could look after the pub all right on Saturday evening, but this time isn't about just shinning it over a little wall onto a roof, is it? I'll tell you after I've talked it over with him.'

'OK.' Sterling knew not to push it, not least because in his experience of Becky and Mike Strange, anything short of outright refusal meant 'yes'.

Back in his office above the library in the square, he plugged in the two-bar electric fire and doodled, waiting. He worked out what he was going to say to Margaret Kingston on Monday about his progress so far, but he needed more evidence. Even what he already had was dodgy. He wondered exactly how he'd explain the expedition to scale the warehouse roof. Even though he had her authorisation to investigate, it was probably still technically breaking and entering or at least trespass. He'd need to convince her that the ends justified the means.

Then there was the invoice. He reckoned he should include danger money, and expenses for Becky. She couldn't be expected to do everything out of the goodness of her heart. He left his desk and went over to the window. Leaves were swirling around the church, and people were scurrying here and there in the wind, those with hats pressing with their hands to keep them on. Freddy the grocer, with his pebble glasses and fingerless gloves, was doing a brisk business in and out of his shop. Sterling knew he was exchanging banter with his customers even without being able to hear through the window and the weather. A tall, willowy woman in elegant black boots and padded maroon anorak, threw back her head and laughed, wagging her finger as Freddy weighed out her fruit and vegetables.

He thought about Hannah Williamson. He'd surely been set up with the girl in the hairdressing salon, and then there was the lunch in the café. His copper's instinct told him that she was a crucial part of something. He liked her. She was bubbly and fun. But she was trouble too. More movement outside caught his eye. At the opposite end of the street from the church, a blind man eased a long white cane with a kind of roller-ball at the tip back and forth over the pavement, like a treasure hunter with a mine detector. His backpack indicated that he might not be local. Sterling watched him expertly find a section of lowered kerb with knobbles and wait to cross the road, his head cocked slightly. From a flurry of passers-by two middle-aged shoppers materialised to assist, and he acquiesced with easy good grace to their exaggerated fussy caution in negotiating his passage to the other side.

Lunchtime was approaching when the phone call came.

'We're go, Frank – I think,' said Becky. 'Why don't you come over to the pub for a bit of lunch? Mike's here, and it's relatively quiet. We can go through things in detail.'

'Great, Becky. Thanks. I'll be about fifteen minutes.'

'See you then.'

As Sterling put the receiver down his mood lifted. Having Becky and Mike on board made all the difference. He didn't lack courage, and he knew he was impulsive, but this next phase needed more – specialised resources, planning, coolness and support. Becky and Mike had all those separately and between them.

'Summarise for me, Frank, can you?' said Mike Strange from behind the bar. Becky leaned next to him, one eye on the conversation and the other on the pub so that she was ready with service.

'Becky hasn't told you?' said Sterling.

'No, I've only just got back. And she thought it should come from the horse's mouth, as it were.'

'OK.' Sterling shifted on his bar stool and began his monologue, flat and Crown Court style, to keep him focused and because he knew that Mike would want it that way. He included what he planned as well as what he'd done. When he'd finished, Mike whistled softly – startling because in Sterling's experience he usually gave no tells.

'The business with the window. I don't think that's going to work. Becky?'

'I agree. The operation you've been describing has its amateurish aspects – after all, education is the main business – but someone will probably go around and do some kind of check beforehand. Also, Frank, drama studios are bare places. You know that from your recce. Where are you going to put yourself? Behind a curtain? In a cupboard that is unlikely to exist, and if it exists is unlikely to be big enough, or in the right place? In the control room? There'll be people in there.

'However we do this, we have to make a lot of assumptions. In the end, balancing everything out, you might not be able to get in at all. But there is a better chance if we do things a different way.'

Sterling took a bite of his sandwich and nodded. They knew what they were doing, Mike and Becky. What he liked about the conversation were the references to 'we'. It looked as though the task force had expanded to three.

An hour later, the planning was done. Sterling's own preliminary efforts now seemed impossibly naïve, while the new approach seemed plausible if breathtakingly ambitious. 'Right,' he said, 'I'd better go away and sort myself out.'

Becky put a hand on his arm. 'We know you've got bottle, Frank, and you'll be all right in a scrap if it comes to it.' She looked at his empty pint glass. 'But how's your fitness?'

'Not bad. I got caught out on another case a few months ago so I've got myself back into shape. I'll do a run this afternoon and another tomorrow morning.'

'Include some sprints,' said Mike, with what Sterling, because he knew him so well, recognised as the barest hint of a wry smile.

Chapter 10

Saturday 10 October - Fireworks

They were in Southwood Beach Parlour, Sterling for the second time in a week. It was the fag end of Saturday afternoon, and they cultivated a perception for anyone looking on that they were three autumn day-trippers having a last coffee before the long trek home. All were dressed in dark anoraks. A keen observer might notice that Sterling's trousers were smart and neatly pressed, and slightly incongruous above his trainers, but everyone was allowed a little eccentricity. The way he scratched at his neat grey beard, which exactly matched the grey of his hair, might have indicated a rash, were it not for the fact that it was false, and expertly applied by Mike back in the pub. It wasn't yet dark, but twilight wouldn't be lasting long under the heavy skies. In half an hour's time, when the sun officially set, it would be still and very dark. 'Just what we need,' Mike had said. 'Hopefully, everything else will fall into place.'

The café was winding up for the day. At 6 o'clock, one of the girls behind the counter went to the door to flip the sign from 'Open' to 'Closed' and turn the lock on the door. She lingered there ready to let the stragglers still inside out into the silent dusk. Sterling watched her yawn, half completed before she put a bored hand to her open mouth. Another girl wiped the tables. The manager, goateed and shaven-headed, looked as though he was cashing up. Whatever their evening plans, thought Sterling, they'd almost certainly be duller than his own.

'We'd better go,' said Becky. 'Timing is everything.'

The girl let them out, and they walked along the esplanade towards the college. Sterling felt the usual tingle before action – the familiar Marchurch Dreamworld sensation – and he knew it would be helpful for whatever he was getting into. Plan A was insertion – he smiled at the term Mike used – at the rear entrance. It was more risky than Plan B, through the door in the wall at the other end of the college, but if their calculations were correct, Sterling would be much closer to where he needed to be for the next phase. The back of the college and the area around it were dark. The task force was benefiting from the recent removal of streetlights and later switching on of the ones that remained. No one was about in the hiatus between afternoon and evening. Becky and Sterling moved up the road, arm in arm, as Mike approached the side pedestrian gate. At the top of the road, they turned around and strolled casually back. Mike had worked his magic. In the inky blackness, Sterling eased inside and made his way to the shelter of Glen Lodge. Once in position behind the hedge, he knew that Becky would re-lock the gate. Phase 1 was over.

He settled down to wait. Their second assumption might be correct. If something were going to happen this evening, it wouldn't be until much later on. He sank to his haunches. He had never minded the waiting when he was on the job. In fact early hours stints in squad cars with Andy Nolan had been amongst the most entertaining of his career. The problems they'd sorted out. The criminal justice system they'd put entirely right. He wondered what Andy Nolan was up to now. It wouldn't be long till he was a detective inspector. He'd always had one of the best deductive minds Sterling had come across in his time in the Kent police.

He checked the grip bag he'd brought with him. Mike had suggested outfits for every sartorial eventuality during the evening, and the advice seemed sound. He looked at his watch. 6:50. It was going to be a long wait.

At 8 o'clock, the screen of his mobile telephone lit up. 'Signs of life at the rear entrance and at the doors of the college hotel building. Stand by.'

Sterling felt another frisson. He, Becky and Mike had been right again. It looked as though Phase 2 was on. He could see nothing from behind the hedge at Glen Lodge, but the others were watching for him. He waited for the next instruction. It came at just before 9 o'clock. 'Dinner jacket and bow tie.' He reached inside the grip bag, got out what he needed and changed quickly, shivering in the windless, cool October night. Doubt began its worming. What was wrong with trying to get in through that back window? This hiding in plain sight business was insane. He steadied himself and started some deep breathing. He had his authorisation in his pocket. He had back up. I'm just going into a small provincial FE college on the south coast, he told himself. It's not James bloody Bond and S.M.E.R.S.H... Get a grip.

The next message came silently up on the screen. 'Lots of activity. Go.' Sterling shoved the bag under the hedge and out of sight and brushed himself down.

He put on the spyglasses, with tiny video camera embedded in the frame, which Becky had supplied. They were tight on his face and the nose clips would soon start pinching, but footage was essential and he didn't intend to use anywhere near the four hours' battery time. He caught the sleeves of his jacket in his fingers and palms and pulled them down. He checked that his bow tie, a clip-on affair, but of good quality, was straight, and looked down at the highly polished shoes that had replaced his trainers. He couldn't see, but he was sure they'd do. After a final deep breath, a poor man's Michael Caine stepped towards the back car park.

Mike was right. It was busy, and could have been like a building site, or a military base, or anywhere where people scurried about, except that everything was in almost complete darkness. As large cars and SUVs came through the gates, only their sidelights continued to show as parking attendants directed them into spaces. No one noticed as Sterling merged into the throng in front of the college hotel in the underpass. In the group, exclusively consisting of men generally older than Sterling, everyone was silent. Occasionally, nods were exchanged, but Becky and Mike were right again. These were not people who were well acquainted. Sterling leaned on the glass beside the doors and tried to make himself as insignificant as possible.

Gradually the hubbub in the car park and up to the hotel dissipated into the air. The automatic doors of the hotel swished open and a tall, elegant, slender woman in a dark blue sleeveless evening dress with a small diamond brooch pinned at the heart and hair piled up in an elaborate braided blonde bun appeared in front of the dinner-suited men. Could this be the Mrs Jenkinson the hotel receptionist referred to earlier in the week?

'Good evening, gentlemen,' she said. 'Many apologies for the short delay. As you can imagine, there is a very small window of opportunity for us to get everything ready. As usual, we have prepared a little surprise for you before the main evening's entertainments. It's very different this time, but we think you'll love it. Don't worry about the 'No smoking' notices around the building. We suspend the normal rules whilst you are here. Now please follow your hosts as we complete our preparations.'

She stepped aside and the group, probably about thirty strong, thought Sterling, entered the large atrium where he had talked to the receptionist earlier. There was an air of submission as the guests allowed themselves, sheep-like, to take waiting flutes of champagne by the inner door and be herded, glasses to hand, into the corridor beyond the hotel area. Sterling tried to keep himself in the middle. So far he was relieved that he had recognised no one. The hosts at the front and back of the group were large and kitted out in ill-fitting dinner suits themselves. Sterling had been cold behind the hedge at Glen Lodge. Now he felt the perspiration trickling in tiny rivulets down his back, and his collar had begun to chafe. He wondered what phase he was in now. What did it matter? Forget the bloody phases.

He concentrated on trying to remember the route he and his fellow sheep were taking. He recognised the internal transition from the Cara to the Lavender Building. When the flock was shepherded into the drama studio and he and his fellow guests were directed to the tiered platform of seats looking down in a semi-circle at the curtain at the back, he knew that another of his hunches had been right. He sank down into the anonymity of a middle row and allowed himself a little prayer of thanks for the dim light. Becky had been right. The fact that something was going on in the college that should not be going on was working to his advantage. Security was loose. There were no tickets and checks, except presumably at the front gate, and he was already inside. The lights, so far, were low. And his glasses, grey beard and hair, expertly prepared, made him a plausible part of the crowd.

On the platform, quiet snatches of conversation and brief exchanges began here and there among the dinner-suited men as the drinks loosened tongues. Sterling stared forward and held himself aloof. His preparations with Becky and Mike had included a cover story. He was a property developer up from Dovethorpe for a bit of fun. But he didn't want to get involved if he could help it. Muzak came from some-where, and then the smoke and aroma of newly lit cigars. Very naughty, thought Sterling – the college a smoke-free zone and all. There would be people busy with the air fresheners later on.

After a few minutes, the muzak faded away, the lights dimmed and a spotlight focused just in front of the centre of the curtains. When Hissing Sid appeared in his own dinner suit, the wind tunnel, swept-back look if anything enhanced by his get up, Sterling instinctively shrank down in his seat, even as he realised that the MC could not possibly see the audience or individuals in it.

'Gentlemen, good evening once again from me, Sidney Brown, your principal host tonight. To those of you who have been with us before, a warm welcome back. We constantly try and improve your experience here, and we don't think you will be disappointed. If this is your first visit, I can assure you it doesn't get any less exciting, and we are confident that you will return again and again. Without any further ado, let the fun begin. Gentlemen, *The Hairdresser*. Enjoy!'

The black curtains drew back at the same pace as Hissing Sid walked off into the wings at the side. The spotlight focused on a black hairdressing chair in the centre of the stage. A large horizontal mirror had been set up at a tilt above and behind the chair like a demonstration mirror of the sort used in college kitchens when lecturer-chefs do demonstrations. To the side of the chair was a trolley of hairdressing implements – curlers, scissors and cans of spray. The muzak began again. Cigar smoke curled up into the criss-cross of lights below the ceiling. There was a rustle of jackets in the audience as men leaned forward. From behind the curtain at the back of the studio a girl emerged in diamanté ballet pumps, black silk leggings and a cashmere top that showed a generous cleavage. Sterling shifted in his seat. More perspiration dribbled down his back, and not because the temperature in the studio was high. He slipped a finger under his collar to try to relieve the chafing. The planners had got another assumption right. It was Hannah Williamson fussing redundantly and over-theatrically around the trolley. But after that it was all wrong.

There was some movement behind the curtain. Hannah went to it and a tall, well-built young man in a white shirt and dark jeans emerged, apparently needing a cut, though his hair was already short and neat and well groomed like a young footballer's. It wasn't long before any perfunctory pretence of hairdressing activity was over. Hannah leaned over and whispered in the young man's ear, her chest pressing against his arm. The scissors were put aside and then they were kissing. The shirt was the first item of clothing to be discarded. A combination of the young man's muscles and its tight fit gave Hannah a momentary struggle as she pulled it over his head. Flames licked extravagantly down from a tattoo on his upper right arm. The muscles didn't end at the biceps and deltoids. The cashmere top was next and the audience emitted a small collective gasp.

As the performance continued, Sterling continued his squirming. He'd expected a smutty kind of farce perhaps. A burlesque show with Hannah in the troupe. At the more risqué end of the spectrum some pole-dancing. Perhaps a striptease. But that was the trouble with assumptions. They could be so inaccurate. For the purposes of the investigation, of course, he had seen enough after two minutes. On the other hand, given the event, the setting and the clientele, there was no chance that he could leave without raising suspicions.

In the darkened studio, he reflected on how people who mattered to him questioned what Angela referred to as his 'moral compass'. It had bewildered his socialist father that Sterling seemed so indifferent to social injustice and inequality. Angela appreciated his support in her battles to defend and develop her library, but wished he'd provide it not just because they were friends. Andy Nolan praised his policing skills but lamented his alleged focus on results rather than victims. They'd got it wrong. This was wrong: college employees – *college employees* – manipulating two young students into a sordid show for a depraved audience. The whole thing was rotten. The problem was … he didn't stop watching.

At the end, the actors having run through their repertoire to its predictable conclusion, two shining faces looked out at the darkened audience. The expression on the young man's was bashful, gormless and relieved, all in a strange collision. On Hannah's there was unadulterated triumph and ecstasy.

Then a movement, easy to spot because of Sterling's heightened sense of awareness and because the room was still and mesmerised, caught his attention towards the back near the door. Johnny Fontana stood there in the shadows. His expression, in the gloom, was much harder to read. Sterling thought he saw longing and desire. But there was also vulnerability as he leaned forlornly against the wall, and most of all, a kind of bitter, knowing jealousy.

Another sound came from an assembled company too stunned to think of applause – this time, a kind of collective sigh that rippled softly through the studio. As for Sterling, he felt his Adam's apple bob as he swallowed and tried to clear the furriness from his throat. On top of everything else, another contradictory thought materialised. Now he knew exactly what Hannah meant by 'liking a man with a bit of go'.

Chapter 11

Saturday 10 October - Flight

The curtains whispered across to meet in the middle, removing the panting participants from view. As they closed, Hissing Sid emerged from the side of the stage to the centre. It looked as though he too was struggling with perspiration, which streaked down the side of each cheek in tiny snail's trails, and with his collar, as he stretched and twisted his neck. His voice, in Sterling's experience hoarse, was even thinner and more strained as he struggled to get his words out. Frequent throat clearing only brought limited improvement.

'Goodness,' he croaked. 'That was quite something. Thanks to Darren and Hannah for getting the evening off with a ...' he paused for a second, as if realising what he was going to say but too late to change course, 'bang.' A ripple of mirth, which gained strength as the men relaxed, washed through the smoky studio, and a rueful smile found its way onto Hissing Sid's features. 'We can provide further, more ... hands-on entertainment in the hotel if you would like a break from the tables, and Hannah herself, one of our stars, will be available. And of course we can provide for all tastes, predilections ... and orientations. Please follow your hosts back to the hotel area.'

Sterling knew he should get out. With Johnny Fontana around, and others here who might have seen him around the college, he could be rumbled at any time, no matter how subtle his disguise, and there might not be a better opportunity. But this was just the starter. Hissing Sid had indicated as much. He allowed himself to be carried along in the slow movement of the flock through the bottleneck of the studio door and back into the corridor.

When they all got back to the atrium in the hotel area, it had been transformed. Now there were card tables set up in rows on one side of the aisle between the hotel entrance and the door towards the studio, and a large roulette table on the other. Smiling, heavily made up young women in skimpy French maid uniforms now held the trays of Champagne, with name badges and the words 'Available for fun' inscribed beneath. Behind the roulette table a bar had been opened, with bow-tied young men ready to take orders. Sterling looked up to the gallery. Each bedroom also had a bow-tied attendant complete with white gloves, and surveying the whole scene, her little empire, was the woman in the blue evening dress. He shook his head with a tiny movement. This was worse than he'd ever expected.

'Something wrong, Sir?' said a French maid.

Sterling looked at her and down at her badge, pinned to the flimsy blouse over her left breast. 'Janeen. Available for fun' it said. Her dark hair was bound tightly in a ponytail that gave her green eyes a slanted look.

'No, um, Janeen,' said Sterling. 'It's just that I haven't been before and it's pretty amazing.'

'Oh, this is just the beginning. It's much livelier later on. Perhaps you'd like to come upstairs with me, relax a bit, get in the mood.'

'Nice offer, Janeen, but I'm booked to join one of the tables. Maybe a rain check.'

'Certainly, Sir.' She smiled brightly and drifted off with her tray. How did that bit work, thought Sterling. Fixed payment for the night? Payment and commission? Commission only? Direct payments from customers and a percentage to the house? It didn't really matter. None of the details of the parallel college really mattered, just evidence.

He made his way to the table nearest the bar and furthest from the hotel entrance.

A croupier welcomed him. 'Are you joining us, Sir?'

'Yes, if you can explain how it all works.'

'Certainly, Sir… What happens is that…'

Then everything changed. The young man's voice came from far away as Sterling tuned it out and addressed a more pressing concern. Johnny Fontana had obviously gone outside and come back through the glass doors. Now he was standing just within the atrium, surveying the whole area, presumably in some security capacity. His eyes fell upon Sterling at the blackjack table at the other end of the room. They narrowed imperceptibly. Sterling could almost see the thought processes behind that hard, cold exterior – 'I know that face' – and then realisation. Sterling had vaguely recognised others in the room who might have seen through his disguise. But no one was as sharp or alert as Johnny Fontana. It was time to go.

'Sir, did you get that? Do I need to say anything again?'

Sterling pushed back his chair. The planning session came back to him. Assumption: you'll get recognised at some stage. Response: scarper (as Becky had wryly put it). The front exit was always out of the question. Security would be heaviest there, and he wouldn't even make it to the car park. It was back the way he came, and the emergency exit from the studio.

Johnny Fontana couldn't have been more than 20, but he had a natural air of authority. He moved quickly, gesturing to two associates and pointing discreetly to Sterling from the other end of the aisle. For all Fontana's urgency, to anyone not involved in the drama he might have been pointing out a Champagne spillage to be cleared up. Sterling considered shouting 'Police raid. Nobody move' on the grounds that everyone would move, haphazardly and in a panic, which would give him more time. But just then, Hannah, in a small, simple black sleeveless mini-dress and heels, made her entrance with a small entourage. There was a surge of people from their chairs and a swell of applause. Sterling slipped behind the retinue and back down the corridor. She'd given him some precious extra seconds. He remembered the way well. As he padded briskly along, he sent out a pre-drafted text message. 'Back door. Now.'

He burst from the corridor into the drama studio. The organisers had thought of everything, because there was a little band of cleaners and other staff in purple and green work-smocks with ECOT emblazoned on the fronts. A girl with a pale face was kneeling in front of the hairdressing chair rubbing vigorously with a large cloth. Everyone looked up from their spraying, furniture shifting and mopping as Sterling moved across the floor, the heady smell of air freshener bringing a tickle to his nose. He struggled at the back with the Velcro strips that held the curtains together, his fingers fumbling. Then he swirled through the curtains as two of Johnny Fontana's henchmen came through the studio door. Sterling crashed against the bars of the emergency doors, which doubled as the entrance for vans and trucks with props for performances. Clearly the college's health and safety culture was intact even for sex shows, gambling and whoring – he'd half expected the doors to be blocked.

He gasped in the sudden cold air and tumbled face first onto the asphalt. The pursuers would be catching up. He scrambled up the bank in the darkness on his grazed hands and knees, knowing and regretting that he'd be leaving tracks in the damp earth, and lurched off behind and parallel to what he assumed was the Lavender Building. If his calculations were correct, he was on the way to the door in the wall. He had long abandoned all thought of assumptions and phases. Now it was about getting out in one piece.

He could see little. Away from the smart and probably well-lit public areas, the college, like all institutions, reverted again to type. The ground felt scrubby, uneven and rough beneath his feet, a mixture of grass and stones. He pressed on, not running but shambling briskly. His pursuers would surely also be unfamiliar with the terrain. He made out the Portakabin looming ahead and knew he was on track. His breath was already ragged, even though he'd only come a few metres. He should have done some extra sprints. His breathing and the thumping of his heart prevented him from hearing if anyone was behind him, or even if they were close. As he reached the back of the Portakabin, he realised with dismay that a fence cut him off from that part of the wall where the door was sited and that he'd have to work his way round the front. At least up this obscure corner of the campus there were no lights and Becky and Mike would be waiting. Johnny Fontana's henchmen, if they caught up with him, would be no match for Sterling and his special forces. With luck the fire in the snug of the pub would still have some life in it. He could taste the Scotch. What a story he'd have to tell.

He stumbled and shuffled around the bulge of the hut and over to the door in the wall, key from his pocket clumsily at the ready. It went into the keyhole all right, but when he came to turn it, no tumblers tumbled, no lock clicked reassuringly – the only sound a forlorn, unyielding rattle. The imagined taste of Scotch turned to bile as he went to work more desperately. A shape took form out of the shadows and became Johnny Fontana, hair gleaming dully in the murky light. Two other figures emerged next to him. Something else also gleamed dully, lower down. Sterling's long experience of patrolling Marchurch seafront told him what it was. At that moment, the others following him up from the emergency doors of the drama studio burst from around the corner and almost cannoned into the welcoming party. After that small drama, Johnny Fontana stepped forward.

'You must think we're stupid,' he sneered. 'Snooping around and assuming we wouldn't keep an eye out for you, last week and tonight. Granted we can't run everything as tightly as we'd like, given the circumstances, but really... Did you think we'd not spot that you'd nicked the door key? This door is so handy for us – of course we'd notice if someone else started nosing around.'

Sterling stood still, trying to regularise his breathing. Then he shrugged.

The young man leant back against the door, relishing his control, twirling his knife. 'We'll have your phone. And those glasses. They're chunky. I reckon there's a recording device in there – a camera or something. I'll need that. I reckon that's all you've got, apart from what you'll say you've seen and heard. We can handle that – the idiot rantings of a loose-cannon private investigator. But it might not come to that. Perhaps a bit of an incentive to keep your mouth shut will do the trick.' He motioned to the heavily built young men beside him, who stepped forward in a hostile semi-circle.

Why did those who gave out beatings ever think they'd shut people up, thought Sterling. Surely it would do the opposite. Not that he relished a kicking in any circumstances. Where were Becky and Mike? Had they got his message?

There was a click and the area around the wall, the door and the corner of the science lab was bathed with harsh phosphorescent light. Sterling put his arm up to his eyes, as startled and disoriented as the young men around him. Yes, he thought. The message had got through. In the same instant as the floodlight came on, the door, instead of just opening on its hinges, crashed from the vertical to almost the horizontal in one violent movement, crushing Johnny Fontana's legs and pelvis and pinning him entirely to the ground. He howled – a confused mixture of anger, pain and frustration. A small, balaclava-wearing figure leapt through the wall, used the door as a springboard and landed next to Sterling, taking his arm and leading him like a blind man towards the bridle path. Sterling heard Johnny Fontana's gasp and curse as the momentary extra weight of the jumper added more pressure to the door, but then he was rallying his troops even while he was pinned to the damp gravel.

Sterling couldn't resist his impetuosity. As he and Becky bypassed the door he stooped down to the young man's ear. 'Yes,' he said. 'I do think you're stupid,' before he allowed Becky to take him swiftly away. They ran up the path, crossed the railway bridge and reached the van parked in one of the quiet side streets away from the college. Moments later Mike appeared with the lighting equipment and Becky drove them all away.

'No problems back there?' she said.

'No,' said Mike. 'It was a risk using the door like that, but the element of surprise neutralised the possible disadvantage of the opposition's greater numbers. The tear gas helped. You'd gone by then of course.'

Sterling smiled in his uncomfortable niche in the back of the van. Assumptions. Risks. Phases. He thought he might try a little gentle ribbing. 'What kept you? I thought I was going to get a nasty roughing up.'

Mike never seemed to get irony. 'We were just waiting to see if that young man would say anything else that might be helpful to your case, Frank. We didn't think it would be too dangerous to do that. Mind you, he may not just have had a beating up in his thoughts. You saw that knife.' Mike was quiet for a moment. 'Although we got out of that OK in the end, that boy is formidable. I watched him from the wall before you came. He knew what he was doing. All the others obeyed him without question. He's young, but I know that type. Competent, well-organised, a natural leader, charismatic even. And ruthless. Completely ruthless. You should watch out.'

Sterling let his body relax into the rattle and rhythm of the van. He closed his eyes. Mike was confirming what Hannah and others had intimated and Sterling had concluded for himself. You didn't control an operation like that, where so many people were involved and a little blabbing could ruin everything, without being strong and intimidating, and paying good wages, but were those things enough?

'He thought I was a one-man band, though, so he didn't get it all right. But I know what you mean. It must be about half past eleven. Do you reckon there will still be a fire in the snug?'

'We can probably revive it,' said Becky.

'Good. And the drinks are on me of course. Mine will be a Scotch. Double. You might need something strong yourself. Becky, this is even more amazing than the warehouse.'

'I can barely wait,' she murmured.

Chapter 12

Saturday 10 October to
Monday 12 October - Sacked

Sterling rolled the whisky round his tongue. The fire was doing well in the grate of the snug and he felt good. Becky shook her head. Even Mike sat still in his chair, looking into his glass as if he couldn't quite believe what he'd heard.

'What now, Frank?'

'Danger money,' said Sterling. 'The bill is going to be eye-watering, bearing in mind what I've been through. And I'm going to have to find a way to thank you for what you've done. Again. But in terms of the case and the college, I'm not entirely sure. I need to bounce some ideas off you, if you can stand it after all the evening's excitement.'

'Go ahead,' said Becky.

'Well, your operation has just been penetrated and the person doing it has just got away. What next?'

'They'd think about what you're going to do and take the appropriate action. What's the worst thing you can do now? Maybe dial 999? But what are you going to say? That there's a break-in at the college? What's a squad car going to find? With a few quick adjustments, a normally functioning training hotel. Also,' – Becky was thinking hard – 'they know you, Frank. You've been going into that college and stirring things up. They know what you're like. A maverick. A bit of a lone wolf. Unorthodox. There are some sophisticated elements in that operation. Good brains. You've been taken on by that principal, so they'll be thinking that you'll report to her as agreed. There are all the PR aspects. If I know the principal and the college, they'll want to avoid scandal. And you'll want your money once you've delivered your report, so you're buying into that. You're probably feeling a bit proprietorial about the case too.'

'How well you know me, Becky.'

'Of course.' She smiled.

'So,' said Mike, 'they'll carry on tonight. It's one o'clock now so there are only a few more hours, and then they'll remove all traces of what's happened. They do that anyway, so there's no change of routine there. They'll probably sort out all the other obvious stuff as well, just to be on the safe side, and they'll start a campaign to discredit you. You'll need to be ready for that. Even the photos and video footage might not be completely convincing. I'll have that footage ready for you tomorrow by the way, ready for when you go and see the principal. That blonde boy... he's a worry. He and his associates have probably done their home-work on you. I'm thinking that you might need to lie low for a bit, maybe stay here in the pub.'

'Maybe,' said Sterling. 'But I don't think they'd have given me anything more than a beating up, Mike. This doesn't feel as though it's an openly violent organisation. It does things in a more sneaky way.

Threats and intimidation. I don't think I'm in any physical danger at the moment.'

'Better safe than sorry. The offer's there,' said Becky.

'OK. Thanks. As usual. You know, we've found out a lot, and we've found out enough for Margaret Kingston to start sorting things out, but I don't think we've found out everything. And we've found out nothing that links Jane Casterton to what's been going on.'

'It's always messy, Frank,' said Mike. 'And it always turns out differently from what you expect. Just reporting back will set things off in a new direction.'

Sterling nodded. Mike was rarely wrong.

Sterling had tried to phone Margaret Kingston on Sunday morning, and sent a text, but there had been no reply. Perhaps she was one of those people who completely switched off at the weekend, which seemed unlikely, or, more plausibly, she was away. No matter. He was seeing her on Monday afternoon. Sunday had been quiet. When he got back from the Cinque Ports Arms, no one had firebombed his house. No one had tailed him down Holy Ghost Alley, across St Peter's Street, down Milk Alley, into No Name Street and past the Guildhall. As he had said to Becky and Mike, what he was up against was threats, intimidation, insinuation. The leaders of ECOT's shadow organisation, whoever they really were, would have realised that they couldn't stop the damage, but they could work to limit it. On Monday morning, when Sterling arrived at his office with the memory stick Mike had given him, he realised how.

On the mat was a small envelope addressed to Frank Sterling, Consultant. He took it up to his office and booted up the computer. First he reviewed the evidence from the spyglasses. It had come out well, jerky in places in the hotel and drama studio and between them, positively chaotic in his escape. He winced as the emergency doors burst open and the ground rose up to meet him as he sprawled. His grazed palms and knees gave a kind of collective twinge. Then there was jagged darkness and his own hoarse breathing until Johnny Fontana's disembodied voice by the college wall, and after that the burst of light that obscured everything. Margaret Kingston would not be able to ignore any of this, or the separate stick of photographs from the sortie to the warehouse in the Horticulture Section. So far so good.

He opened the mystery envelope, and a new memory stick clattered onto his blotter. He reflected that he might have been more careful. Supposing it had been some kind of letter bomb? He clicked it into the computer. It only contained one file, entitled 'A Message for Frank Sterling'. 'Oh-oh,' he muttered softly. He had never been one to put things off. He clicked twice and the display started with a caption.

'THINK, Frank.'

The caption faded and a blurred picture gradually came into sharp resolution. He leaned forward. Surely not... Yes, he was looking at Hannah Williamson, and she was cutting his hair. Pictures never lie. They really were getting on famously. The editing was artful as she snipped and they laughed and smiled together. He knew what would come next. There it was. Hannah leaned in, pressed her ample cleavage against his arm, did a little half-hearted snipping and whispered in his ear.

The editing went from artful to brilliant. Now she was slipping off her clothes, the same outer layers, the black silk leggings and the cashmere top, in the drama studio as in the hairdressing salon – the same lighting and the same barber's chair as well. The transition was seamless. When she clambered on to the naked youth and began her energetic riding, his fiery tattoo was nowhere to be seen, nor any other evidence in the rest of the performance that it was he and not Sterling enjoying, and giving, vigorous attention. So that was why Sterling had been guided to the chair in the corner of the salon away from other distractions and under the bright lights. Sterling knew he had been played. Now he realised exactly how. He felt no rancour towards Hannah. She might have been part of the play but he didn't think she'd be aware of this.

The scene faded. Sterling leaned forward again. New pictures segued into view – headlines from local newspapers a year or two back. 'Cop denies using too much force in arrest', 'Officer in trouble – yet again'. Someone had done their research and succeeded in digging up some dirt. The clip ended with another caption. 'KEEP QUIET, Frank. It can only get worse. If this goes viral....' and then faded completely away. Sterling pushed himself back in his chair and rubbed his eyes. They were good. You couldn't deny that. But they didn't dig deeply enough. A few weeks later after the first headlines, the new ones were 'Burglar's allegations of brute force by officer dismissed' and 'Officer commended for bravery in uneven fight'. And anyway, the psychology was all wrong. Sterling didn't give a damn what they did, and he was pretty sure he could prove it wasn't him in that clip. Then something else occurred to him. If they were using this ploy on him, they were probably using the same technique elsewhere.

He unplugged the memory stick and slipped it in his pocket. He had time to sort out his report and invoice before he went back over to ECOT to see the principal. He made sure there was a danger money premium and something for Becky and Mike's trouble. The unease was starting up again, like a persistently returning headache. He'd be glad when this case was over. He spell-checked what he'd written, printed two copies and set off for the Southwood train.

He was cautious on the journey. Of course there was the usual unease, but overlaid on top of that were thoughts about what Johnny Fontana and his minions might have in mind for him. Someone had delivered the memory stick, so they knew where his office was. At the Ramston and Southwood stations, he kept alert and away from the platform edges. On the tramp from Southwood station, which he now knew so well, no one followed him or threatened attack in any of the alleys. As he approached ECOT down the incline, there was no welcoming party at the gates or the front door of the main entrance. It was as if the shadow organisation had shrunk back into itself, with its leaders content to believe that their threats would be effective.

Adele was at her desk in her office in the Tuckett Building. Her eyes were as red-rimmed as ever, but she managed a smile when Sterling appeared through the door. 'Mr Sterling, nice to see you again. The principal is just finishing something off and then she'll be with you.'

When he entered the big office ten minutes later, she was at the window. As she turned to face him, she seemed to be wringing her hands. She drew a breath. 'Good morning, Frank. Shall we go to the sofa?'

'No,' said Sterling. 'I think I should have this chair at your desk, and I may have to come round to show you something on your computer.

'Intriguing,' said Margaret Kingston.

'I've done a report as promised, but I'll give you a longish verbal overview, and hand the paperwork over afterwards.'

'So you've finished your investigation....' There was a note of hope in the principal's voice.

'Kind of. Let me talk you through what I've found out.' He put his file on his side of the desk and clasped his hands in front of him. He knew he could do it without a single note. 'You were right, Margaret. Something is going on here, and it's probably much worse than you imagined. I don't know everything but I know enough to tell you that you've got a parallel organisation working on this site, a kind of large, malignant parasite. When you engaged me last Tuesday, I went for a walk around the college, and even that early I started finding things. For example, there's a door in the side wall that looks rotten but is actually very well maintained. It's used as a convenient entrance and exit. Another example: the vending machine at the bottom of this building – it's probably been changed now, but there was a metal panel bolted across the bottom of the display window. The row of goods it covered up I'm pretty certain contained drugs of various descriptions. My hunch about fancy cars and misdeeds is also probably right, though I don't have direct evidence for that.

'Now for specific things that I do have evidence for. I went to the Horticulture Section and had a look at that green warehouse in the corner.'

'It's empty,' said the principal. 'We didn't get the European funding. And it may have asbestos in it.'

'No,' said Sterling. 'It's not empty. Last week it was full of cannabis plants growing in perfectly controlled conditions. Then there's your training hotel area in the Cara Building and the drama studio in Lavender. On Saturday night I gatecrashed an event there. Or rather, events. A sex show in the studio, card and roulette tables in the lobby-cum-atrium area, and a brothel in the bedrooms in the gallery upstairs.'

Margaret Kingston got up and began pacing up and down between the desk and the door. She put her fingertips to her temples, as if all the information was giving her a bad headache. 'Lord. Who's involved?'

'I'll come to that. First, the evidence.' Sterling got out the memory stick that he and Mike Strange had downloaded photos and video clips onto. 'Here. Plug this in.' He opened two files and he and the principal sat together in front of her computer. The first file showed some photographs from the top of the warehouse structure. Sterling had been careful to do them in sequence, showing the roof, the panels and the skylight that hadn't been covered up properly. There could be no doubt about where the cannabis was growing. 'The head of the Horticulture Section....'

'Pat Manton, Section Manager,' said the principal.

'That's her. She steered me away from that building, although that doesn't prove she's involved.'

Then he opened the video file. Mike Strange's spyglasses had produced good sound and pictures as

Sterling had gone into the hotel, filtered with the crowd into the drama studio and taken in Hannah's performance. In the atrium, Sterling looked around, up and down and left and right, the camera in the glasses making it obvious what was happening and where. His encounter with Janeen came through clearly in the computer's speakers. Sterling felt himself flush. Mike should have edited that bit. Through the spy-lens, Sterling seemed to be taking a very keen interest in Janeen's breasts. 'Looking at the name on her badge,' he murmured softly. The principal seemed too rapt to notice. At various stages during the screening, she gasped and muttered. 'My God,' Sterling heard her say. 'Mrs Jenkinson, in an evening dress. Dear Jesus, Hissi....' She stopped and glanced at Sterling who tried to stay poker-faced. 'Sid Brown.' As the screen showed Sterling's flight, cinema verité-style, through the corridors back into the drama studio, out of the emergency doors and up to the back gate, she looked at him again. 'This was dangerous,' she said, and he nodded. When she saw the encounter with Johnny Fontana she looked hard at the screen. 'Student?' she asked, and Sterling nodded again. The end was dramatic, a burst of light too bright for the camera to assimilate, and then blankness.

'You can't have got all this by yourself.'

'No, but you don't need to know about my associates. There was no law-breaking on our part, and I had your authorisation.'

The principal nodded. She got up and started to pace again. 'I need to think. She told me... God, this is ten times worse than I was led to expect. Who else do you think is involved apart from those in the film?'

'What, you mean staff? Employees?'

'Yes.'

'Well, without evidence, it's a minefield.'

'Never mind evidence for the moment, Frank. You've done a good job in a very short time. Clearly you're competent, and because you're competent, and because of your reputation, I trust you. So, who else is involved?'

'Your caretaker, probably. I've got an idea who's behind the technology – one of the technical support officers. Other support staff. But they're small fry. Even those you might call the more senior people in the video clip – none of them is the head honcho.' Sterling paused. He wasn't sure how she'd take what he was going to say next. He could hear the usual rumbles outside the office. Someone was singing a re-released pop song accurately and tunefully outside. It sounded like *The Joker* and drifted faintly in. 'The blonde student in the video clip: his name is Johnny Fontana. He's young, but in spite of that I'd put him at number two in this parallel organisation. He's like a sergeant major. He's an enforcer. Charismatic. Well organised. Ruthless. People, even older people, are scared of him. And I've seen him with someone who fits the bill as the number one.'

'Jane Casterton,' said Margaret Kingston.

Sterling was still.

'It is, isn't it?'

'Off the record, and in the absence of direct evidence, since she certainly wasn't around on Saturday night ... Yes.'

'I knew it. She pretends to be supportive. She pretends to buy into my plans. And all the time there's this ... filth.

I need a drink,' she said abruptly. 'I suppose coffee will have to do. Would you like one, Frank?'

Adele came in with the tray, and the principal and Sterling graduated to the sofa. When Adele had gone, the principal was muttering to herself and twisting her fingers in agitation. She turned to Sterling. 'What's the legal position, Frank?'

'Where do I start? It's obviously illegal to have a cannabis factory on the premises, and it's certainly illegal to distribute drugs on a public campus via a vending machine, if I'm right about that. The sex show is hardly at a private party. I expect that is about public lewdness. You obviously don't have a gambling licence, do you? So that's very dodgy. And there'll certainly be no minute anywhere giving the green light to a brothel in the hotel. Those boys and girls, probably students here – 'available for fun' – they're being recruited and pimped, so there's that. Honestly, the list is so long, you'd need a criminal lawyer to get to the bottom of it. And remember, I think there's more.' He fished in his pocket for the second memory stick.

'More. Jesus. As if this isn't enough.'

Once again, the principal and Sterling hunched in front of the computer. 'Isn't that you having a haircut?'

'Yes,' said Sterling grimly. 'In your hairdressing salon upstairs. Keep watching.'

The principal flushed. 'Isn't that you…?'

'No, not anymore. Do you see what's been done here? A clever editor has taken footage from my haircut and fused it with the sex show on Saturday evening. That's why the girl is in the same outfit. It's been very skilfully done, but you can see differences if you look very closely. I was set up in the salon for exactly this purpose, and the people behind this found apparent skeletons in my cupboard to go with it. So you can add blackmail to all the other stuff. And think about it, Margaret. It's not just a small-town PI who's being blackmailed. There'll be others, including if necessary the blokes in the hotel on Saturday night – footage from cameras in the bedroom, whatever. The sex show will have been turned into a film clip. Think of all those lucrative revenue streams – blackmail, gambling, prostitution, porn – everything overlapping. In fact, it's probably more lucrative than running the college.'

The principal smiled wryly. 'The blackmail … it's not stopping you, is it, Frank? Here you are, presenting your report.'

'That stuff can't hurt me. It wouldn't be difficult to prove that it's not me in the later bits of the footage, and the headlines aren't accurate.'

'How does that matter, Frank? It's not about facts, or the truth. It's about what people can be led to believe.'

'My business is based on my reputation as an investigator, the results I get, and often word of mouth. I don't give a tinker's damn. Anyway, I react badly to intimidation.'

Sterling closed the blackmail file, took out the memory stick and put it back in his pocket, while Margaret Kingston returned to her favoured position at the window. He reflected on how tiny she was, but even in those circumstances strength and determination radiated from her. She turned back to the investigator at her desk.

'Yes, Frank, you've done an excellent job. The evidence looks solid and a good number of people are directly in the firing line. But this shadow, parallel organisation – the people behind it will have battened down the hatches, won't they?'

Mike Strange had said something similar in the snug on Saturday night. 'I think so. They'll have had time to clear out the warehouse and the vending machine. The training hotel will have been sorted out on the night. The technology stuff will have been wiped or removed to somewhere safer.'

The principal smiled a small, tight apologetic smile. 'So in a way, you've made yourself redundant.'

Sterling bridled, disbelieving. 'What, you don't want me to carry on?' He tapped the report and the memory stick he'd left on top of it. 'This is just the tip of the iceberg.'

'I don't disagree, Frank. But I've got the PR aspects to look at, the politics and so on. I've got to look at the big picture and find the best way out of this huge sorry mess. Of course I'll be making maximum use of what you've given me in college procedures, and of course I'll have to call the police in.'

He shrugged. He was sure he could have done some more. He had the knack of getting to the bottom of things. 'Well, you're the pay mistress....,' he said lightly, determined not to show his disappointment. 'Speaking of which, if I'm not carrying on, you'd better have this.' He took out his invoice from his jacket pocket and laid it on the desk, pointedly crossing out 'interim' and replacing it with 'final'.

The principal looked at the bill. 'Goodness, it mounts up quickly. My budget is going to take a hit. The Wednesday and Saturday totals are really high.'

'Danger money,' said Sterling, flatly.

'Ah,' said Margaret Kingston. 'Got it. Well, given the situation, fair enough.'

Chapter 13

Monday 12 October and Tuesday 13 October - Reconnection

Since he'd still got his visitor's pass and authorisation (in case I need to call you back in, the principal had said) he thought he'd pop down to the pottery and see Ellie Laski. If his presence in the college unsettled anyone in Shadow ECOT (as good a description as any), that would be a bonus.

He went down the stairs to the lower ground floor and towards the back door. He looked at the vending machine. Now row L was visible, L1, L2, L3, L4 and L5 stocked to the brim with Twix, Snickers and Mars bars, and a selection of crisps. Sterling looked closely and found what he was looking for. There were the screw holes, two on each side of the machine, which had been used to keep the metal plate in position. The empire strikes back... It was amateurish, but probably effective.

Ten minutes later, the pottery students did their usual imitation of a torrent as the first afternoon class ended. Sterling waited till torrent had become trickle and tapped on the open door.

Ellie Laski's head appeared from behind the open door of a kiln. 'Frank Sterling,' she smiled. 'Trailblazer extraordinaire. Come into the warm.'

'Thanks, Ellie.'

'Coffee?'

Sterling thought about her first offering. 'I've just had one, thanks.'

'OK. You can watch me drink mine.' She sat down a moment later with her mug. 'What on earth have you been up to, Frank? I assume it's connected with your activities. This place is awash with rumour, and astoundingly jittery. I could hardly get any work out of anyone today, and I'm famous for my classroom discipline.'

'I've noticed,' said Sterling. 'I have been busy, but I can't really tell you anything. You'll probably know more in the next few days. I've finished here. I just came down for a chat.'

'I'm glad you did.' She looked at him over her mug, a shy, uncharacteristically uncertain gesture. 'It's been crappy here over the last few weeks, and now it's as if a storm is brewing, and there's going to be a downpour. Some of us are going to get drenched.'

'How so?' said Sterling. He hadn't known Ellie Laski long, but her confident, assertive manner had just disappeared.

She looked away, up at the garden gnome with the fishing rod that looked down boss-eyed at the room. 'Oh, you know....'

'Not really,' said Sterling. He clasped his hands together under the table and made himself quiet.

The pottery teacher shook herself, drained her mug and stood up abruptly. 'I've got to get ready for the next lot. Last lap this afternoon.'

'Right,' said Sterling. 'I'd better make a move too.'

She walked him to the door. 'See you again soon.' It was mostly a statement, with a hint of a question.

'Yes, certainly. After the dust has settled. That would be very nice. Perhaps when you've got some more time.'

'You know where I am.'

Sterling nodded and made for the station. Johnny Fontana, the-boy-who-was-everywhere, was at the main gates with his henchmen. An onlooker would have assumed he was waiting for a lift. His cold blue eyes fixed Sterling with a malevolent glare. This time he said nothing, but on his face was a look, almost a smirk, that said well, the blackmail ploy hasn't worked but we've got everything under control. Sterling made himself stroll with a nonchalance he didn't feel across the road and into the alley next to the 1960s flats. He was more at ease when he was out of sight. This saga was going to run and run, even without his involvement.

On the viaduct into Ramston station, just before the change of trains for Sandley, he looked out under the grey October sky and even greyer slates of the town to the derelict grain mill to the south, a molar stump rising above the other buildings. Something Margaret had said stuck out like that stump. Amidst her agitation, there was an expression or a phrase – more than one perhaps – that wasn't quite right. He worried at it, but it would not come back to him. So long as he kept it in mind, experience told him that his subconscious would at some stage dredge it up. Something else irked him – the sacking that had come from nowhere – and the act and its abruptness were unsettling.

The next day, Sterling the erstwhile commuter reconnected with Sandley. He caught up with his correspondence and messages. He got out the polish and duster for his office and did some desultory tidying up. He went to the bank to pay in the cheque the college accounts office had made out for him. He contacted the people who might have work for him and arranged appointments, but though the work would pay, it looked dull. He was restless. The ECOT problem nagged away at him. There was another concern. He'd phoned Hannah Williamson, but her phone was going to voicemail and she wasn't returning his messages. Sterling felt a low-level edginess. He had created havoc on Saturday night. There must be a connection.

He went down to see Angela. He knew that she'd been at a conference for a couple of days. It was early afternoon and the library was busy, but when he put his head around the automatic door he could see her in her office behind the counter, tut-tutting, shaking her head and then tossing sheets of paper aside. She put her head in her hands. Sterling was about to withdraw when she looked up and saw him. Her impatient expression didn't change, but she motioned him in. Sterling could hear a hubbub in the children's area. A tall, gangly, dark-haired young man was reading to a group of toddlers and their parents, his voice full of excitement and mystery. His long fingers turned the pages as his eyes scanned his audience with an evangelising intensity. He too spotted Sterling at the door and acknowledged him for a short moment before his gaze returned to his excited listeners.

'Alright, Angie?'

'No, I'm bloody well not alright.' Angela Wilson never swore.

'Anything I can help with?' Normally, help went in the other direction, so Sterling looked on this as an opportunity.

'You can join my commando unit for an assault on County Hall. The mission will be to burn it to the ground. I also need a cyber-attack on the county's website. You might have some contacts with the hacking fraternity, or maybe even the hacking sorority, for that. I want to kidnap the whole of the Library Committee and hold it to ransom. Actually, why stop there? You can develop plans for snatching the government minister responsible for libraries.'

'OK, I can fit all that in. Do we need a manifesto or a ransom demand?'

'Leave those to me, but we'll need to release a video clip. You'd better be the cameraman.'

'Got it. I wonder if I can ask why I should be assisting you in this – just for motivational reasons really.'

'Of course you may, Frank. It's connected with the many years I spent working for my degree, getting a postgraduate library qualification and then actually being a librarian. In this role, as you may vaguely know, I am responsible for leading and managing the poorly paid staff of this library. Working with my similarly embattled colleagues across the county, I have to manage metadata, build databases, manage our internet area and sort out, supervise and edit content. For that I must have advanced information and communication technology skills. I supervise the cataloguing, indexing, stock selection, conservation and preservation of books. I oversee information retrieval and management and knowledge management. I apply long developed customer and community engagement skills. I collaborate with the schools, college and adult learning sectors.'

'Right. I am definitely in,' said Sterling. His loyalty was blind and unquestioning.

'I haven't finished my rant,' said Angela icily. 'To resume. So it irks me beyond bearing that the county wishes to dispense with a vital cadre of library assistants and replace them with volunteers. Not that I have anything against volunteers.'

'OK.' Now there was an inkling of where things were going.

'My own little complement is excellent – helpful, reliable, dedicated. I welcome their contribution to my little operation. But they are, or should be, in addition to regular, trained and salaried library staff, and not some kind of cheap, unskilled replacement so that the council and ultimately the government can save a bit of money. Actually, it probably wouldn't save money in the end. They still have to be trained and managed, and the shock to the service and plummeting standards would cause havoc.' She sighed. 'We'll have to start a campaign, another one.'

Sterling pictured turmoil. Police in riot gear in serried ranks cowering under a hail of rocks and missiles from an apoplectic elderly population outside closed libraries up and down the country, demanding entry. Parents and toddlers lying in roads blocking traffic. The bloodied faces of teenagers alleging police brutality. Shaky, blurred mobile footage of flare-ups and violence.

Library managers, their faces covered, denouncing the government on television. The Prime Minister at Question Time, embattled, perspiring, calling for order and calm, and promising a review.

'Enough of that. There's a union meeting coming up. We'll go on from there.'

'Well seriously, Angela, if there's anything I can do....'

'Keep borrowing. A couple of books a week. DVDs. Come down and do some research or read the papers. Tell everyone. Footfall and activity are key.'

The images in Sterling's head faded. This was humdrum, but no less important because of that.

'How's your ECOT thing going, Frank?' said Angela, switching suddenly.

'Got sacked.'

'What? Why? Hadn't you made any progress, or did Margaret think you weren't worth it?'

'Neither of those really. Given the timescale and the circumstances I did really well, and I had plans to take it even further, because I don't think we know the half of it, but Margaret had different ideas. She thought she had enough. "I'll take it from here" was her attitude. So....' Sterling shrugged.

'I can't say I'm that surprised, knowing Margaret.' There was a queue developing at the counter, and Angela's library assistant was beginning to struggle. 'I've got to go. Tell me all about it over a drink later.'

'Wilco,' said Sterling. He stepped out into Market Street. A walk around the town would clear his head. He set off up Milk Alley, crossed St Peter's Street and ducked into Holy Ghost Alley. He'd go down to the Strand and continue his walk by the quayside.

In the watery October sunshine, Sandley proved again why he had settled here, from the barbican guarding the bridge over the river to Earlsey to the Art Deco cinema in Delf Street at the other end. The town was shaped like a semi-circle, with the quayside and the river to the north acting as its diameter. He decided to walk along the circumference, starting outside the high walls of the Secret Garden and from there along the outer town path. Along the path he could see the tall chimneys of the Salutation hotel, and on the other side the weeping willows along the river, swaying docilely in the autumn breeze. He hadn't made a bad choice to leave the force. He could do as he pleased. There were no punishing shifts, no red tape, no bureaucracy and stupid rules to fall foul of (and fallen foul he frequently had). There were more visceral, complex reasons too. He couldn't take the waste and excess of a large organisation anymore. He was no active environ-mentalist, but he wanted to do no eco-harm. His current work made the best of his skills and diminished his weaknesses, chiefly a hot-headedness that got him into trouble.

But It was often too hand-to-mouth to be comfortable, and very occasionally he missed the banter and comradeship. He was nearer forty than thirty now, divorced these many years and orphaned even longer, and the future was uncertain. He left the back walls of the Secret Garden behind, and crossed the road leading down to Lower Sandley on the coast. Now the path curved round on top of an embankment like the earthworks of a hill-fort, with the town tucked behind. It made no sense if it was about flood protection. The danger to low-lying Sandley was at the diameter by the river, not on the circumference. He could see the tower of St George's Church just beyond his office, as the crow flies no more than four hundred metres away. Immediately below, the green keeper at Sandley Bowls Club fussed about on the too-good-to-be-true green surface, finding fault that ordinary mortals would never see. Sterling crossed another outward spoke, this time the road towards Deeping to the south. He beat down to the Pioneer supermarket and the winery next to it, tucked under the bank. He shopped in this part of town when he was flush. It happened rarely. Enough walking. He'd head back to his office down Delf Street.

As he passed in front of the supermarket doors, someone tapped his arm. 'Frank,' said Jack Cook.

Sterling remembered painfully how their last meeting had ended – in the kitchen of Jack's café, Jack pinned by his throat to the wall, his chef looking on, murder in Sterling's heart and throttling hand. He nodded and made to pass on.

'Frank,' said Jack again. 'Don't rush off, mate.'

Sterling turned to the heavyset man in the untidy overcoat in front of him. The gap in Jack Cook's left eyebrow, hairs burnt off by some flying hot fat, was still there. His face was still ruddy from hot kitchens, a rich diet of his own home-made cake and evening pints in the pubs round Sandwich, even the Cinque Ports Arms when the mood took him. 'I'm not your mate,' said Sterling.

'OK. OK.' Jack put up his arms in surrender. 'Look, I really cocked up that time.' He was referring to a case where he'd lent Sterling a car and then betrayed him by fitting it with a tracking device. 'You know what that woman was like. I was too stupid and I got carried away. And for what? Nothing.'

'Nothing?' said Sterling. 'That was not what you implied at the time.'

'I was taken in myself, Frank. Promises were made but the benefits never materialised. None of them. Look, I'm sorry. I was an idiot.'

Sterling's dead father had had many mantras, most worthwhile. One was, 'Don't bear a grudge'. His grounds appeared to be both moral and pragmatic. Grudges diminish those who hold them, and besides, why have bad blood when the alternatives could be useful? Maybe Jack Cook could help Sterling again in the future. Maybe he'd lend him a car again if he really needed one.

'Alright,' said Sterling.

'Excellent,' said Jack Cook. 'It had been nagging away at me. Why don't you pop into the café sometime soon for coffee and cake? On the house of course.'

The fare at the café was much, much better than anything the poor tired little supermarket next door could supply, and Sterling had missed it. His father was clearly right about grudges. 'Alright,' he said again. 'And you can buy me a pint sometime.'

'Glad to,' smiled the café owner. He made off to his car. 'See you soon,' he said over his shoulder.

Sterling completed his walk in ten minutes, along Delf Street, past the cinema where every so often he and Angela sat in moth-eaten seats amidst faded, chipped colonnades watching the latest film offerings, and into Market Street. He'd cleared his head. He'd enjoyed the freedom of his hometown. He'd had the unexpected pleasure of an apology, the resolution of a grudge and the promise of free food and drink. He'd decided to leave the ECOT case behind, and even Hannah, if he couldn't get any answer to his calls, would have to take her chances. He was ready to move on. But then, as he clumped up the narrow stairs to his office, through the cheap thin door, he heard the telephone begin to ring.

Chapter 14

Tuesday 13 October and Wednesday 14 October - The Golden Tick

'Sterling.'

'Mr Sterling, it's Adele here, from college. At last you're in. And your mobile was switched off.'

'Hello, Adele. What can I do for you?' said Sterling, though he could already guess.

'The principal would like you to come in.'

'I got the impression I'd finished.'

'Ms Kingston thought you might say that. She asked me to say that there have been further developments.'

Sterling knew he couldn't turn work down, and knew he didn't really want to, even after clearing his head, and now he was in the driving seat. 'Well, the meter's running, Adele, right from when I step out of my front door and get on the train.'

'Yes, she thought that might be your position. The terms are the same, and expenses of course. She wonders if you can be at her office for 9:30 tomorrow morning.'

'That's fine. I'll be there then. Is there anything I should know before I arrive, Adele?'

'She asked me to e-mail you the college's disciplinary procedure, which I've just done, so you can familiarise yourself with it. You may be called as a witness.' There was a moment of silence. 'She's said nothing else,' said the secretary in her cool, professional tone. Then she dropped to a whisper that Sterling strained to pick up. 'But between you and me, all hell has broken loose here. Some would say' (she dropped her voice even lower) '"shitstorm". So get ready for bedlam.'

'Thanks, Adele.' Sterling smiled into the receiver. 'Noted.'

There was someone new in the principal's office at 9:30 on Wednesday morning: a tall, slender, confident-looking woman in a well-cut dark mauve trouser-suit, with high, delicate cheekbones and a no-nonsense air. Sterling had long ago jettisoned feelings of unease or dread. He'd got too far in for that. Now he was intrigued about where things would go from here, especially as tension crackled in the air. Margaret Kingston was behind her desk. The tall woman moved from the old mantelpiece and sat on the sofa. Her leg had a nervous twitch. College sounds seeped as before into the office. A door opened and closed. There was a tramp of feet on the staircase and then other, less identifiable noises. An oblique shaft of sunshine, like a spotlight, bathed a glass paperweight on the desk, as if elevating it to a kind of holiness, and there was a glint of rainbow.

'Thank you for coming in, Mr Sterling,' said the tall woman.

So, you're in charge, Sterling mused. Interesting.

'Let me introduce myself. I'm Zoë Westhanger, and I'm chair of the college corporation. After you briefed Margaret on Monday, she and I got together and she gave me, and my fellow corporation members, a full update in an emergency meeting that evening. We were shocked to the core, Mr Sterling, at what you'd found out, and at the longest meeting we've ever had, we decided to take decisive and comprehensive action to sort things out and get the college back on track.'

Behind her desk, the principal looked on, stony-faced. Sterling could sense a wave of something – disagreement, perhaps resentment – pulsating from her tiny frame. He imagined the lead governor could feel it too, but she seemed brisk and strong herself.

'So we decided on a swift disciplinary procedure. In connection with that, we needed to identify as many of the people involved as possible – staff and students. I hesitate to call them culprits because there has been no process, but we could at least suspend those who seemed to be involved pending investigation. The external members of the corporation, including myself, have little to do with the day-to-day running of the college or with staff and students, so our best bet was to get the internal members – the staff and student ones, and the directors in the SMT – to see the evidence you gathered of Saturday's shenanigans. We did that on Tuesday morning.

Sterling didn't like where this was going. 'You mean you involved some of the people who might have been involved in the scamming in the first place, and you didn't go to the police.'

'Mr Sterling,' said the chairwoman, as if repeating his name gave the chosen course of action legitimacy, 'we couldn't plausibly have excluded any senior post-holders without creating even more problems. As for the police, there will no doubt be a time to involve them, but we have to do as much as possible in-house first. We have the reputation of the college to consider.'

Yes, saving your own skin. The principal's skin. Everyone's skin. Those were the first things people considered. Sterling could barely repress a tut-tut.

'We managed to identify a list of employees and students registered on courses from the video footage. In fact one director was particularly helpful. It was Jane Casterton who managed to identify the key people.'

God, thought Sterling again. No wonder the principal was angry. She'd been overruled and outmanoeuvred. Jane Casterton. They'd put the fox in the chicken coop. Sterling shook his head slightly and waited for the chair of the corporation to continue.

'We immediately moved to suspend them subject to further enquiries and the full staff and student disciplinary procedures, including the horticulture section manager, on the basis of your photos. One or two students have not been on the premises since the … incident on Saturday night. We've tried to contact them by telephone, but in the end letters were sent out.'

Sterling plumbed his memory for some phrases that used to do the rounds during his time in the Kent police when there had been an operational cock-up. It was about pursuit of the guilty and punishment of the innocent. No one was exactly innocent in this whole fiasco, but some were guiltier than others, and those with the dirtiest hands were looking odds-on to escape. Jane Casterton was cutting people loose and covering her tracks.

'Let me guess,' he said, looking at the principal. 'Suspended from the staff, as well as Pat Manton, Sid Brown and the woman Jenkinson, as they were on the footage. And among the students, Johnny Fontana, Hannah Williamson and the lad Darren. And I bet Hannah Williamson and Darren are the students you can't contact.'

Zoë Westhanger exchanged a glance with Margaret Kingston, a glance that said, 'he knows a lot'.

'That's right,' said the principal, 'though in the case of Fontana it turns out that he isn't registered as a student or employed as a member of staff, so we've just banned him from the premises.'

Suspicion and mistrust hovered in the air. Sterling began to feel angry – with the manipulators in front of him and the situation they were trying to manage. 'Hasn't it occurred to you that you haven't been able to contact the missing students because they've been taken out of circulation?'

'Much more likely, Mr Sterling, that they've jumped before they were pushed.'

'These are kids, Ms Westhanger....' He stopped in mid-sentence. A phrase that he or the chairwoman had used triggered the memory of a training course in the police. He thought of the content and then the title came to him: safeguarding – protecting children, young people and vulnerable adults from harm and abuse. It came back to him in harrowing detail; especially the girls abused for years by predatory gangs and not listened to. 'You're seeing them as delinquents but they are actually victims. Kids come to college to learn, not to be recruited – by college staff – for sex shows and gambling and brothels. That's one point. The other is that you don't seem to be addressing who might be behind all this and what else is going on.'

'Well, we'll look at the first point' – Zoë Westhanger glanced towards the principal, who nodded – 'although none of the students we identified are minors. On the second – not so, Mr Sterling. We're addressing everything. That's why we've called you back in. We do want to get to the bottom of everything illegal and unacceptable that's been going on here, but we need to do it in a controlled way that minimises the damage. We need what you've already shown yourself to be – an effective investigator who can show some discretion.'

Sterling wondered if he could still manage the second requirement.

'Also....' Zoë Westhanger paused. 'We've run into some problems with the disciplinary procedure. Some of those who have been suspended are contesting the allegations against them very strongly. There is now some union involvement. We've got bogged down.'

Now Sterling smiled inwardly. He knew all about union involvement, and at the sharp end. If the union people in this were good, like his Police Federation rep Jim Selsey, they'd mount an effective rear-guard action. They'd require court-standard evidence. It was ironic – the criminals protected by the comrades. 'What do you want me to do?'

'We think the evidence you've produced from the Saturday night goings-on will stand up to scrutiny. We'll face down any legal challenges from that. Proving who managed the cannabis production is the priority. In fact all traces of cannabis have been removed, and Pat Manton, whom you've mentioned, has denied all knowledge of it, maintaining that the building was locked at all times. Beyond that, we also want you to get to the bottom of all other irregularities and present us with a report at the end. At that point we'll involve the police and give them all the evidence we've got.'

In the lobby, business concluded, Sterling stood and considered. There was a smell of polish and coffee in the air, together with other, Victorian influences, since it was such an old building. A lecturer squeaked and clicked across the smooth floor in fashionably heeled shoes, nodding to Sterling as she lugged her bag of notes and equipment. After the hubbub of recent class changes, all was calm. The attitude of the college powers-that-be nagged at him. Margaret Kingston didn't want him involved anymore, whilst she and Zoë Westhanger didn't seem to care about Hannah Williamson's and her show-partner's disappearance or whether they were offenders or victims. He made for the stairs. One person would have the full picture. It was time for confrontation.

He paused at Jane Casterton's door on the first floor and took a breath. He could at least show a little restraint. But there was no answer to his sharp knock. He tried the door. Locked. In his ex-policeman's gut, rarely inaccurate both on the job and currently, something felt wrong. Back downstairs in the secretaries' office, Jean, the surly girl who managed the curriculum director's diary chewed her gum with a grudging insolence, like everything else she did. She clicked on her mouse and looked at the computer, the effort exhausting.

'She should be in. She's got no appointments anywhere. Wednesday is her catch-up day.'

'Have you got a key to her office?' Something in Sterling's voice alerted Adele.

'Here,' she said, offering one on a small bunch.

'Follow me,' said Sterling to the two secretaries.

At the door on the first floor, the surly girl protested half-heartedly. 'Should we be doing this?'

'Well, you're here to see I don't run amok, aren't you?'

He turned the lock and could hear the tumblers. The door opened to a small, gory hell. In some places it looked as if a pointillist had been in action, with tiny dots of rusty brown speckling the room, especially in the upper areas. But the overwhelming impression was of large red daubs of blood everywhere else – on the carpet, on the desk and on the wall behind the office chair. In the middle of it all, the subject of a sustained, remorseless and frenzied attack, was Jane Casterton. She was lying, arms stretched flat in front of her, face down on her desk, as if she'd come over sleepy and decided to have a rest. The scene might even have been tranquil except for the blood and scatter of papers all over the floor, and most notably the Investors in Quality figure embedded in her skull – a large, golden, upside down tick.

Even though Sterling was shocked he let his training take over. He took everything in with a professional eye, but there was a parallel track in his thinking. All that planning downstairs. All that rubbish about the reputation of the college. All the steps to avoid unwelcome publicity. Well, everything had changed now, including his own part. Never mind about digging up more dirt, and getting evidence for a disciplinary procedure, and exercising discretion at all times. Now it was a murder enquiry. Now the police had to be brought in.

Although he filled the doorway, he could sense Adele and the surly girl glimpsing the room in gaps around his torso. He could sense too the wellings of a scream from the girl. 'Shut up,' he said pre-emptively, and she gulped. 'Both of you, stand back and don't touch anything. I'm going to check for a pulse and we'll take it from there.' He went in, did what he had to do and then shut and locked the door. 'Right. She's dead, but we still need an ambulance. We also need the police. I'll do all that. Right, let's go back downstairs.' The secretaries were rooted to the spot. 'Chop chop,' said Sterling harshly. He turned to the girl. 'Follow Adele's lead. Keep shtum about this, or you'll get into trouble.'

Chapter 15

Wednesday 15 October - Re-acquaintance

Sterling summoned the emergency services on the way to the principal's office. He paused outside until he'd finished, then knocked briskly on the door and entered straight away, motioning Adele and the sulky girl to follow him in.

The principal and the chair of the corporation were having what seemed to be a robust conversation.

'I thought we'd concluded our business, Mr Sterling,' said Zoë Westhanger, not bothering to conceal her exasperation.'

'We had,' said Sterling. 'But something's come up and it won't wait. I'm pretty certain we can add murder to the list of crimes and indiscretions in the college. Someone's done in one of your curriculum directors.'

'Jane Casterton,' whispered Margaret Kingston.

'Correct,' said Sterling. 'I've phoned for the police and an ambulance. Only Adele and Jean know what's happened, which is why I've brought them in.'

'You might have waited, Mr Sterling,' said the chairwoman. 'Then we could have decided how best to proceed.'

'Not with a suspicious death, Ms Westhanger. That trumps everything, even PR and news management. You'll need to prepare for a media frenzy.' He looked at the secretaries. What had just happened confirmed what he already knew: Adele was a cool customer and good in a crisis. Jean on the other hand was close to hysteria. 'Jean,' he said in a softer voice. 'It's been a shock. Sit down on the sofa. We'll get you a drink.' Unbidden, Adele sat next to the girl and put her arm around her shoulders as the sobbing began.

Sterling drew the other women into a huddle away from the sofa. 'The police will want to interview them or take statements almost before they do anything else. The same with me, for that matter. I've locked the door to Jane Casterton's office, so a forensic team will be easily able to do its work when it goes in.'

The principal gathered herself. The new crisis was energising her. The steamroller was back. 'You need to carry on looking after the college's interests, Frank,' she said in low, urgent voice, so the secretaries would not hear. 'While you're doing that, I'm determined that it's going to be business as usual here even while the police go about their work. We've got courses to run and students to educate. Obviously, tell the police all you know, since it's probably strongly connected with Jane's death, and they'll have to know about all the other stuff anyway. We'll carry on with Pat Manton's disciplinary hearing as she and her representative are kicking up so much of a fuss. It's scheduled for 10:30 tomorrow and we'll call you as a witness for that, so you'll need to be around. I think Adele has sent you a copy of the procedure. The others – for staff and students – are not so urgent because – how do they say it in the police? – we've got them bang to rights.' She rapped the desk, as if chiding herself. 'Scrub that, in the light of your point about safeguarding, Frank. We'll reconsider the students' cases. Your terms will be the same as before. OK?'

She looked from Sterling to the chair of the corporation, as if facing down any hint of disagreement. 'We don't try and massage this, Zoë, or everything will come back to bite us. This is what I propose we agree with the police in our first press statement – something to the effect of, "There has been a major incident in the college involving the death of a senior member of staff. We believe it may be connected to serious incidences of indiscipline and even criminal activity on college premises. We are conducting our own internal investigations and disciplinary procedures, and at the same time we are cooperating fully and openly with the police at all times. The college corporation and senior management are shocked at this turn of events but are determined to treat the interests of students and their learning as our top priority." I'll also get an e-mail and messages out to all the staff and the student body to give a broad outline of what's happened and that it's going to be business as usual.'

Whilst Zoë Westhanger nodded, Sterling had almost tuned out, buoyed by what was happening. In effect, not only was he back on the case, and on the same terms, but he'd been given carte blanche to proceed in the way he thought most suitable. There was no shortage of lines of enquiry, and many might lead to similar results, but already he knew his first and most important focus. Hannah Williamson and the boy

Darren were in trouble, and finding them was the key he chose to unlock everything.

They could hear the sirens getting louder as they approached, and when they stopped, the principal's office was bathed in a flickering blue light. 'Will you show the officers and the ambulance crew Jane Casterton's office, Frank?' said Margaret Kingston.

'I think that's best,' said Sterling. 'Then when the scene has been officially secured I expect the investigating officers will come down and talk to us after they've set all the police things in motion.'

The young police officers trooped in. Their smooth faces and clear, eager eyes made Sterling feel his age. He had been like that not so long ago. There was a twinge in his left knee. He was beginning to creak. This is what happened as you drifted to 40.

'We've had a report of a suspicious death,' said the young woman.

'Upstairs,' said Sterling. 'I checked the woman's pulse, and she was certainly dead. It was a formality really, since there was a statuette buried in her skull. Then I locked the room and informed the principal and the chair of the corporation.' He nodded towards the women in turn. 'These two secretaries were with me,' – he motioned now towards the sofa – 'and I expect they'll prepare statements when they've got over the shock. We've asked them to keep quiet, and they're staying in here for now.'

'And you are....?'

'Frank Sterling. I'm a consultant working for the principal.'

'Right,' said the young woman. 'A consultant. And how did you come to find the dead person, Mr Sterling?'

'We'd been in a meeting down here and then I went up to ask her something. The door was locked. I smelt a rat. I came down for a key, went back up and there she was.'

'OK, well, I'm sure that the investigating officers will want to interview you, so don't go far.' She motioned to her colleague. 'We're going up to cordon off the scene. We'd better have a key and you'd better come up and show us.'

When the ambulance had arrived, and the forensic team and all the camp followers associated with major crime, converting the college frontage into a teeming anthill of activity, Sterling was kicking his heels in the secretaries' office, coffee supplied by the redoubtable Adele. She'd been busy on his behalf in a different way as well. There had been no guff or logic chopping about data protection when he'd asked for the contact details of various 'persons of interest', as he'd phrased it. He knew that the police would not be sharing any forensic details about Jane Casterton with him, or even any other information about their investigation, but he had plenty of other possibilities. Let them establish time of death, blood trajectories, presence of fingerprints and all the other things associated with violent death. His parallel investigation could be just as effective, and he'd had a head start.

He arranged his appointment on his mobile as he loitered beside the ambulance. He'd catch a train after the investigating detectives had seen him. He looked beyond the low wall into Ramston Road. Already there were gawkers. A tall man in a cloth cap almost bumped into a lamp post as he walked past, a lead pulled taut at an angle forwards from his hand by a dog (Sterling assumed) hidden by the wall. Two pushchair handles in a young woman's hands moved along the top like a shark's fin in the ocean. A young man in a pitcher's cap took in the scene with the video camera of his mobile phone.

Adele came out for Sterling. Her step seemed lighter and more carefree than he remembered, and her eyes somehow less red-rimmed. If she'd been shocked, she'd made a quick recovery. 'The detectives have been to Jane Casterton's room, spoken to all their colleagues and finished there. Now they are in the principal's office. They've asked to see you.'

'Right,' he said. 'Let's get it over with. Then I can get on.'

As soon as he went in, he knew how it was going to be – both in this meeting and how he needed to proceed – and he saw it with a welcome clarity. Now he knew there would be few overlaps between his activities and what the police were doing. He'd be left alone.

The sleek, slim, short man sitting on the principal's sofa reddened slightly. 'Frank Sterling,' he muttered. He might as well have added 'Just my luck'.

'Inspector Andrews,' said Sterling, demoting the little Napoleon who had been such a thorn in his side in a previous case, and when Sterling had been on the force.

'That's "superintendent", Sterling.'

'No need for introductions, then,' said Margaret Kingston. Even in the crisis, she picked up the atmosphere and smiled tightly.

At least the roly-poly, decent, honest Detective Sergeant Murphy was with Andrews, and not the hard-bitten cynic with the nicotine fingers and sceptical eyes who sometimes accompanied him. 'Bill,' said Sterling.

'Frank,' said Murphy subversively.

The little man on the sofa tutted. 'Well, where's there's sh....' He stopped himself. 'We'll need to interview you formally when forensics have finished. You'll need to give us an alibi, if you have one, when we establish time of death.' If anything, he was more insulting then he had been during previous encounters.

Sterling struggled to keep his temper. 'I know the drill,' he said. 'In the meantime, whilst you go about your more pressing business, perhaps it would be helpful if I updated Detective Sergeant Murphy before I go on my way.'

'Who said you're going anywhere?'

'So, you're arresting me.'

The two men stared at each other.

'Give Murphy your mobile number and make sure we can contact you at all times,' said Andrews. 'Sergeant, you might as well get a preliminary update now.' He dismissed the men by turning his attention to the principal and chair of the corporation.

In the small telephone room Adele had found for them in the elevated walkway, Sterling shook his head. 'I really don't know how you put up with it, Bill.'

'Pension in three years, Frank. I'm on minus 34 in terms of months. When it's that close, it's surprising how much you can put up with.'

There'll be no pension for me, thought Sterling. Not till I'm 70, the way things are going. 'Right. An update. Fasten your seatbelt. It's going to be a rocky ride.'

'Bloody hell, Frank,' said Murphy when the account had finished. 'You've got the knack. What a mare's nest. In all my years, even my time in London, I've never come across anything like this. But why weren't we called in earlier?'

'You would have been, but they were trying to manage it. Of course, you can't postpone reporting a murder, especially when there's a body with something buried in the skull.'

'And this girl, Hannah Williamson. You reckon she's been disappeared, and the young bloke.'

'Yes, and while you and Napoleon go about your official business, that's what I'm going to look into.'

'Nap... the Super will want to start at the murder. He won't be interested in the tittle-tattle you've provided.'

'Tittle-tattle? Please.'

'Well, that's what he'll call it. But I'll make sure it's factored into the investigation, and we'll follow the leads. I am renowned around Marchurch for my tact and diplomacy, so I'll make the best of it when I introduce it. The one thing you haven't done is say who you reckon bashed in the victim's skull.'

'That's because I don't know. Plenty of people would have wanted to. But who would have been able to, and who would have had the opportunity? That's not the only thing I don't know. I suspect that there's loads more to come. Right, I'm off, unless you object.'

'We'll see you soon, Frank. I'll let you know if we do need to interview you formally.'

Chapter 16

Wednesday 15 October - A Darker Turn

It was true that Sterling had lived with his father in a good number of the dilapidated Kentish coastal towns, but only from Ramston southwards. He knew Marchurch and its suburban satellites, stretching northwards in a long and tapering tail that clung to the shoreline, from his time as a young police officer on the seafront beat. He looked out from the window as the last bungalows of the Marchurch hinterland receded from view and dykes criss-crossed the large expanse of polders over which the train was clattering on its long embankment. Another large, parallel levee between the low-lying land and the North Sea beyond it carried a bridle path from the island to the mainland, and on it a solitary cyclist clad in garish Lycra and helmet laboured against the wind. The bike wobbled as he stood on the pedals and hunched further over the handlebars, the saddle jerking from side to side with his effort. A tiny, weather-beaten chapel greeted the train at the end of the farmland, and then the bungalows and houses started again as it reached the settlements beyond Earlsey.

Sterling struggled to understand why no one else was concerned by Hannah Williams's apparent disappearance. He hoped the visit to Whithampton a couple more miles up the line would give some answers. Using the Google map Adele had thoughtfully printed for him, he left the small station and plunged down into the Victorian terraces between the railway line and the town. Albert Street was exactly as he had imagined – a mid-Victorian terraced cottage in a long row of Kentish brick. The houses might once have been identical, but now some were whitewashed and some had the original brickwork, and all had different doors and styles of double-glazing. He looked at the address he had again, and knocked at number 32.

There is a constituency that believes that some people become more handsome or more beautiful with age. Faces that are narrow in youth can fill out. Noses that are prominent can go into proportion as the years pass. Hair that is fine can thicken, and if it goes white can gradually come to suit the complexion of its owner. In men, beards can add shape and character. In women, eyes can mellow. If in the passage of years life has been happy, it can be reflected in face, voice and demeanour.

The woman who answered the door to Sterling must once have been pretty. Now she was beautiful, with a slender face and tiny, slender fingers on the door handle. Black leggings and a turquoise blouse emphasised her slim and well-proportioned body. She looked as though she might be about his own age. Mentally he did the sums. She must have been young when she had Hannah. She smiled as she opened the door and ushered him in through the narrow hallway to the sitting room with a friendly sweep of her arm.

'Mr Sterling, I presume. Sorry for the muddle. It's my half day today, but I haven't had time to tidy up.'

'Don't worry,' said Sterling. He perched himself on the sofa. It was one of those places where every surface was covered with something – a spider plant on a small table in the front of the window; figurines on the mantel shelf over the fireplace; as it clearly wasn't considered cold enough for a fire, a silk screen in front of the hearth; photographs of family members on a small dresser; and pictures on every wall. He recognised amongst them a reproduction of the famous Vettriano – servants with umbrellas and dancers in evening dress on a watery, windswept beach. More of a minimalist in temperament himself, Sterling wondered what the room would look like without the muddle, and, ever practical, what dusting and housework in such a house would be like.

He accepted a cup of tea and waited for Mrs Williamson to settle in the armchair opposite.

'So, Hannah,' she said. 'It must be important for you to come up here and see me personally. On the other hand, you're not the police, so it can't be too bad.'

'Are you expecting something bad, Mrs Williamson?'

'I don't know. Where Hannah is concerned, lots of things are possible.'

On the train up, Sterling had been wondering how much he could say. Having met this woman, he knew he could be honest. 'I think she's in a spot of bother, and the college has suspended her, although that might be under review.'

Mrs Williamson's face fell. 'I'm afraid that sounds like my girl. I love her to bits. She's my oldest, and she's always been a sunny, cheerful girl, but when she, you know, grew up, that's when the trouble really started.

She discovered boys when she was 14, or they discovered her. Whichever way round it was, she never looked back. Now she's 18 going on 38. I thought I knew the ways of the world but she's left me far behind. What's she done this time?'

Sterling leaned forward and clasped his hands together. There was no point in dressing things up. He talked about the sex show and put it in the context of what was happening at the college, including Jane Casterton's murder, but he didn't mention her role in the attempt to blackmail him. He liked her after all, and she was being used. As he talked, his eyes fixed on a whorl on the multi-coloured carpet, he sensed the woman opposite tensing. In his peripheral vision she seemed to be wringing her hands.

'I don't think she's been seen since Saturday. She's not answering her mobile. The college hasn't been able to contact her.' Finally he looked up, just as Hannah's mother's face began to crumple, tears flooding down her cheeks.

She got up so abruptly that Sterling recoiled as if he was about to be set upon. But Mrs Williamson went over to the window and turned her back to him. He watched the tremor in her shoulders as she struggled for control, and heard her gulping attempts to stifle the sobbing. He waited, still and quiet.

'Sorry. Sorry, Mr Sterling. She's such a lovely daughter and I can't bear the idea of anything happening to her. The trouble is I'm not surprised about what you've said. Her father was the same. He loved sex, but unfortunately not just with me. He was a charming man, mostly, but it never worked out between us. He left when Hannah was pretty young. So she had his absence to contend with, and that's where I'm told the problems started.'

'Who told you, Mrs Williamson?'

'The family psychiatrist we started seeing just after she turned 15. Can I trust you, Mr Sterling?'

'Yes. She cut my hair at college, and I liked her. I wouldn't be here if I wasn't concerned. The more I know, the better I'm going to be able to help.'

Hannah's mother nodded and clasped her own hands over her knees, as if she was about to recite. Facing Sterling, it looked as though she was engaged in a religious rite with him. She drew in a deep breath and then launched off. 'Some people would call my dear daughter a nympho, a slag or a slut, Mr Sterling – stupid, ignorant, men's words – but of course it's much more complicated than that. It's more accurate to say that Hannah has a mild sex addiction, which the psychiatrist believed stemmed from when her father went. She had plenty of love and affection from me and all the rest of her family, but we couldn't fill that emptiness. As I said, after puberty, it kicked off. In earnest, you might say. And the trouble is that she's a very pretty and bubbly girl, which means that sex isn't hard to find.'

'It explains a lot, Mrs Williamson.'

'I hope it does. Did she....? Did you....?

'Yes, she did come on to me, but nothing came of it. It was blatant, and I got the feeling, rightly as it happened, that she was put up to it. Anyway, I'm not here to tell tales out of school. When did you last see her?'

'Not since Saturday morning, but I'm afraid that's not unusual. She's 18, Mr Sterling, and sex addiction or not she's her own person. I've long given up on curfews or threats to kick her out. She said she'd be staying with friends this week. She does that often. I couldn't stop her even if I wanted to, so I never gave it any more thought.'

'No ideas where she might have gone? No call? No texts?'

Hannah's mother shook her head. 'No. It sounds really serious. You've got me worried, Mr Sterling. What should I be doing?'

'Report her missing, Mrs Williamson. Because the college is so occupied with the fallout from the murder of the member of staff and all the other shenanigans, it hasn't focused sufficiently on Hannah and Darren and the other students. And to be honest, the police are pretty much the same. Their energy is on the murder. If you go to the police here in Whithampton, the wheels will start grinding and her missing status will become official. As she doesn't seem to have been seen since Saturday, they won't be able to fob you off with any nonsense about how she hasn't been gone long enough.'

'I could have done more for her, but she's always been too confident.' The woman stopped twisting her hands in her lap and looked directly up at Sterling. 'How much danger is she in? You don't think....'

'I don't know anything, Mrs Williamson. Now that I'm clearer about things from this end, I'll redouble my efforts to find her. Refer the police to me, and I'll update them fully. Tell them to make the link between Hannah and the murder investigation. In cases like this, it's not too many cooks spoiling the broth, it's the opposite in my view – and in my experience as well.'

'I'm not that hopeful about the police. Promise me you'll find her, Mr Sterling.'

Sterling went back to his training, all that time ago and repeated regularly up to the time he'd left the job altogether. There was a golden rule, drummed into family and victim liaison officers, and anyone else dealing with a misper, or rape, or burglary, or GBH, or murder, or anything criminal at all, or, when it came down to it, simply anything at all. The rule was, 'Make no promises'. There was never any guarantee of a good result. It was the same with private investigations. Even the most skilful operator, and Sterling thought he would not be a fraud in such a fraternity, could make no hard and fast commitments. He looked into Hannah Williamson's mother's eyes, brown like her daughter's and still awash with tears. He remembered Hannah's carefree laughter and sheer vivacity.

'I promise,' he said.

Technically, he could get out of it. There was a strong chance that he'd find Hannah. But the really pertinent question, given the goings-on at the college and the stakes, getting higher all the time, was whether it would be dead or alive. In these circumstances, urgency was less important than thinking things through and making the right decisions. Hannah Williamson's mother had no more beans to spill. He was going back through Marchurch. There were people there who almost certainly knew something useful.

As the train pulled into the station, he got out the next set of Adele's directions. Marchurch had changed from when he was on the beat there. Although at the bottom of Station Approach Road the man in the sou'wester, metal weathered to a coppery green, still stared resolutely out to sea, with his hand shading his eyes, a new budget hotel had appeared, and beyond it towards the town and the beach an unfinished building programme of shops and apartments in the continental style – all curves, whitewashed walls and solid glass-metal doors. Sterling turned right and right again into All Saints Avenue, past the multi-storey car park and the block of flats it serviced and under the railway bridge with the line that would take him over to Southwood and Ramston and beyond them to Sandley. A left turn soon after took him into the road he wanted, Tivoli Park Avenue, with its semis on the seaward side and a large, leafy park on the other. On the short journey, Sterling had gone through a small segment of the class system – from the bed and breakfasts around the station and the flats of the middle-class aspirers to the established middle classes away from the town.

Mrs Jenkinson had done well for herself. Her semi gleamed in the October sunshine. The front area was paved over in an expensive and tasteful scheme of pale brown slabs and in front of the garage was a new model SUV. As he approached the front door, Sterling noted that although it was only two o'clock in the afternoon, all the curtains were drawn, both in the upstairs and downstairs windows. He could hear the bell tinkle within the house when he pressed the button by the front door. The notes were familiar. When he pressed again, the tune came to him: Amazing Grace. But there was no reply.

Sterling stood back and looked around. The old intuition again: something didn't feel right. He glanced to the houses on either side, and then back to the road. It was the dead time in the afternoon – after retired people had gone in for lunch and before it was time for the afternoon school run. He edged towards the side gate beside the garage and rattled the handle. The gate was locked but not so high that he couldn't get over in a well-practised combination of clamber and vault. The garden at the back was immaculate, even in one of the year's most untidy periods, and fortunately for Sterling, well protected from the neighbouring houses by shrubs, fences and trees. Just as at the front, all the curtains were drawn, but in a careless, seemingly hurried way out of keeping with the state of the rest of the house. Sterling cupped his hands over his eyes and tried to peer in through the French doors, but there was no convenient gap to look through this time.

He sat on the step, quiet and concealed from prying eyes. He had a decision to make, and he made it quickly. The padlock on the garden shed was solid enough, but the hasp and the metal plate it was attached to were flimsy. Sterling left the padlock alone and set to work on the plate with a screwdriver from his emergency kit, part of him lamenting how little attention householders paid to effective crime prevention, another part glad. When he'd removed the plate and padlock, he slipped into the shed and cast around for a suitable tool, picking a spade from what was on offer.

Sterling used the bottom edge of the spade as a crude lever on the lock of the French doors and there was a tearing, rasping sound of weary protest as it gave way. In a few moments, he had managed to ruin doors and spade beyond any prospect of repair. He listened for a burglar alarm, and heard nothing, but that didn't mean there wasn't some alert now being activated in his old nick beyond the seafront. Whatever the situation, he didn't have much time, and slipped swiftly and quietly inside.

The dining room was empty. So was the kitchen. So was the sitting room. So was the rest of the downstairs area. His gut was wrong. He went light-footed up the carpeted staircase. No, his gut was right. In the main bedroom, a study in white and pink, he found Mrs Jenkinson. The high heels and dark blue evening dress from Saturday night had long been put aside. Now she was wearing a cream blouse and light green slacks, and her blonde hair spilled down just below her shoulders. On her feet were a pair of fluffy pink slippers in the style of clogs. In normal circumstances he would have noticed the clothes straight away, and the footwear perhaps later. But here the circumstances were as far from normal as they could possibly be. The footwear was just below Sterling's eye line, because Mrs Jenkinson was hanging from a noose on a hook in the ceiling.

He quickly strode over and felt a bare arm. She had long expired because rigor mortis had clearly set in. He calculated that she had been dead for at least four hours. Still … he couldn't leave her strung up like that. Never mind the unsentimental matter of forensics, it just didn't seem right. He slipped back downstairs, rummaged in the kitchen for a knife and returned to the bedroom. Righting the tipped-over chair near the body, he clambered up and started hacking at the rope. In the final moments before the strands parted, he conducted a clumsy danse macabre with the stiff corpse before he manoeuvred it over to the bed and laid it down as gently as he could manage.

The noose was classic, but you could get instructions for that from any internet search. The rope could have come from the garden shed. Her face, when he could bring himself to look properly, told him nothing. Violent death was never pretty and it was true in this case as well.

Sterling put his hands in his pockets and took another tour of the house. It was as smart and well kept as the garden. In the lounge, the white leather three-piece suite showed no particular signs of occupation, and there was no sign that the straight-backed chairs in the dining room had been moved from their precisely arranged places. In the kitchen, the worktops and sink area were pristine and completely empty. He took a tea-towel, draped it over his hand and clicked open the dishwasher, which was also empty, apart from two dirty cups, saucers and teaspoons and a small matching plate. Still using the tea-towel, he went through the cupboards and found a biscuit barrel with a Cotswolds scene on the lid – a miniature railway train wending between the stone cottages. The crumbs from the plate matched the Nice biscuits in the tin. He closed the cupboards and the door of the dishwasher and got out his phone.

The call handler went through her 999 spiel, and Sterling went through his – smoothly because of the practice. When it was finished, he sat down on a chair in the kitchen to wait. What a mess. He tried to think straight. It looked like suicide, but so much had been happening. For him to find one body was possibly acceptable, but to find two … He knew he'd be spending most of the rest of the day, and probably longer, in Marchurch nick. He was no closer to finding Hannah than before he came up this way, no closer to knowing who'd bashed Jane Casterton's head in, and no closer to having answers to all the other questions that still ricocheted round his head.

Soon he heard the police and ambulance sirens. Then he heard the doorbell chimes. He thought of Mrs Jenkinson lying dead upstairs. Nothing amazing for her, not now, and little in the way of grace.

Chapter 17

Wednesday 15 October - Stranded

Marchurch nick hadn't changed in the way the railway station quarter had. It was a square, squat 1960s building with a large annex at right angles and in the same style. The pub next door, The Black Spot, in which he'd spent many a post-shift drinking session, still looked exactly the same, a little faded and louche, but welcoming enough. He went into the station around the back with the young officers in their squad car. Security was still tight, the netting up to catch the Molotov cocktails and the barbed wire rolled up on the high wall looking as forbidding as ever. He was led past the custody and booking area towards the front. It didn't look as if the place had been decorated and he remembered the dingy green. Even the chip below the custody sergeant's desk was still there, where a young drinker from London whom Sterling had subdued and arrested had lashed out in anger and frustration all that time ago. As he passed along the corridors, no one recognised him and he recognised no one in return. How long was it since he had been based here and bashing the beat in Dodge City, aka Marchurch seafront, on summer Saturday nights? 10 years? Longer? He hadn't missed it.

The officers put him in an interview room just behind the reception area at the front. That had been redone. There were electric sliding doors to get in, but the reinforced glass plating on the inside windows and doors segregated the police from the public, including, Sterling knew from experience, prospective assailants.

'I'm gasping for a cuppa,' said Sterling to one of the officers. 'Milk, no sugar.' The young man nodded. This was a witness interview, not an arrest. He could be considerate.

After half an hour, Andrews and Murphy appeared. Andrews got straight to it. 'Why shouldn't I arrest you?'

'What for?' said Sterling. 'I reported an incident that had happened hours before, whether it was suicide or murder dressed up as suicide. I felt her body. Rigor mortis had really set in – forensics will tell you that. Say that I'm involved. I go and visit, she lets me in, I string her up, go away, come back and break in, get her down and then phone you lot. Or I string her up and wait for six hours and then call. And if I hadn't broken in, who knows when she would have been found.'

Andrews glowered. Behind him, Murphy put a hand to his mouth to hide a smirk.

'OK, Mr Sterling, let's start again from the beginning.'

'Inspector, I told Detective Sergeant Murphy everything this morning at the college.'

'Tell me. And it's "Superintendent".'

'Right,' said Sterling. He supposed he ought to be thankful that he was being taken seriously. 'Another cup of tea would help things along.'

At the end of the first round of questioning, Sterling moved on to the events of the day. 'I advised Hannah Williamson's mother to inform the police officially that her daughter is missing. You lot, and the college, can't go on ignoring that. She hadn't seen her, and she didn't know where she was – just that she was going to be away for a few days. When I'd finished in Whithampton, I reckoned I'd got time to call on Mrs Jenkinson on the way back down. There was a good chance she'd be in because the college had suspended her. It was obvious when I called that something was wrong, so I found a way in. I was right too. And that takes me up to when your blokes brought me over here.'

The questioning continued from the afternoon and into the evening. Sterling refused to budge from his justification for cutting the body down. During it all, Andrews became more attentive, though never respectful. At the end, he was his usual provocative, pig-headed self, in Sterling's view.

'Don't go far,' Andrews finally said, 'and don't think for a moment that you're in the clear. If you find out anything more, make sure you tell us.'

Murphy walked Sterling to the front door. 'So you'll be carrying on looking for the girl and the boy, Frank.'

'Yes. It'll keep me out of the way while you carry on with your murder and suicide investigations, and I expect it will help you in the end – not that that idiot deserves it. Tomorrow I'm involved as a witness in a disciplinary procedure at the college – the woman who allegedly ran the dope farm – under the 'business as usual' banner. Waste of my time in the circumstances, but "he who pays the piper....", or in this case, "she".'

Murphy gave him a sly glance. 'A disciplinary procedure. You'll know the ropes then, Frank.' Sterling's disciplinary brushes and Federation Rep Jim Selsey's rearguard actions were the stuff of legend in some police quarters.

'Funny man. How have you been getting on today?'

Murphy looked back over each shoulder. 'It's the old wall of silence at the college, Frank, all "see no evil, hear no evil, speak no evil", and we're obviously waiting to hear from forensics. So we're up against it. There's no CCTV round Casterton's office, so we've drawn a blank on that too. That's why the Super's been swallowing his pride and taking you seriously.'

Sterling reflected on the grilling. 'So that's what it was.'

It was cold and windy outside the station. The woebegone shrubs in the bit of greenery beyond the parking spaces wobbled and swayed. There was more than a sniff of rain in the cold air. Sterling looked around. 'Where's the car to take me home? It's past 11. There'll be no trains now.'

Murphy looked shamefaced as he clapped him on the shoulder. 'Sorry, mate. His Nibs,' he said, no longer bothering to hide his contempt, 'said no car. Misuse of public money. You'll know where the taxis are down by the amusement arcades.'

Sterling walked down the narrow railed path to the road. 'Bastard,' he muttered. 'If there had been a little more consideration, a little more respect, I'd have gone beyond the facts to the hunches and the gut feelings.' But there was a bonus: the slights and scepticism delivered by Andrews had cleared Sterling's conscience. The police would have to get on without his full cooperation.

Down the hill to the garish, tawdry temptation of the seafront lights, he wondered how much the taxi from Marchurch to Sandley was going to cost. The college was in line for another hefty hit.

Chapter 18

Thursday 16 October - Discipline

Sterling had better things to do than be a witness in an internal disciplinary procedure, which was a bizarre, irrelevant sideshow given that there had been two deaths the day before, both of which he had discovered, and both connected to the web of crime at the college. But he had business in Earlsey, including on the campus, so it wasn't greatly inconvenient. He read through the disciplinary procedure given to him by the indefatigable Adele so that he could prepare. Fifteen pages. They were all the same. The police one was even longer. His own experience told him why. If all the "t"s weren't crossed and the "i"s not dotted it was open season for the employment lawyers and union reps. He'd been confident enough of his own innocence in the course of his escapades not to worry about the minutiae of process, but he'd known disciplinaries stretch out for months because of procedural or documentary errors and shortcomings. Still, he was just a witness.

Adele was there to meet him in the lobby. The red rims previously around her eyes had almost entirely disappeared, and her blonde hair had been retouched and seemed fuller. Lipstick and mascara, never in evidence before, had removed the faded look.

'Mr Sterling, the principal would like you to pop in before you go up to the boardroom.'

'Thanks, Adele.' He turned back to his de facto secretary before he approached the principal's door. 'How did you know I'd be coming through the door just then?'

'You don't have a car. The 8:20 from Sandley arrives in Southwood at 9 o'clock. It takes twelve minutes to walk through from the station. 9:12. Here you are.'

'You're wasted doing this.'

Adele smiled and looked down.

'Good morning, Frank,' said Margaret Kingston from behind her desk. After the arm-wrestle with the chair of the governors and the arrival of the police yesterday, the principal was back in charge. There might have been a full-blown crisis pulsating through the college, and the bodies were stacking up, but she was the one dealing with it all. Authority suited her and sat easily on her small shoulders. 'Are you ready for the disciplinary procedure?'

'Yes,' said Sterling. 'It's really no big deal, saying what I saw and did. If you're chairing it, should we be having this conversation?'

'Don't worry, Frank. I'm not trying to manipulate things. I'm more interested in an update about how you've been getting on.'

'I need an update from you as well, Margaret, if I'm going to be effective in representing the college's interests.'

'OK. I don't mind going first. Well, the police have done all the forensics. They've been questioning everyone in this building, establishing timelines and movements, etc. I've told them what you've found out and what the college has been doing about it. It seems to match with what you've told them according to the sergeant, Murphy, is it? They reckon a man did it – you know, Jane – the force and the anger and so on.' She gave Sterling a look he couldn't read – pursing her lips together and looking beyond him to her right. She's pleased, he thought. Is that it? Then she changed tack. 'That superintendent … how can I put this? He's a numpty. He's got all this evidence – not directly about the murder, I grant you, but pretty relevant however you look at it – and he's insisting on starting from scratch. It's almost as if anything you've found out is disqualified. Apart from you and me – again, this is what Murphy said – no one else has been very forthcoming.'

'Numpty is about right,' said Sterling. 'There's something else, Margaret. Clearly you haven't heard yet because it's probably only going to be in the local news shortly. Someone else from the college has died.'

The principal closed her eyes and sighed heavily, a reaction indicating she was thinking more of the ramifications for herself and the college than concern for the dead person. 'Tell me.'

'I went up to Whithampton yesterday to speak with the daughter of the missing student, Hannah Williamson, who I believe is one of the keys to all this. It wasn't much help, not directly anyway. But on the way back I thought I'd call in to see Mrs Jenkinson while she was on suspension as she lives – lived – in Marchurch. When I got to the house, I knew something was up. I was right. She was hanging in her bedroom.'

'Suicide?'

'It looks like it, though the police will be having a close look at it. I spent yesterday evening in Marchurch police station. I expect the police will want to talk to you and people she was close to at college.'

'I didn't know her that well. She was in charge of housekeeping in the training hotel – and of course the other, less salubrious things – just below programme manager level, so there were no direct meetings. Poor woman. Running a brothel on public sector premises is a pretty awful thing, but to go like that.... I'll have to think about a press release. When the nationals get hold of this, all hell will break loose.' She spoke with relish, as if she was spoiling for a fight. 'Anything else to report, Frank?'

'I'm still worried about the girl, and the boy Darren. They're my focus. But once I've found them, all the dominoes will fall.'

'Well, you know what you're doing. We'll review again in due course.' She stood up briskly. The meeting was over.

Adele brought Sterling a cup of coffee as he waited outside the boardroom between the staffroom and the Learning Resource Centre. It didn't look as though there were any other witnesses. He leafed through the disciplinary procedure again, concentrating on the parts he thought would be relevant. There would have been an investigation, so there would be an investigating officer. The issue was so serious that Pat Manton had been suspended, so he re-read the section on suspension, and the part on formal procedure. Then he turned to disciplinary action itself. If the manager of the horticultural section were found guilty, the college would be skipping all the stages. She could forget a verbal warning, a first written warning and a final written warning. It would be a cut to the chase: summary dismissal for gross misconduct. The list of offences normally regarded as grounds for summary dismissal was impressive, but it didn't include running a dope farm – or, not on the table this time round – pimping, prostitution, brothel-keeping, sex shows, and running an illegal gambling club.

Sterling couldn't suppress a small smile. Usually, these meetings were about sledgehammers cracking nuts, but the college's disciplinary armoury was puny in relation to the scale of law breaking, like a sandcastle in a tidal surge. There was another thing. The evidence was there all right, but was it enough? Still, he was just a witness, and he had other fish to fry.

The heavy board room door opened, and a tall, gangly man with worry lines permanently etched on his face summoned Sterling in, indicating a high-backed, throne-like chair near the door. The room was old-fashioned, and dominated by a huge conference table of dark oak – just the kind of set-up Margaret Kingston would be itching to sweep away. Sterling glanced around at the portraits lining the room – all men, all white, all former principals. The bald head of Eddie Prestwick, his arms clasped at his desk, stared out with a faintly bewildered look. Sterling could see his own edgy reflection in the table surface, and a smell of French polish brought on the possibility of a sneeze. At the head of the table, the man joined Zoë Westhanger, the chair of the corporation, and to her right the principal, whose tiny frame barely emerged from the level of the table, so that for a moment there was the illusion that she was a small child observing grown-up proceedings.

Further up from Sterling and between him and the panel of three, the Investigating Officer, whose ID card identified her as Programme Manager for Social and Health Care, sat fidgeting with her long brown plaited hair, her fingers slipping restlessly through the single braid. Her bony face was tense and anxious. Sterling hadn't met her before but she had interviewed him on the phone as she looked at the photos he had taken of the dope factory. Opposite Sterling sat Pat Manton, her eyebrow twitching manically in her freckled face. Next to her was the union rep, Sterling assumed, a hard-bitten looking man in a crumpled brown suit concentrating on an untidy array of papers in front of him, an education union's Jim Selsey.

The chair of the corporation did brief introductions. 'Right, Mr Sterling. Let us have your account.'

For about the fourth time, Sterling recounted how, just over a week ago, he'd been on the roof of the green building in the corner of the college and the horticulture section, and what he'd found. 'You'll have seen the photos,' he said, and then nodded as the photos came up on the screen through a laptop and USB connection.

'Ms Manton is responsible for that whole area,' said the Investigating Officer, 'and she holds all the keys.'

'Ms Manton, Mr Mulryne, do you have questions for Mr Sterling?' said the chair of the corporation.

'Certainly,' said Mulryne, the union rep.

'Mr Sterling, those photos were taken on the roof of the warehouse, so you must have been on that roof.'

'Correct.'

'And it looks very much as though they have been taken in darkness.'

'At about 3 in the morning, yes.'

'And did you see Ms Manton around that area, or on the premises, at that time.'

'No.'

'And can you explain what you were doing there at that time?'

'I'd been to the horticulture section earlier on in the day and I was suspicious about the building. Ms Manton knew who I was and I had the feeling she had steered me away from that particular place.'

'So you resorted to some breaking and entering later on?'

'It wasn't breaking and entering. I had full authorisation from the principal. She thought something was going on. I found out what – or a bit of it, anyway.'

'So we're expected to accept evidence from a kind of fishing trip at the dead of night....' The union rep let the words hand in the air.

Sterling stayed silent. There was nothing to say to that.

'OK, Mr Sterling. Perhaps we can accept that there was a cannabis-growing operation in that part of the college, although there's only dubiously obtained photographic evidence and the building is now empty. But can you say with certainty that my union member here was connected in any way with that enterprise?'

'Not with certainty, but....'

'Thank you, Mr Sterling.'

'Finish what you were going to say, Mr Sterling,' said Zoë Westhanger.

'Well, just that I'd have thought it difficult to run a dope factory in those circumstances without the manager knowing. There would need to be all sorts of to-ing and fro-ing – supplies, nutrients and so on in, produce out.

If she didn't know, the people who set it up were brazen. If she did, it all becomes more plausible. And then of course there's the matter of technical knowhow. What I saw was a skilled, well-organised business.'

'But,' said the union rep, 'you can't be certain.'

'No,' said Sterling.

Chapter 19

Thursday 16 October - Crushing

Outside in the corridor, Sterling sat down to collect his thoughts. The union man was good. He'd concentrated on the three weakest parts of the case against Pat Manton – the way the evidence had been collected, the lack of actual cannabis plants, and the tenuous link between Pat Manton and the operation. She did it, but probably the evidence wasn't strong enough for a proper court. If the panel decided to dismiss her, Sterling reckoned there would be an appeal, and beyond that legal action. She was gutsy, and she wouldn't flinch. He himself had enjoyed being a witness and for once not the subject of disciplinary action. He'd enjoyed the court work when he'd been on the job, as that question-and-answer session had reminded him. As for the cannabis farm on college premises, well, it was brazen and wrong, but he couldn't summon up the anger he felt when he thought of Hannah and Darren, and all the other kids corrupted by the goings-on in the training hotel. The cannabis was probably too strong and pure, and therefore dangerous in the vending machines and on the street, but wasn't that a case for legalisation, quality control and regulation? You couldn't stop drug production, but education professionals corrupting students....

He looked at his watch. It was approaching 10:30. He couldn't remember the timetable for class times and breaks, but now he was in the college he'd go down and see Ellie Laski. The pottery classroom was quiet when he arrived and when he knocked he prepared himself to be disappointed. The door swung open abruptly.

'Frank. Welcome again. Never mind about trailblazing or path finding, since you've come on the scene it's been chaos here. Murder, rumours, swarms of police. Is it like this wherever you go?'

'I have my moments. Haven't you got a class?'

'It's a very welcome free period. Come in. Coffee?' She strode on long legs back into the heart of the room to where a kettle and mugs sat next to the kiln.

'OK.' Adele's offerings were always much better, but ambience was going to be important here. He perched next to her on a stool and looked at the brown muck in a mug that had seen cleaner days. 'Do you have a little more milk, Ellie?'

'Mr Fusspot.' She splashed some more carelessly in. 'So, what's new?'

'Another death, actually. You'll hear anyway I expect. Whenever the principal has to do a press release I imagine she round robins all of you. Did you know Mrs Jenkinson in the Hotel and Catering Section?'

'I knew what she looked like. The rumour mill had it that she'd been suspended for as yet unspecified naughty activities. Bloody hell, Frank. Is it her?'

'Yup. I went to see her yesterday and found her body. It'll be on the local news by now, I should have thought.'

'What happened? Was her head bashed in like the evil Jane Casterton's? Another murder? God, this place is getting dangerous. Maybe I shouldn't have come down here.'

'She was hanged. Whether she did it herself or someone else did it and staged it as suicide I don't know. The police are obviously looking at it.' He summarised what he'd found out about what was happening at the college – he'd done it often enough that it came naturally – and focused on the crude attempt to blackmail him.

Ellie Laski sipped her coffee. Her hair fell forward across her face. Sterling could see the soft, pale brown, unlined contours of her neck. Her slender fingers grasped the mug in both hands. It was completely quiet in the pottery classroom. Sterling sat still and became aware of the musty, dusty smell of clay. He knew he was on the right track.

'Why did you tell me this?'

'Well, I'm kind of thinking that we're mates. We're on the same wavelength. Independent-minded. Questioning. Maybe a bit sceptical.'

'That might be part of it, Frank, but you're a sly one. You don't give out all this inside information, and the personal blackmail stuff, just off the cuff.'

He put his hands up. 'OK. I guess you're right. I've found out everything I've just told you but now I'm struggling. I go to see someone yesterday and she's dead. The police are struggling too – my contact called it a "wall of silence" last night. It wouldn't matter so much, but the stars of the sex show are missing, and I'm worried.'

The potter carried on looking down at her mug of coffee. When she looked up her eyes were shining, but not from happiness. 'I was being blackmailed too, Frank.'

Sterling held her gaze.

'I didn't tell you everything about why I came to be an art lecturer in an obscure FE college in the southeastern corner of England – from one of the best secondary schools in Birmingham, where I was the youngest assistant head teacher they'd ever had.'

'And therefore well steeped in the jargon,' said Sterling.

'Inevitably.' She smiled through her tears and dabbed at her eyes with a piece of coarse industrial paper from a nearby roll. 'I was under pressure and overworked, and I did a really stupid thing. There was a young teacher at the school on teaching practice, and I was responsible for mentoring all the trainees. He was struggling, and I spent a lot of time helping and sorting things out – not that I know anything much about History, which was his subject. One thing led to another, and we started a … relationship.'

'What was wrong with that? Presumably he was over 21, and he wasn't a pupil. The mentorship thing might have been a bit of a problem, and I imagine you had to do an assessment of him that could have been influenced by what you were doing, but really, in the scheme of things….'

'If only it had been just that. It was a crazy time. I was stressed and here was this young bloke and it was like a whirlwind – exciting and fun and carefree. So carefree that I booked out one of the school minibuses for a weekend camping away together, and in a total panic lied when I got found out. Stupid. Stupid, stupid, stupid. Everything turned to shit after that, especially the relationship. The union got involved and a solution was negotiated. I resigned instead of getting sacked, and got a satisfactory couple of references. This was the first job I got after all that. Then, after about a month, this was in my pigeon-hole.' She opened a drawer in her desk, fished around at the back, her arm entirely obscured up to the elbow, and took out a memory stick.

Sterling looked at it. It was the same make as the one delivered to his office. 'What's on it?'

'Someone managed to get all the correspondence from the disciplinary process, including the letter where I admitted breach of trust and misuse of school property. If HR here got hold of it, I'd be out. They told me to 'stand ready', whatever that means. I've been on bloody tenterhooks ever since, waiting for the demand. I can't lose this job. I've settled in down here by the seaside and there are no other options.'

'Well, Ellie, your secret is safe with me, and the way things are going, none of this is going any further. Jane Casterton was the mastermind, and now she's gone, everything's falling apart. If you and I have been targeted for blackmail, that suggests it's widespread, with someone in charge of the research.' He paused. A candidate for that had just occurred to him. 'But I don't think blackmail, or the intimidation I've seen around the college, or the cash washing around, is enough to keep people in line. There's got to be something else – something I'm missing. Do you know a blonde boy around college – Johnny Fontana?'

'I don't teach him, but everyone knows Johnny Fontana. There are lots of boys with dyed blonde hair in this place, but only one Johnny F.'

'He's the one I need to catch up with, but he's one of the ones who's been suspended – or rather, banned from the premises – he doesn't seem to be registered as a student. Anyway, I don't think he'd tell me anything even if I caught up with him.'

'Talk to Hissing Sid, Frank. I know I told you to watch out for him, but there's always been something about him apart from his creepiness.'

'Yes?'

'I told you before – somewhere in there is a human side.'

'I was going to see him yesterday after I'd seen Mrs Jenkinson, but obviously I got diverted. I might do that after I've finished here.'

He stood up. 'Right. Thanks for the coffee. Thanks for telling me … you know…. It will really help.'

The potter stood up as well. She was at least as tall as Sterling, perhaps even half an inch taller. 'I'd better get on.'

They each shuffled awkwardly from foot to foot. Then Ellie Laski took Sterling's elbow in her hand and brushed his cheek with a clumsy kiss. 'When things have settled down….'

'Sure,' said Sterling.

After that conversation, he knew where on campus he needed to go next. Then he'd catch up with Hissing Sid in Marchurch. He started down the tree-lined roadway towards the bottom of the college, but had only gone a few paces when a young girl approached him. She looked familiar, with long black hair streaked with purple, Doc Martens and a black goth t-shirt, inscribed 'Angel Girl' over a purple butterfly, and tucked into a black mini-skirt. Her black tights had small holes up and down each leg, and little mounds of sun-starved flesh poked through like tiny blobs of lard. The refectory, last week, that was it. She'd helped him with the tray.

Eyes down on the path, she offered him an envelope with his name on it in crabbed, mean capitals.

'Thanks,' he said. 'Who gave you this?'

She shrugged, gave a smile halfway between unease and shyness, and moved off, her boots indicating a hint of pigeon-toe. He opened the envelope and drew out a small sheet of paper. A short unsigned sentence was printed in the same scratchy, ungenerous hand. 'Need more information? LRC, 817.124 Runciman, flyleaf.' Sterling looked at his watch. It was a diversion, and back where he'd just come from, but there was time. He stomped back into the Tuckett Building, past the newly respectable vending machine and up the stairs from the lower ground floor to the ground floor, past the principal's office, the secretaries' office and the boardroom and into the Learning Resource Centre.

A librarian at the desk looked up brightly as he entered and he nodded. Although the Tuckett Building was old, probably late Victorian, the LRC was bright and open and modern. There were one or two students scattered around, including some sprawled on the easy chairs around the area, but few books. Instead, fingers tapped on mobiles and tablets, their owners as likely to be on Facebook as typing essays. An assistant was in intense conversation with a student in front of a screen, their heads almost touching. Angela Wilson had taught Sterling well, and he knew the classification system from Sandley library. But this was no old-fashioned library. Beyond the computer stations, the study desks and information boards, the shelf stacks all seemed to be bunched together in clusters, with no space in most cases for getting at what was in them. Up close, the stacks had electronic arrows and buttons in panels below the information framed in numbers and letters at the sides. It was about saving space, Sterling realised. You could fit more books in your LRC if you could move the stacks and not have permanent spaces in between them.

He looked back at the desk. He was going to need help with the system, but then he realised that there was already a gap where he needed to go – down the 800 aisle. 817 was halfway down, and 817.124 Runciman on one of the top shelves. That was when the whispering started, or perhaps it was a slight whirr. Sterling concentrated on reaching up for the book, anxious for the help to his investigation that it might contain. After the whisper was the bump. The act of outstretching his arm spread-eagled him against the 800 stack as the neighbouring stack nudged into his back. Although it was a nudge and not a cannon, at about one mile per hour, it was relentless and indeed painful despite that. He was too surprised to think of calling out. His face, pressed against a row of books in front of him, made a kind of imprint as they moved backwards as far as the next stack would let them go. He felt squashed and then breathless as the rogue stack drove into him in deadly near-silence, grinding softly as it met resistance. He felt an overwhelming claustrophobic panic as the tonne of metal, cardboard and paper squeezed inexorably on. He'd been on duty, as a young policeman, at football matches when there had been mangling and trampling. So this is what it was like at the receiving end.

He began to drift in and out of a black-edged consciousness. There was a ringing in his ears, and giddiness around his temples. He gathered himself to shout before all the air was forced out of him. Libraries were silent, solitary places, where people spent most of the time looking down, immersed in their own little worlds. He'd heard people say that as you are dying your life flashes back before you, but that wasn't what he was experiencing. All he saw was Angela tut-tutting and complaining that this was the kind of thing that gave libraries a bad name.

Just as he was finally losing hope, a face appeared at the gap in the stacks. Sterling's own face, jammed up and forced sideways in a grotesque distortion, must have triggered the look of dismay and fear from two metres away. 'Jesus Christ,' said the small mouth, and then disappeared. A second later, the gentle grinding stopped abruptly, and a second after that, the huge weight oppressing Sterling began to ease as the stack moved away. He sank to the floor like melting ice cream, the only difference being the gulps of air he was forcing in whoops into his lungs. Next to him, the Runciman book, entitled, with macabre humour, *A Crushing Disappointment* fell open to reveal a blank flyleaf. Before he blacked out, more from shock than physical injury, he couldn't help admiring how enterprising and ingenious the attempt to get rid of him had been.

Chapter 20

Thursday 16 October - Westgate Villa

He came round in a small office-cum-staffroom behind the front desk, not unlike the one in Sandley library. In one half, there were easy chairs arranged in a half square, a sink and a kettle, and on the draining board a mug inscribed 'OVERDUE: better books than babies'. In the other were desks and a chaos of books and papers.

Somewhere in a corner of his mind, he remembered half getting up, half being pulled up, and stumbling out of the stacks with his arm over the shoulder of the petite, brisk woman with overlapping front teeth whose face had appeared at the moment of crisis and was now standing over him.

'Thank goodness,' said the same woman. 'A little longer and I reckon you'd have been a goner. Here, drink this.' She pressed a tumbler of water into Sterling's hand. 'There's enough going on here without an accident in the Learning Resource Centre.'

A short, wide middle-aged man in a grey workshop coat was conducting a first aid examination. He thrust two fingers in front of Sterling's eye and asked

'How many fingers?' Sterling considered resistance but it was easier to submit. 'Hmm, accident,' he said. He started to say 'I don't think so' and then stopped. There was no advantage in making a fuss and telling Andrews and Murphy, and going through all the rigmarole of reporting and explaining would disrupt any momentum he was gathering. 'It was a good job you came along.'

'A student alerted me. I wouldn't have noticed otherwise.'

'Small girl? Pretty, in a gothic kind of way? Black hair, purple streaks?'

'That's her,' said the librarian. She gave Sterling a curious, almost suspicious glance. 'How did you know that?'

'I saw her just before I went between the stacks. She must have seen what was happening. Is she not out there?'

'No, once I'd got you out and in here, I noticed she'd gone. You need a medic to check you over.'

The first aider nodded in agreement.

Sterling stood up, testing his limbs and the rest of him. 'No, I don't think it's necessary. I've got to get on. You'll need the company who supplied those stacks to check them out.'

'I've already roped them off and put notices up,' said the librarian. 'There are supposed to be fail-safe mechanisms to stop this sort of thing happening.'

'There's probably a problem with the sensors,' said Sterling. He knew where in college the technical expert resided who could have done the tampering. Now getting to his next destination was more urgent and fuelled by anger.

The librarian looked at him. 'Are you sure you're OK? I'm going to have to do an incident report, and I'll say someone almost got crushed.'

'And I'll have to fill in my forms,' chipped in the first aider. 'You leave here at your own risk.'

'Do what you need to do. I've got to get on. You can contact me through Adele in the principal's office.'

Sterling shambled away from the LRC, down the stairs to the lower ground floor and through the back. He could feel the aches and bruises coming up, but gradually the shambling turned into a brisker, more even pace. He'd been naïve. Because no one had come near him since his escape on Saturday night, he'd thought he was untouchable. Not just naïve. Sloppy. The shock and anger, if not the physical discomfort, had subsided when he reached Glen Lodge at the far end of the college, but he was still ready for a confrontation. It wasn't to be. The Z4 roadster was not in its parking spot, and Glen Lodge itself was locked up. Glen Havers had got himself a reprieve, but there would be a reckoning – Sterling would make sure of that.

He called the direct line Adele had given him. 'I'm down at the rear entrance, Adele. Can you get me a taxi to take me over to Marchurch?' The pace was quickening. The time for trains was over.

'Hang on,' she said. In two minutes she was back. 'There'll be one there in five minutes.'

'Thanks. The next thing is more difficult. Can you see if you can track down a girl for me, a student? I don't have her name but she's a goth, or she dresses like one. She's small and pretty, with dark hair and purple streaks. She's wearing black tights with holes in them.'

'That's going to be more difficult, but I'll put feelers out. You'll probably get a list of ten and you'll need to narrow it down.'

'I have every confidence, Adele.'

'Apart from that, how are you getting on, Mr Sterling?'

'It's bruising, Adele, and progress is slow.'

'For the police too,' she said softly.

Hissing Sid's house was at the end of Byron Road in what was known as Marchurch's poets' quarter, a gracious little Victorian end-of-terrace with a wide, generous bay window. Sterling knew the road because he'd once had to visit to tell a couple their daughter had been stabbed in one of the eruptions on the seafront. She hadn't pulled through. The house backed on to the park at the back and nestled cosily in the corner. The brickwork had escaped the fashion for pebbledash late in the last century and had recently been repointed. It looked as though the sash windows were the originals, but Sterling could see the secondary glazing arrangements behind them, and the subtle way the Victorian method of getting air to circulate through the tops and bottoms of windows had been preserved. Just under the roof was a small plaque that announced "Westgate Villa", and underneath that "1897". Even in the 19th century, builders were full of hype. The house was neat and well proportioned, but describing it as a villa was a stretch.

He asked the taxi driver to wait and rang the bell. Hissing Sid's lupine face appeared through the gap between door and jamb. When he saw who the caller was he made to push the door closed but Sterling was ready. He put his shoe in the space at the bottom. 'We need to talk, Mr Brown. Things have got wildly out of hand. Jane Casterton and Meg Jenkinson are dead.

Hannah Williamson has gone missing, and the boy Darren. The police are struggling. So am I.'

The two men locked eyes. Then the older one turned around and retreated into the house, leaving the door ajar. Sterling went over to the taxi-driver and paid. 'I'll be here for a while, so there's no need to hang around.' Then he went back and entered the house. He found Hissing Sid in the front room with the bay window, staring in a sprawl from a black leather armchair into what looked like an original Victorian fireplace.

Sterling looked around. There was a matching sofa against the inner wall, opposite the window, and above it a scene of nineteenth century Marchurch, a gentle seaside idyll before the march of the railways like long spidery fissures over the countryside. On the mantelpiece over the fireplace was a small carriage clock, all gilt and glass, and on either side of that some photos in frames, including a younger Hissing Sid from the 70s, far more mod than rocker, and a pretty woman with a dark beehive and a big smile in a floral mini-dress, hanging on to his arm.

In the corner between the fireplace and the window was a large black plasma television. There were good odds that Hissing Sid spent much time watching it. On a kind of small stand by his armchair were a remote control device and a kind of revolving tray with partitions containing nuts, sweets and chocolate. The ceiling still had its original features – heavy rose mouldings and coving. The room was a curious clash of old and modern, overlaid with a faint air of decay and lack of interest, and, if you looked closely, bodge. Tiling in the fireplace had been chipped and not quite cleanly repaired. The Marchurch picture hung slightly askew from a makeshift nail. There was evidence of housework, but equally evidence, in stray patches of dust, of carelessness. It was the room of a person for whom making an effort was an effort.

Sterling perched on the sofa and Hissing Sid's eyes swivelled around to him.

'Well, you've really stirred things up. I've had the police here and they say there'll be charges. They told me not to go anywhere. Where would I go? My home's here in Marchurch. I barely leave the town except to go to work. I haven't got a car. I haven't been out of Earlsey for years. At least they haven't tried to pin Jane Casterton on me. Yet. God, what a mess.' He passed a hand across his eyes, as if warding off a migraine. 'All I ever wanted to do was be a hairdresser. Own my own salon, or maybe a couple, here in the town. I grew up here and never wanted to be anywhere else.'

Sterling felt a curious affinity with the hometown loving, go-nowhere man. Birds of a feather in one small sense. He remembered his walk around Sandley, when he'd been sacked.

'It all went to pot when Yvonne fell ill. There were bills and we were going under. I cut corners. Diverted cash where I was working. I spent four months at Her Majesty's pleasure in Standford Hill, on Sheppey. That was years ago, but of course Jane Casterton found out, and established that I hadn't mentioned it in my college application. Another month and the offence would have been spent. Of course, that cut no ice with her.'

'So,' said Sterling, 'you're saying that she recruited you by blackmail.'

'That's how she did it with virtually everyone, except Johnny bloody Fontana. Everyone's got some secret somewhere. I had no choice. None of us did. She was a terrible, terrible woman, all the worse because to her it was all just a game – a twisted consolation because she never got the top job. She wasn't even interested in the money. Then, when it all started falling apart, she started cutting us loose, those of us fingered by your evidence. Me, Meg Jenkinson, the others. Meg met me in a pub a few weeks ago. She wanted out and was looking for a way. I told her it would be by doing time or in a body bag. She got the body bag.'

'Johnny Fontana,' murmured Sterling. 'He was suspended too – or at least banned from the premises. He didn't seem to have been currently enrolled.'

'He'd have been all right, student or not,' said Hissing Sid bitterly. 'He didn't have to be on site to work the puppets' strings.'

Sterling sat back into the sofa, which squeaked as he shifted. He'd heard that story before. He wanted to say 'Spare me the hoary old justifications and excuses. Spare me the sob story. Spare me the miserable bloody back-story. Really, please, just spare me. Everyone has a choice. No one has to set out on a path of procuring, pimping, compering a sex show and all the other pecca-dilloes. Sterling remembered a case here in Marchurch where a man had put out his girlfriend's eyes. 'She made me,' he had whined. 'It was her fault. She goaded and goaded.' Jesus.

But he knew better, and patience was best. The police had their forensics, their resources, their databases, and all their people scurrying around, whilst he'd been getting good at the confessional, especially in this case.

'Do you reckon Fontana did Jane Casterton in?'

Hissing Sid shrugged. 'Possibly, but I can't see it. They were close, and there was nothing they'd fall out over.' His focus drifted off into the distance again.

'Hannah, Sid,' said Sterling softly, 'and Darren. What's happened to them? What happened last Saturday night?'

'Hannah....' said Hissing Sid. 'A beautiful girl. A sweet girl. She loves sex of course, never mind who with. And showing off. That's why it was so easy to recruit her. She got the boy Darren involved. They had something going. He wasn't that keen but she sold it as a bit of fun for a lot of cash. Hannah's different from lots of those other girls, with their eyes on the main chance. She didn't know you were being filmed when she cut your hair. Maybe she knew something was going on, but not what exactly. She recognised you on Saturday night, just after Johnny Fontana had. Maybe it was the haircut. Anyway, you ran off out the back right past her. When Fontana came back, we'd just got everything settled down for the night. We'd reassured the punters, and we were carrying on. But Hannah was getting lippy.' Hissing Sid looked sideways at Sterling. 'She was worried about you. Fontana took her to one side but she kept on kicking up a fuss. All the kids were getting jittery again, so Fontana took Hannah and Darren out. It was all very discreet, but he didn't mess about.'

'Well, I reckon that's the last time anybody saw them. Where did he take them, him and his goons?'

'You've got to understand....'

Sterling waited for another tangent.

'Jane Casterton did what she did, and got what she got, through a massive network of blackmail. She had someone doing research just for that. Then there were the big cash payments and intimidation, which is where Johnny Fontana came in. But you don't keep the wheels on and prevent gossip, blabbing or grassing just by that stuff. There were rumours of something else.'

The clock ticked on the mantelpiece. The sofa squeaked again as Sterling leaned forward.

'We were in cells, Mr Sterling, like the official cost centres of the college. No one except the principal and the finance director really knows what's going in the college for each cost centre. The programme managers know their own budgets but nobody else's. It's divide and rule. It was the same with Jane Casterton's black ops. No one knew what anyone else involved was really doing – only when it all came together in events like Saturday. Only Jane Casterton, and maybe Johnny Fontana, knew everything. That way if anything went wrong it could be contained.'

'The rumours,' said Sterling.

'People are scared of Johnny Fontana. He's a bully. It had nothing to do with me, but I heard here and there that if anyone wasn't falling into line, wasn't paying for the drug supplies, was doing some skimming, wanted to stop … you know, doing the entertaining, and threats weren't working, Fontana would take them somewhere and….' Hissing Sid stopped and mopped his forehead with a handkerchief from his pocket '….torture them. I heard a name. The Box.'

'Where is it?' said Sterling.

'I don't know. I kept out of all that.'

'You must have some idea. How could something like that be a secret?'

'What she did, she did for years. There are plenty of secrets. I don't suppose some will ever come out. If it exists, The Box is probably near the college, or maybe in it. She liked to keep things tight and close.'

'Who might know, apart from Johnny Fontana and his mates?'

Hissing Sid flapped his hands. 'I've got no idea. I don't want to know. Nothing good will have come out of The Box.'

There was nothing else for Sterling in the interview. Hissing Sid probably knew more than he was telling, but that would be for another time and for someone else – probably the police. Blackmail, threats and now the possibility of torture. Sterling needed to find Hannah and Darren fast, and now he had another lead, tenuous as it was. He got to his feet.

'I'm glad it's falling apart,' said the man in the armchair. He looked old and tired, the collar button of his shirt undone and his tie awry on his chest. 'It was getting worse and worse. Once you were in it, you couldn't get off the treadmill. I'm finished now – finished at the college, finished here – but you know what, it's a relief.'

'There's mitigation,' said Sterling. They'd all be going for that, all the people who'd finally be charged. He wasn't sure why he'd said it. The man in the chair was listless and apathetic, but Sterling remembered the cock of the walk in the college, compering the sex show and lording it over the hairdressing salon. 'I'll be making tracks then,' he said.

Hissing Sid said nothing. He picked up the remote control as Sterling left the stuffy room. As Sterling closed the front door he could hear the babble of a quiz show on the television. If Hissing Sid was hoping that Hannah and Darren could be found safely, he wasn't letting on.

Chapter 21

Thursday 16 October and Friday 17 October - Carrot-top

There was a pub a few houses along from Westgate Villa – the Lord Byron Arms – one of those neighbourhood Victorian pubs set among terraced houses, now fast disappearing as people drank beer from cans more cheaply at home. Its faded sign flapped and creaked in the wind. Opposite was a path that Sterling was sure led down to the park. From the park he'd be able to get across to Rhodes Square, down to and along the front and up the slope to the station. He strode down past a broken, empty half-pint vodka bottle labelled with silver Cyrillic script on a red background, and ragged scraps of paper from a discarded red top. The unkempt ground was half-pebbled, half-mud until the neatness and order of the park.

As he cut through to the square, he tried to process what Hissing Sid had said and what he might have missed out. It was worse than Sterling had thought. Hannah and Darren had disappeared on the Saturday night, not before the attempt to suspend them at the beginning of the week. He hadn't heard anyone mention 'The Box' before, but what Hissing Sid said was plausible, and if Johnny Fontana was involved, he should follow it up.

As for the shadow enterprise at ECOT, blackmail, cash and threats would have done much to keep it hidden but flourishing, like a parasite on its host, but abduction and torture would reinforce *omerta*. Johnny Fontana was the man with the secrets, but he'd never help Sterling, even if Sterling could find him. Who else would know about The Box and where it was? He'd have to find someone in Johnny Fontana's entourage, someone he could put pressure on.

In the blustery mid-afternoon, the lights outside the arcades and bingo rooms had none of the allure of the night-time. They simply looked faded and tired, as if going through the motions like the bored men and women in the change booths and the number-callers. A couple of women, perhaps mother and daughter, sat on stools with their bingo screens, looking down with glazed eyes. The older woman watched as Sterling passed, an unlit cigarette poking out from the corner of her crinkled mouth. He was glad to get on the train to Ramston, change for Sandley, and out of Earlsey. He wasn't going to find Hannah and Darren by rampaging around ECOT like a bull in a china shop.

He hadn't been in his office since Monday, but it felt like longer. He opened the window to get rid of the fustiness, turned on the bar-heater and booted up the computer, slipping into the port the memory stick on which he'd copied Saturday night's exploits. He watched everything again carefully. It was just after he'd been speaking to Janeen when he found what he was looking for. He telephoned Adele and 20 minutes later she called him back. 'Thanks, Adele,' he said. 'Likely I'll see you tomorrow.' An intuition had been growing in his head. In his policeman's gut, there were lurches and butterflies. Tomorrow was shaping up to be a breakthrough day.

At the back of the college, the Z4 roadster was in its space by Glen Lodge. Sterling went through the front door and along the rickety corridor. The building was silent and when he entered the technicians' office without knocking, the television screens mounted on the walls above and beyond the counter were blank and grey.

Behind the counter there was still junk and chaos. Glen Havers looked round from behind a computer screen amidst the disorder, his face registering surprise and perhaps dismay.

'I can't talk to you now,' he said. 'I've got a meeting.'

'The principal's not coming. I'm here instead. I need a word.'

Havers's hand went to the phone.

'Don't bother, Glen. Adele will say the same as me. We fixed it together.'

'I talked to you the other day. I've got nothing more to say.'

Sterling vaulted over the counter in one deft movement, his left hand and arm acting as a pivot on the well-scored surface. Although he was two metres away, Havers recoiled at the sudden, abrupt movement and Sterling's approach towards his personal space. Sterling flopped in one of the high-backed chairs in the clutter, rocking and swivelling as he settled. 'That's a nice motor outside, that Z4, Glen. What, less than two years old? Pretty much top of the range.'

'So?'

'Well, on your money, in a college, not even on the teaching staff....'

'Sod off, Mr Consultant. What I earn, what my finances are, what kind of car I drive – none of that has anything to do with you.'

'But getting squashed by a shelf-stack in the resource centre – because of faulty sensors – and being on the wrong end of a crude blackmail attempt – using one of those memory sticks....' (Sterling pointed to a box on a nearby desk) '.... now that *is* my business. And it's not just me, Glen, mate. All sorts of people are stepping up with their blackmail stories. There's a researcher here in ECOT, beavering away, digging up the dirt, but only a technical wizard could do some of the things I've seen – the downloads, the attachments, the video clips.'

Havers's bent nose seemed even more out of true as sweat gathered over his top lip. He sat upright in his chair, his palms flat on the work surface in front of him.

'I expect you've been very careful, Glen. There'll be a box of surgical gloves somewhere in this junk shop, and other precautions I can only dream about. You'll have closed things down as best you can, but your card is marked, old china. When the police really get their arses into gear, when they've gone past Jane Casterton and Meg Jenkinson – their specialists are going to swarm all over your little operation. However efficient you've been, they'll find something – here, at home, on your hard drives, on the researcher's computer, around college – files, bugs, cameras, sensors, fingerprints, websites. Blackmail, porn, illegal surveillance, attempted murder. Bloody hell, Glen, reeled off like that ... You're in deep shit.'

'You know fuck all,' said the technician, but his voice sounded high-pitched and hollow.

'I know enough – and you know it – but I'm not really interested in all that.' Sterling swivelled and rocked. 'What I'm interested in is The Box.'

'Jesus,' said Havers. There was no denial there, only recognition. 'What box? I don't know anything about any box.'

Sterling stood up suddenly, swept a mug of pens and pencils violently onto the floor and loomed over Havers in his chair. 'Come on, Glen. Don't bullshit me. I can go up to the Tuckett Building, find one of the police investigations team and really land you in it.'

'I don't know anything. You're well out of order with all these stupid accusations. Fuck off. I've got work to do.'

There comes a point in interrogations, Sterling knew from long experience, when you know you're not going to get any further. Wheedling won't work, nor sweet reason, nor intimidation, nor violence, which is not only out of the question but often counter-productive. In Glen Havers's case, that point had been reached. Now he was defiant, and Sterling could see where it came from. Havers was terrified – much more terrified of someone else than he was of Sterling and his threats.

'This isn't over,' said Sterling as he regained the area in front of the counter and moved off into the corridor. His last view of Havers was of a man staring at a computer screen, eyes brimming and with a tremor in his outstretched hands. Sterling moved from Glen Lodge, through the Cara Building underpass and up the slope. If Adele had got it right, the gardeners would be working in front of the Tuckett Building, so he walked around the bottom by the pottery and up towards the main entrance. The front car park, with spaces normally reserved for senior staff, corporation members and important visitors, had its share of police cars, and it was obvious that Andrews had established a base inside. He'd have thrown his weight about and got the facilities he wanted – access to refreshments, a decent interview room and all the other requirements for running an on-the-spot murder investigation.

From beyond the main entrance, Sterling could see a head of close-cropped, light red hair bobbing and ducking as its owner worked with a spade and wheelbarrow.

'Got a moment?' said Sterling as he approached.

The young man looked up suspiciously. He had the pellucid white colouring common to some people with red hair, and a sharp, triangular face, wide across the forehead and with a narrow, pointed chin.

'What's it worth?' he said immediately, leaning on his spade and clearly savouring the diversion.

'Maybe something,' said Sterling. He got out a small roll of cash. 'You're not from around here.'

'Manc,' said the young man, eyeing the money.

'I was watching a video last night,' said Sterling, 'and I think there's a shot of you in it.'

'Yeah?'

'Last Saturday evening, down in the training hotel. It looked like you were doing security.'

The young man smiled slyly. 'So that's what this is about. Well, it can't have been a very good shot, 'cos I'm still here. Anyone they identified they suspended.'

'It was your hair,' said Sterling, 'from across the room.'

The young man ran his fingers over his scalp. 'Carrot-top,' he said. 'Some people love it; some people don't. It doesn't bother me either way.'

'Moving on. Johnny Fontana,' murmured Sterling.

'Johnny,' laughed the young man. 'Of course it would be about him. Mr Big Shot. Mr Scary.' With his fingers he put speech marks round the "Scary".'

'That's not how people usually react.'

'Look, I just wanted to earn a bit of extra cash. No one frightens me. He knows that. Anyway, this is my last day. I've been down here six months, which is well long enough, so tomorrow I'm off. I'm only staying today to be sure to get all my wages.'

'Easy come, easy go, then,' said Sterling. 'Right, Saturday night – there was a disturbance – remember? Johnny went off after somebody with a couple of his blokes round the back of the building. I don't think you were with him then, but later on he took away two young people.'

'I had nothing to do with that,' said Carrot-top sharply. 'I was just security, for one night only.'

'I'm not saying you did. I just need some information.'

The young man shrugged.

'The Box,' said Sterling. 'What do you know about it?'

'Ah, The Box.' Carrot-top laughed again. 'The Big Man's alleged torture chamber. Bag of wind.'

From what Sterling had heard, he wasn't so confident. Another thought came obscurely to him. Could he refer to him as 'Carrot-top?' Was it PC? He'd had a client who was hot on that. They were still occasionally in touch.

He'd ask her, if he remembered. 'Do you know where it is?'

'I know where it's *rumoured* to be, but that's the kind of information that will cost you.'

Sterling peeled off a note. The young man looked on impassively. Sterling peeled off another and then another. The young man nodded slightly and tucked them away quickly away. Then he jerked his thumb at the Tuckett Building. 'It's right behind you, allegedly. Lower ground floor. You didn't hear it from me, and I very much doubt it will be worth anything.'

'Thanks anyway,' said Sterling. This had been by far the quickest and least complicated way of getting what he wanted to know, involving a straightforward transaction with a reasonable if mercenary source, but he wondered how it was going to go on his expenses claim form. He pictured Margaret Kingston in her office, going through it line by line and quibbling. He looked at Carrot-top and smiled.

'What?' said the young man.

'I was thinking how ludicrous it would be to ask for a receipt.'

'Too right, pal,' he replied, and went back to his digging.

Chapter 22

Friday 17 October - The Box

The police were still everywhere around the main entrance, with cars and people and milling about. No doubt there was still crime scene tape round Jane Casterton's office on the first floor. Sterling nodded at one or two officers and went to the secretaries' office.

He approached Adele's desk. 'How are you fixed right now? I need someone with a bit of spunk,' he said softly.

Her computer screen flickered in front of her, light and shadows playing on her face. 'Willing to be diverted,' she said.

'Follow me – we're going downstairs. It could get a bit dodgy. Are you all right with that?'

'Sure, Frank.'

'Good. As I thought, but tell someone you trust.'

Together, they went down to the lower ground floor, home of the pottery, the vending machines, classrooms, the caretaker's cubbyhole, and Sterling's hunch.

'What are we doing?' said the secretary.

'Finding lost kids; keep your wits about you. Like I said, this could get dodgy.'

They walked up and down the corridor that bisected the rooms either side, Sterling muttering and eliminating possibilities as they went. Then there was only one place left. He ducked into the caretaker's space, too small and inappropriately equipped to be dignified as an office – cubbyhole was a virtually perfect description. Behind the makeshift desk and pegboard and all the clutter was the heavy-looking door solidly built into the wall that Sterling had seen on the first day of the case. It was clear that the dimensions of the cubbyhole did not match the length of wall in the corridor. Sterling knew the door was locked before he even tried the handle, and was not surprised.

There was movement behind him, next to Adele at the desk. 'What's going on here?' said the caretaker. His rheumy grey eyes were magnified behind spectacles speckled with grit, or perhaps fragments of skin from his dry, scaly forehead. The bitter expression on his pink, blotchy face was clearly its default position.

Sterling pointed at the door. 'We need to go in there.'

'Why?' said the older man. 'No one but authorised personnel.'

'I'm authorised,' said Sterling. He pinned the caretaker to the wall behind him and pushed a fist close to his face.

A sour look flitted across the caretaker's features. The jig's up, it seemed to say. 'It was nothing to do with me. I had no choice.'

'Key,' said Sterling.

The caretaker pointed shakily to a key at the bottom of the pegboard.

Sterling took the key and unlocked the door.

'Frank,' hissed Adele as she peered into the corridor. Sterling noticed that it was the first time she'd used his forename. 'Mr Smith – the caretaker – is walking off.'

'Let him go. Where can he hide? This is more important.' He swung open the unlocked door, which was as heavy and solid as it looked, and with a frisson of fear and expectation stepped through. In the cavern before them was a hotchpotch of tables, broken chairs, old overhead projectors whose poles and mirrors tilted at tortured, broken angles, and discarded Banda machines. A lingering, pervasive smell of duplicating fluid took Sterling back to his early school days, the term after primary school when a history teacher was still producing his own handouts. He had sniffed the sheets with his friends and joined the giggling, Banda fluid making the Norman Conquest giddily alluring. But it wasn't the depository of broken furniture and lost technology that caught their attention – it was the breeze block-style construction, drab and grey in the gloom and about the size of a shipping container. Sterling did rough calculations in his head. The principal's office upstairs on the ground floor must at least overlap with some of this.

'Wait there,' he said to Adele, almost physically stationing her by the wall next to the heavy door and giving her the key. Sterling approached The Box. There were no padlocks on the locking bars. The people controlling it were obviously confident about the effectiveness of the outer door – the door to the cavern. Sterling looked back at Adele. She leaned rigidly against the wall and nodded. His heartbeat thumping in his ears, Sterling fumbled at the bolt slides, which squeaked and rasped in the gloom, and slid down the bars. The doors pulled noiselessly open and he was straight away assailed by smells, and not the scented candles and patchouli of a gift shop. This was more piss and shit, sweat and fear, and something else. He reeled back and put his sleeve to his mouth, groping for and then finding a light switch just outside the door. The Box was bathed in an unforgiving, harsh light.

As Sterling's eyes were getting accustomed to the change, a voice, full of anger and defiance, called out from underneath some covers a metre or two into the inside. 'Fuck off, Johnny.'

'It's not Johnny, Hannah. It's Frank. Why are you hiding in here?' I thought we had a date.'

Hannah Williamson emerged quickly from under a grubby duvet, trying to get to her feet but under-estimating lack of practice and shakiness. She lurched stumbling and laughing towards Sterling and tripped into his arms, pulling at him and almost causing him to topple on top of her.

'Steady on, girl.'

'Frank.' She buried her head in his chest and held him close and tight. Sterling looked down on her greasy scalp. There was a powerful smell of dank hair and stale sweat. She was still in the black, sleeveless mini-dress of Saturday night but the sex-diva had long gone. This was just a frightened, dirty, woebegone girl. He could feel the increasing convulsions of her small body, as laughing turned to sobbing.

He waited until the weeping and shaking had abated, then gently took her by the shoulders, pushed her away an arm's length and looked her up and down. 'Right, let's look at you. Any bones broken? You look a bit thinner but that's all.'

'I'm OK, but....' Her eyes started filling up again.

Sterling looked further in. There seemed to be two sections to the basement prison – Hannah's quarters, an untidy mess of duvet covers, a pillow or two, a bottle of water knocked over in the excitement of rescue and in one corner by the doors a slop bucket. Sterling had seen many things on the job and even as a PI. Just yesterday he'd cut down a body hanging from a noose, and the day before there was Jane Casterton with a golden tick embedded in her skull. But he'd never seen anything like the torture chamber in the back section of The Box. There were shackles on the side wall and the back wall, and a tray of vicious-looking instruments on the other one. Opposite the shackles and next to the tray was a large armchair, used, by the look of it, for viewing and decision-making.

None of that induced the sudden gagging that rose up from his guts into his throat and emptied vomit onto the shiny floor – what did that was the naked shackled body slumped in the corner, back to the wall. Sterling recovered himself enough to go down on his knees and feel on the neck for a pulse – he'd been doing that a lot lately. The flame licking Darren's arm looked as diminished as the boy himself – less vivid, less vibrant, less vital. Over his sad muscled body was a mass of stabs and cuts and burns. Sterling could still see the dread and pain in his scared dead eyes. He looked round The Box. Darren would have screamed and screamed, but the soundproofing on the floor and doors and walls would have masked a constant raging torrent.

Sterling stood up. He'd become aware of another presence.

'Well, this is cosy,' said Johnny Fontana. He was standing in the lip of The Box in a long leather coat over his skinny jeans and blue brothel creepers. 'The old dodderer told me you'd come in here. You're doing my job for me, Sterling, finding my little box of joy and letting yourself in without a by your leave. The next best thing after your little near-death crushing experience.'

The bulges in his pockets could not be just his hands. Sterling moved across to Hannah in her living quarters.

'That's far enough,' said Johnny Fontana sharply.

'When's it all going to stop, Johnny?' said Sterling.

'Oh, it'll be stopping soon, mate. You've cocked things up royally since you came on the scene. Everything's fallen apart. But there's time for a bit more mischief before I'm on my way.'

'Like Darren?' Sterling cocked his head back towards the prone, bloodied form. 'That was going too far. What did he do to deserve that?'

'The bastard was punishing me,' said Hannah bitterly.

Johnny Fontana's eyes flickered.

'Punishing me,' Hannah continued, 'because the big shot Johnny Fontana, Mr Enforcer, lording it over all the poor scared students with his cowardly little army of bullies and toadies, can't get it up. You can't do it, can you Johnny?'

'Shut up, you little whore – opening your legs for any bloke who comes your way.'

'Yeah, but with you it was a waste of time, wasn't it? And effort. My wrist still aches. Not Johnny Fontana. Limp Dick Fontana.'

'Shut up. Shut up.' The young man was shaking his head violently, as if overwhelmed by tinnitus.

Yeah, thought Sterling. Shut up, Hannah. You don't get away from wasps by giving the nest a good poke. In the circumstances, she was showing amazing courage and spirit but her judgement was terrible. He concentrated hard. He'd noticed something odd in Johnny Fontana's stance. A vague memory stirred that he tried to bring in to focus – an incident on Marchurch seafront, source of many of his worst experiences. The same stance; a terrible outcome. Slowly, smoothly, casually, he slipped off his jacket. That was OK – the natural thing to do – after all, The Box was hot and foetid, and his smell of his own bile and vomit had added to the poisonous atmosphere.

There was a blur as Johnny Fontana's left hand came from his pocket with a stoppered bottle a little smaller than a pint milk bottle. With his right hand, Fontana whipped off the stopper, and then everything seemed to go into slow motion as the steaming liquid hissed jaggedly through the air. Sterling held up his jacket like a shield over Hannah and himself, ducking over her and then propelling himself in a clumsy hybrid between a sideways tumble and a forward roll as he felt the acid eat and burn the thick material. He heard Hannah gasp behind him, but it seemed more like surprise than pain. The momentum of the roll cannoned him into Johnny Fontana, who crumpled at his legs under Sterling's 170 pounds. There was another bonus as the bottle shattered on the floor of The Box, dousing Fontana's hand in the acid residue and provoking an animal scream. An unexpected coup de grace followed: Adele moved from the cavernous shadows with a broken table leg and started raining blows on the screaming boy.

But it still wasn't over. Fury and agony gave Johnny Fontana new strength. He sprang to his feet, pushed Adele violently enough that she toppled backwards and landed awkwardly on her backside, and stumbled off through the cavern towards the corridor.

Sterling creaked to his feet. The bruises from the shelf crushing would be overlaid by new ones from his graceless gymnastics. He checked for casualties. 'Hannah, any acid on you?'

'No, I think I'm OK.'

'You'd know it if you weren't. Adele?'

'Well, I'm going to have a bruised bum.'

'Could have been worse.' He looked at her – there was fire in her eyes, and all diffidence was gone. 'You did a good job. Secretary, back-watcher, attack-dog.'

'Blackmailee,' murmured Adele. 'So you see, I had a sort of vested interest in looking after you.'

'Ah,' said Sterling. They looked at each other for a long second. 'Well, none of my business.... Look, can you see to Hannah? Take her upstairs and tell the plods about Darren and everything else that's been happening down there. Fontana had a limp after that pasting from you. I'm going after him.'

'Be careful, Frank. Got your mobile?'

'In my jacket.'

They considered the smoking, corroding mess. Sterling gingerly tipped it upside down and the phone fell out of the pocket, bent, melted, misshapen and curiously foetal. He looked at Hannah. 'Better that than....'

'Take mine,' said Adele. 'You're bound to need it.'

Sterling eased into the corridor. Fontana would be out of here as quick as his sore legs would take him. But had he really shot his bolt? Sterling edged along, alert to ambush.

Chapter 23

Friday 17 October - Pursuit

Sterling became more confident away from the hell behind him, trotting briskly along the lower ground floor past the vending machines and bursting into the blustery sunshine. Beyond the corner of the pottery, he saw the blonde head bobbing irregularly, moving down the tree-lined roadway and through the underpass towards Glen Lodge and the rear entrance of the college. As Sterling reached the back car park, he saw Fontana disappearing into the road.

He quickened his own pace. The boy was injured, but Sterling wasn't feeling too bright himself. The effects of the crushing in the Learning Resource Centre were emerging more obviously in stiffness and bruising and he couldn't get Darren's mutilated body out of his head. The road to the seafront was nondescript enough. On the college side were solid Victorian piles, some turned into flats, some bed and breakfasts and some holding out in the form of family homes, as originally intended. Opposite were Edwardian villas, all red brick and robust, whitely painted verandas. Here and there was infill – late 20th century houses and the occasional small apartment block.

Sterling shook his head at the ordinariness of it all, compared to the carnage and mayhem in the buildings above and behind. In front of him, looming dominantly over the sea, were Grantville Mansions, and a railed walkway joined them to pleasure gardens across a gap in the cliff. Johnny Fontana paused half way across, one arm cradling the injured other, and caught notice of Sterling as he reached the entrance of the mini-golf. Fontana's eyes flashed wildly and his coat billowed and flapped in the gusty conditions. He got out his phone and punched in a quick-dial number. Talking agitatedly into the phone at his ear, and jabbing the air urgently with his right forefinger, he hauled himself on and plunged into the gardens. As Sterling followed he could see Fontana's head appearing and then disappearing amidst the tarmacked paths, the short railings and the palm trees.

A feeling began to nag at Sterling, more insistent even than the stitch in his side. The distance between him and his quarry seemed to be staying a constant 50 metres. He wondered if he was chasing or being led. The gardens ended. To Sterling's right and beyond the railings was the long sweep of Southwood bay under the cliff top he was lurching along, and to the left pubs, hotels and restaurants. He was enveloped by a large bright gaggle of young boys and girls, chattering and giggling in some European language – Italian, he guessed. Their olive-coloured, open, smiling faces made a cheerful contrast to out-of-season Southwood. 'Possiamo andare' said a tall girl with a long nose and clever eyes, and like a school of fish, the group began to move off. Emerging from the gaggle, Sterling stumbled on as the wide, generous cliff top promenade narrowed into an alleyway of tired shop fronts, some boarded up ready for winter.

Sterling started and reeled at the burst of machine gun fire that erupted suddenly from ahead. He ducked into a doorway. He couldn't have been shot. If he had been, he would have known about it. But Fontana had led him into a trap. After the machine gun were the bleeps and pings. A gnome-like man in a sheepskin coat with heavyset eyes paused from locking his door, looking over the top of his glasses. 'You wouldn't believe how many people get caught by that.' It was too much effort to smile. He jerked his head to the small arcade sandwiched between a coffee shop and his own gift shop. 'I've told them and told them. Some old geezer's going to get a heart attack down here. Council's not interested.'

Sterling took his hand from his racing heart. 'Did you see a young bloke come down here – in a long black leather coat? Blonde hair.'

The man motioned with a backward thumb towards the road at the end of the alley. 'Went right down there.'

'Thanks.' Sterling passed the arcade where a delicately pretty young Italian girl, possibly from the same crowd as those he'd already encountered, was seated in front of a large screen, shooting everyone and everything to oblivion, three boys clustered around watching spellbound, and not just at her gaming prowess. Where was Johnny F going? Unless he was going to clamber up the long steep steps and around towards Marchurch there was no way out. The Palace Cinema, its blue and white décor framing a grey flint stone facade, was showing a cartoon matinee. For a moment, Sterling thought that Fontana might have slipped in there, and then he saw the familiar figure limping and shambling past the waterside pub and clapboard seafood restaurant next to it, heading beyond the harbour master's building towards the canopied fish market at the end of the jetty.

Away from the shelter of the buildings in old Southwood – the cinema, the Pavilion on the Sands and the shops and flats – the wind whipped up, and Sterling tasted the tang of salt as he was buffeted in his own shuffle and shamble to the harbour wall. The day darkened suddenly and then he was soaked by a heavy squall coming off the sea, but he was concentrating too much on the fish market and his quarry to be troubled. Johnny Fontana was sitting with his back to the raging sea on the top crossbeam of the railings that followed the curve of a small bulge in the jetty next to the fish market. On the bay side of the jetty the water was calm and almost placid. He held his damaged hand in his good one and was hunched against the sharp wind. Now he looked far smaller than the six-footer swaggering about the campus.

Sterling approached cautiously. There had been acid in one pocket. A gun was unlikely in the other, but the boy was dangerous.

'You've really messed things up for me, you bastard,' shouted Johnny Fontana. The roar of the wind and the sea and the slap of rain on the tarmac made his voice seem thin and come from further away. He glanced out to sea and then back. 'I'd have loved to see that bitch girl's burning face. After that stupid boy, it would have been the icing on the cake. Still, nowhere to go from here, eh?'

'Nope. I expect the secretary is taking the police down to the basement as we speak, and I expect Hannah is getting ready to give her statement. You might as well give up now.' Sterling's own voice was hoarse and faint, as if it was someone else's.

The boy spat, the wind whisking the spittle away towards the harbour master's building. He was good looking, and his profile showed a straight nose perfectly in proportion with the rest of his face. Sterling hadn't noticed before, but his hair grew low on his forehead, and was thick and abundant. There were little flecks of foam and droplets of seawater amongst the blonde strands.

'Nowhere to go, mate, like I said. But that doesn't mean I'm giving up.'

'What are you doing then?' Sterling swept his arm around the scene. 'This is pointless.'

A heavy-set elderly woman in large, red-framed glasses, wrapped, zipped and buttoned up in a large beige raincoat under a matching sou'wester approached with her dog, a lively golden Labrador. 'You should move away from those railings, young man,' she said in a loud piercing voice that cut through the wind and spray. 'The tide's very high today, and the wind is making it worse. The waves are going to start coming over any time.'

'Fuck off,' said Johnny Fontana.

The shocked woman turned open-mouthed to Sterling, who made a calming gesture with the flat downward palm of his hand, frowning and nodding reassuringly. The woman withdrew but Sterling could sense her hovering a few metres behind him.

'Come a bit closer, Sterling. I can't hear properly in all this wind.' Johnny Fontana took a long kitchen knife from his coat pocket and tossed it into the sea behind him.

Sterling edged forward. Supposing that wasn't the only weapon?

'There's nothing else. We'll have our little chat and then go and see the plods. It'll be a relief actually. I'm really fucking tired.'

'How'd you get into it all, Johnny?' This was gold dust. Sterling might even steal a march on the idiot Andrews.

The boy hunched up on his perch, continuing to nurse his damaged hand. 'If you're good at something, people notice. Jane Casterton noticed. It all went from there, ever since I started at college a couple of years ago. When I finished my course,' – he smiled wryly – 'she took me on for her little operation and trained me up. You don't just learn in the classroom.'

'Meg Jenkinson, Johnny. Did you have anything to do with that?'

Fontana sneered. 'That cow. She did very nicely out of those Saturday nights. She got a good house, a decent car. But at the first sign of trouble, she panics. She says she's going to the police. I tried to persuade her to shut up, but when she said she wouldn't....'

'.... you fixed it so it would look like suicide....'

'My, aren't you quite the detective?'

'What about Jane Casterton?'

Fontana's face changed. The sneer went and was replaced by a look Sterling could not read.

'Something went wrong,' said Sterling. 'You argued. You lost your temper. The statuette was there....'

Fontana's eyes flicked from Sterling up and to the left – a millisecond – and then back. 'Not quite the detective after all. Why you'd ever think that....' His eyes rolled back in his sockets, and then he hugged his arms and toppled back into the roiling sea behind him, like a deep-sea diver minus the gear and flippers. Sterling rushed to the edge of the jetty.

'The lifebelt,' shouted the woman in the beige raincoat. 'Throw him the lifebelt.'

Sterling wrenched the red and white ring from its housing and tossed it into the sea. He knew it was pointless. Over the side, he could see, and possibly even faintly hear, Fontana being tossed and thrown against the hard surface as the waves thundered, eddied and frothed in the autumn wind, the boy just allowing the sea to take him like a rag doll. In a brief second, foam against the jetty went from white to pink to red as Fontana's head was dashed against it and blood poured from a multitude of wounds. The lifebelt bobbed and floated purposelessly in the near vicinity.

The woman stood next to Sterling by the railings. 'Why on earth did he do that? A boy like that. To throw yourself into the water. I've dialled 999. They're sending everyone, they say.'

'Long story,' said Sterling. 'You'll read about it in the papers – national as well as local, I imagine. We'd better wait here.' It was over, or at least, something was over. There were aspects to this case that still weren't adding up.

'You again,' said the young police officer. 'We've had more action with you around than for the last month. Don't go away. We've already got your particulars but I'm guessing we'll need yet another statement. A pony to a quid you're totally mixed up in this. Just give me a brief summary of what happened.' She and her colleague were taping off the fish market and constructing a makeshift little entrance way.

Sterling told her what he'd found in the college and what had happened in the basement, how he'd chased Johnny Fontana down to the harbour, their final conversation and then how Fontana had tipped himself in the water. 'I reckon he had no choice. It was that or a whole life tariff, nailed on.'

The young police officer nodded, and then motioned the woman in the beige coat and sou'wester to come forward. 'Were you present as well, Madam?' she said in a more courteous voice. 'Can you wait while we take your details and a preliminary statement? Then later on someone will call and get something more detailed.'

Behind them, between the fish market on the jetty and the harbour master's building, a fire engine and ambulance were stationed side by side. Another little gaggle of nosey-parkers, just like at the college when Sterling had found Jane Casterton, had gathered in the time-honoured way, near but not with Sterling and his companion, as if instinct told them that he and the woman were more than mere bystanders and somehow tainted by involvement. A small dog had got loose and was darting around and yapping. The Labrador looked alert and inquisitive, and then lost interest.

The little audience watched as a cluster of firemen wrestled with a long hooked pole. After a lengthy few minutes of apparent squabbling, impatient, agitated raised voices and pass-the-parcel with the pole, a stocky young man in the party, his helmet pushed back to give him a louche, rakish air, finally made secure contact.

As he hauled Johnny Fontana's battered, lifeless body from the sea, his colleagues, lying flat on the asphalt, grabbed collar and sleeves and anything else available. Soon they had sufficient purchase, by hand and hook, to drag the drenched bundle up the stone wall and onto the jetty, which they managed, after the initial roughness, with a kind of respectful tenderness. The paramedics sprang to their work, which didn't take long. Even from where he was standing 10 metres away, Sterling knew they were dealing with a corpse. He had a glimpse of Johnny Fontana's battered, bloodied head and face before the body bag came out and was zipped up.

'That policewoman was much less brusque with me than she was with you,' said the woman.

'Yes, another long story. Forgive me for saying, but you don't seem that ... put out by what's just happened.'

'I've seen a lot of death and drama, one way and another. In another life. So you could say I'm a bit blasé. No, that's too casual. Inured is better. Well, I look forward to hearing the story some time, Mr....?'

'Sterling. Frank Sterling. And you are....?'

'Rosemary Richardson. I live up the hill on the back road to Marchurch.' They shook hands formally. 'Well, I suppose I had better get on. Such a shame about that poor boy. He must have been very angry and upset.'

'You could say,' said Sterling. He was thinking of Darren, Meg Jenkinson and Jane Casterton, the crime wave at ECOT and all those who would be ruined by it. Johnny Fontana had created a ruthless, murderous havoc. He called out to the female police officer. 'Officer, I'm going back up to the college, which is where I was before I came down here. You know who I am and everything else. I can explain fully to Detective Superintendent Andrews or DS Murphy. OK?'

She waved him away. Her colleague, a quiet, unassuming-looking young man, a head taller, was continuing to make notes in his notebook.

Sterling padded away from the harbour and back the way he had come. From the cliff top promenade, he looked down at the scene – the unleashed dog, now just a speck, still darting and yapping, the incident tape flapping and fluttering, the ambulance backing gingerly out of the jetty area, the firemen and the police officers in a huddle sharing some information, the nosey parkers beginning to get bored and drifting off. Rosemary Richardson had been right. The tide was coming right up now, and spray was exploding just where Johnny Fontana had been sitting. To Sterling, the case felt as if it was over. Job done. But at the same time he knew it wasn't. What would Angela call that? It came to him. Paradox.

Chapter 24

Friday 17 October - Review

When he'd found Jane Casterton, he'd set in train a flurry of activity that had completely dominated the Tuckett Building, but that seemed to be nothing compared to the latest hornet's nest. As he passed through the college's main gates, he was like a salmon struggling upriver against a strong current as students swarmed from the college like bombed-out refugees. The front car park outside the main entrance was again dominated by squad cars and ambulances. The incident tape now stretched across the whole driveway leading up the slope.

'I need to go up there and speak to the officers in charge,' he said to the policeman at the tape.'

'No one past this point without say-so from DS Andrews.'

'He's the bloke I need to see.'

'Name?'

'Sterling. Frank Sterling.'

The jobsworth looked at his clipboard. 'You're not on the list.'

'Look, this is directly related to the torture chamber in there. Which I found just an hour ago.'

'You're not on the list.'

'Jesus,' muttered Sterling. He put up his hands and turned away. He didn't care about sharing what he knew, but he wanted an update from the other end. He'd created a crime scene and an incident scene in the last 90 minutes, and he wasn't being allowed access to either. An idea came to him. He retreated down and around the building so that he was at the back entrance on the lower ground floor. Unsurprisingly, since The Box was at the other end of the corridor, the doors were closed and barred. But the door of the pottery gave out directly onto the path down to the other college buildings. He knocked and heard Ellie Laski's voice inviting entry.

'Frank. An unexpected pleasure, but what have you been up to now? Yet again, the place is crawling with police, paramedics, the whole lot.'

'I'll tell you in a minute. Have you got an internal phone in here?'

'Sure. Over there. There's an extension list next to it.'

'Thanks.' He went over and realised that he didn't know Adele's surname. 'What's the principal's secretary's surname?'

'Coppersmith.'

He dialled and waited.

'Principal's office.'

'Adele?'

'Frank. Are you OK? Where are you?'

'I'm fine. Things seem to be working out. Actually, I'm back in college – in the pottery with Ellie Laski at the bottom of the building. Can you come down?'

'Possibly. It's kind of lockdown here, but I think I'll be able to wangle it. You've stirred up another...' she paused and giggled - this time, Sterling sensed, more from a nervous reaction to recent events than amusement, no matter how plucky she was, '... shitstorm. Give me ten minutes.'

'I'll put the kettle on,' said Ellie Laski knowingly.

Fifteen minutes later, there was a soft knock on the pottery door. Adele looked around the pottery. 'I spend all my time upstairs in that office I never have time to go anywhere else. This is interesting.'

'Do you ladies know each other?' said Sterling.

'Vaguely,' said Ellie Laski. She held out her hand and the two women shook delicately as Sterling completed the introductions.

'Ellie, art lecturer, meet Adele, principal's secretary. Adele, Ellie.'

They settled down at one of the tables with mugs of coffee. Sterling considered warning Adele about its quality. She'll find out soon enough, he thought. There was an air of awkwardness about the classroom.

Sterling tried to break the ice. 'Ellie's given me some important information about what's been going on. Adele's....'

'.... your de facto secretary,' said Adele.

'Oh really?' said Ellie. 'Well, I'm not surprised. He's got the knack of getting people on his side and doing things for him.'

Some female solidarity seemed to be developing – things communicated and understood beyond the words. Sterling didn't mind. It didn't disadvantage him – quite the contrary. 'I suppose you are, Adele,' he said. 'Pity it's only temporary. How are you bearing up after The Box?'

'That place along the corridor is The Box, is it? Well, it's not just The Box, Frank. That's the second time I've been with you when you've found a body, remember. But I'm OK. I only got a glimpse of right inside, and I was busy, if you remember, beating the boy – what was his name? – Johnny Fontana, with a table leg.'

'Saving our bacon in the process. So, what's been going on up here?'

'Well, I did what you asked and took the girl upstairs. Poor thing, she was in a state, although she's spirited, I'll say that for her. Then I told the officer on duty roughly what had happened and called the ambulance. The officer took her details and a preliminary statement, and then she went off to hospital in the ambulance. The paramedics reckoned the hospital would keep her in overnight for observation. I gave her mother a ring and brought her up to date. She was very relieved, and is going to the hospital. I told the officer that you'd gone off after the boy. Then he and I went down to the basement.'

She smiled. 'Up to that point, he wasn't taking things that seriously – a dirty girl and a cock and bull story – but he was pretty lively when he saw Darren in that torture chamber. Since then, Andrews and Murphy have come back and the place has been swarming. The principal's shocked because The Box is partly under her office. That's bad enough, but she didn't hear anything either. What about you, Frank? I'm guessing that you caught up with Johnny Fontana.'

'He went down to the jetty and I cornered him there.'

'The jetty,' said Adele. 'That's a dead end.'

'In more ways than one. It was weird. He seemed to wait for me to catch up. Then we had a little chat. He owned up to a few things – mind you, there were some things he obviously couldn't deny – and when he'd finished, he flipped himself off the railings and into the sea. I don't know if he drowned or if he bashed his head in on the harbour wall, but he's certainly dead. In other words, he topped himself.'

Ellie Laski had been sipping her coffee and listening. 'I just can't believe all this. You're going to have to go through it much more carefully. I'm totally lost. Am I right in saying there's some kind of torture chamber down the corridor with a dead body in it, and that you've rescued a girl from there, and that you chased the boy responsible for it and he's committed suicide? All in the last few minutes? God. The principal sent her programme managers around to say the college is closing for the rest of the week. I'm beginning to get an inkling why.'

'So she's finally admitted defeat,' said Sterling. 'If you ask me, she should have done it as soon as we found Jane Casterton. Right, I can't remember who knows what, so here's an update for both of you.'

After that, the three of them sipped their coffee in the quiet room under the gaze of the garden gnome with the fishing rod.

'What?' said Sterling to Ellie Laski when he saw her secret smile.

'I'm just thinking that the police have taped every-where off by the main entrance and down here on this floor – authorised people only – and here we are so close to things and they don't have a clue.'

'Everything they do is cack-handed. Andrews is an idiot.'

'You're not actually a consultant at all, Frank, are you?' said Ellie. Both women gazed at him.

'Not really. Well, not an educational one, anyway. You both knew that a long time ago. I'm more of an … investigator.'

'Well, you've found a lot out, that's for sure,' said Adele, 'and things will never be the same around here. It amazes and terrifies me that all this has been going on in the college and loads of us knew nothing about it. A whole shadow organisation running gambling, a brothel, drug production and distribution, blackmail, intimidation. A torture chamber down the corridor. An acid attack. Murder. Suicide. My God, when I just say it all it seems totally outlandish.'

'Think about it, Adele,' said Sterling, 'and you'll realise it's not that weird. Murders and suicides happen every day in every part of the country, so I don't need to go into that. But what about that French politician bloke, ex-government minister, the one accused of rape, attending sex parties in hotels in northern France? So hotels, like the training hotel here, are often used for that kind of thing. Johnny Fontana's 'box of joy', as he called it – well, remember Josef Fritzl in Austria, who built an underground chamber in his house and kept his daughter and their family there for the next twenty years. The Kampusch case in Austria, and the Dutroux business in Belgium, where predators kept their victims imprisoned in secret rooms for years without getting caught, show how easily people can get away with stuff. Johnny Fontana's box was much less sophisticated than the dungeons in those cases. Chucking acid: well, Hannah and I got lucky, and you certainly helped there, Adele, but what about that poor girl in London whose face was scarred forever by her alleged mate? What about the Bolshoi Ballet case in Moscow, where a dancer arranged an acid attack on a director?'

'Yes, Frank, but all in one place,' said Ellie. 'Come on, that's incredible.'

Sterling shrugged. 'OK, so it's been bad at ECOT, and probably on a larger scale than elsewhere, but you go anywhere and to any organisation, and there'll be skulduggery. Trust me.'

'Skulduggery,' smiled Adele. 'So that's what this mess is. But how come no one said anything?'

'The three wise monkeys,' said Sterling. 'I've seen it so often, particularly on the job. See no evil; hear no evil; speak no evil. Aka *omerta*. Don't take this as a criticism, but you've both been blackmailed, and you both kept quiet. You're not the only ones. Others were intimidated. A few were probably tortured or physically assaulted. See?' He drained his coffee. 'I'm off. There's nothing more to be done round here, at least not by me. Doubtless, the plods will want to catch up with me yet again when they've got through all the current confusion. I think I'll go over to Marchurch Royal Infirmary to see how Hannah is.'

Chapter 25

Friday 17 October - Arrest

He knew the hospital well. His wife, long gone, had had a spell as a nurse here, and he'd often picked her up and dropped her off for her shifts. Then there were the work-related visits, interviewing the casualties from seafront brawls, separating them from each other, and occasionally being one himself. He touched his nose. The surgeon had reset it well and straight. Sterling remembered all the long strips of lint stuffed in each nostril after the operation to keep everything steady, the dryness from breathing through his mouth and then his impatience. He'd started to pull the lint out and had been astonished at how much there seemed to be. When the consultant and his acolytes had come on their rounds, he'd tried to stuff it back up his nose. Two mucus- and blood-stained ribbons had been hanging down over his mouth. He could still picture the doctor's look, a mixture of knowing and quizzical.

That was the time Andy Nolan had brought in a secret hip flask of vodka, because 'that's what you do when your mate's lying injured on his back in hospital'. Andy wouldn't do that now – now that he was going up through the ranks and there was more to lose.

Sterling didn't mind hospitals compared to schools and colleges. There was the smell of course – there was no escaping from that – but hospitals were somehow more straightforward. Something was wrong with you and you got it fixed, end of story. He knew that was an oversimplification, but education was altogether more complicated, and then there was ECOT, in a league of its own.

The receptionist looked down his list. 'She's in Mulberry Ward in a separate room. You go through that door, over the walkway....'

'Thanks,' said Sterling. 'I know the way.'

Hannah's mother was sitting in a chair by her daughter's bed. Hannah herself lay asleep, only her head, her shoulders and arms visible. She'd obviously been cleaned up, and her hair had regained its usual glossiness. A drip had been set up, and a tube was delivering something or other into her bloodstream via her wrist. She looked small and vulnerable, more girl than woman, but at least tranquil and peaceful. Sterling thought of another girl and another rescue case and the feeling that came from that. Here it was again – tenderness.

'Mr Sterling,' said Mrs Williamson. 'You kept your promise. A secretary at the college phoned me – Adele – and said you would be coming over. I'm afraid Hannah's been sedated. She won't be awake again for few hours.'

'It doesn't matter,' lied Sterling. 'I really just wanted to check that she's OK.' He felt himself slipping into the stilted conversational mode used by rescuers and relatives of victims.

'She's fine. In fact, she's in surprisingly good condition, the doctor said, considering what she's been through. A little dehydrated. Some weight loss but not much. After they showered and cleaned her up she was quite cheerful.'

'Excellent news.'

'We owe you, Mr Sterling. She told me a little bit about what happened, and said that you were the one who found her. Goodness knows how she'd have got on without you. Thank you.'

'She's a nice girl, Mrs Williamson. A credit to you. I'd got fond of her in a very short time, so obviously I did my best.'

'A credit in some ways. We need to sort things out, she and I, when she gets out of here. Things can't go on as they are. And I gather that there was someone else in the dungeon you found Hannah in.'

'Yes,' said Sterling. The woman clearly only knew the bare bones. Best that it stayed that way. 'A boy. Dead.'

'How awful.'

'Yes, the whole thing is pretty dreadful. I can't really say any more than that, Mrs Williamson. It will all come out eventually, but the police are currently very active, and they won't want details getting out – or at least, only the details they're ready to release. Hannah might say something to you. The key thing for us is that she's safe and recovering. Can you tell me what the schedule is from here?'

'They're going to keep her in overnight for observation and so on, and make sure she's stable, and then she'll be coming home with me. They tell me she'll need a rest for a few days.'

'Right, well, I've got her mobile telephone number. Can you give me your landline number? I'll give her, or you, a ring in the next day or two to see how she's getting on.'

'That's very kind of you, Mr Sterling. I did get the impression from the secretary that you were the one who was taking Hannah's disappearance the most seriously, and of course you did come up to Whithampton. I might be complaining to the police after all this.'

Sterling nodded. He had beefs with them of his own.

When does irritation and resentment bubbling up from a festering grievance become full-blown rage? In his case, Sterling knew the precise moment, the moment in the snug of the Cinque Ports with Angela when his sip took his pint to below the halfway mark, when the guffaw of Jack Cook's voice (Jack newly restored to his preferred pub after his long exile) drifted over from the bar, when a log in the grate shifted and let out a fizzle of sparks, and when Andrews, another man in plain clothes Sterling didn't know and a couple of sturdy uniformed officers marched over to his table and arrested him.

'Frank Sterling?' said Andrews redundantly. His attempt to avoid smiling turned his expression into a smirk.

'No, sergeant,' said Sterling, continuing the demotion he'd begun a few days before. 'I'm Lobby Lud but you don't get your five pounds.'

'I have a warrant for your arrest, on suspicion of the murder of John Fontana today at 2:30 p.m. You do not have to say anything, but it may harm your defence if you do not mention, when questioned, something which you later rely on in court. Anything you do say may be given in evidence.'

Scenarios drifted into Sterling's mind's eye. He was leaping up and kicking out, scattering his tormentors like confetti, springing to the door and bursting out into the inky night. He was challenging the smug superintendent. 'Arrest me and you'll never get out of this without terminal career damage. It's ridiculous. You're making a mistake of biblical proportions.' He was seeing the doubt and anxiety in his persecutor's eyes.

He rose from the table, leaving his glass and Angela's solicitous eyes, which had the effect of doubling his discomfort, and held out his arms for the handcuffs. Denial, histrionics and ranting would make no difference at all. He called over to the bar. 'Becky, I'm going to need a brief.' He turned to the man with Andrews and said, 'Which nick?'

'Dovethorpe,' he replied. Becky nodded.

'And can you find Rosemary Richardson? She lives up the Marchurch road in Southwood – she's a witness.' This time, Becky gave a tiny thumbs-up.

The car outside the pub drew away from the kerb and headed southwards. Sandley slipped quickly away. 'There was no need for that,' he said, bitterness supplanting rage. 'Arresting me in the pub in front of my friends. Humiliating me. I don't hide where I live and where I work. You could have done it nice and quietly.'

Andrews put his arm around the back of the driver's seat and turned to Sterling from the front passenger seat. 'We do our jobs as we see fit. Anyway, that's the very least of your worries, Sterling. The way things are looking, you're going away for a long time. We'll get down to the station, and look at it all in more detail.'

'I can't wait,' said Sterling. He sat back awkwardly, his handcuffed hands behind him making sitting almost painful. Soon the metal would be chafing his wrists and he'd be getting heat-burn. He wondered where Murphy was. His absence made Sterling uneasy.

Dovethorpe police station, of all those in the east and south Kent coastal towns, was the one Sterling knew least well. It was a solid, square, post-war red brick building with large vertical rectangular windows on both floors, enclosed by low, no-nonsense black railings that might have inhibited a determined assault by a mob or gangs of organised criminals for about 10 seconds, unlike the more sophisticated Marchurch nick fortifications. The car swept in through the side gates and around to the custody entrance at the back. There was a kind of TARDIS effect as the premises behind the frontage proved much more extensive than first impressions implied. Perhaps he'd been brought here to achieve maximum disorientation. The security gates clanged shut behind him and he was guided up to the custody desk where a bored sergeant with a clipboard made him empty his pockets. Behind Sterling, slumped on a bench, was a young man in a patterned red and green hoodie, baggy jeans and yellow and white trainers, whose arresting officer was engaged in an intense conversation with a tall, grey man in a shabby pinstriped suit.

'Sign here for your belongings, which I'm going to put in a locker while you're here.'

Sterling made sure he squeezed up his signature close to the last recorded item, his house keys, so nothing could be added. The dodges were coming back to him.

He answered questions about his health and cooperated when his fingerprints were taken. Then he was taken to the cells, his belt removed and his shoes placed outside the cell door.

Inside, there was a bed with a thin blue mattress and a couple of threadbare blankets. Previous inmates had graffitied on all the walls. 'Trust no one' said one effort above the bed, in incongruous copperplate handwriting. There was an odour of staleness, waste and decay. Sterling made his anger fade. There was no use for it in the present circumstances. He sat on the bed, pulled his legs up and closed his eyes – not to sleep but to think. There were things that didn't make sense, and the clues were somewhere in his head. They'd leave him to stew for a few hours, and Becky would need time to find a solicitor. If he did things right, that would suit him.

Chapter 26

Saturday 18 October - Interrogation

He'd done some thinking, but then he'd gone to sleep. He woke to the sound of the slat in the door at the top of the cell being pulled open and then shut and the key in the lock turning and rumbling.

'You've got a visitor, Mr Sterling,' said the custody officer. 'While I'm here, do you want anything to eat and drink?'

'What about a menu first?' said Sterling.

The policeman didn't bother to react. The joke was stale 5,000 days before. 'I'll bring some tea and toast.'

He ushered a man in an elegant, well cut dark navy suit and highly polished tan shoes into the cell. His face was pink and well scrubbed, with a small, sharp, pointed nose. He carried a small, battered leather attaché case whose colour, though not its condition, matched his shoes and the thin tie over a brilliant white shirt. Becky had not troubled to engage the local duty solicitor.

'Mr Sterling, I'm John Evanston. Our mutual friend Becky Strange called me last night and said you were in a spot of bother. I'm a solicitor specialising in criminal defence and I've come down from London this morning.

There was no point in getting here before now. The timing indicated that they'd bang you up, soften you up and start the interview process this morning. I can advise you about legal procedure now, and I can also represent you as things unfold today and over the weekend. If you want me to represent you, we need to talk generally about what happened whilst exploring what will be your best defence. Becky's given me a bit of background. You were in the police yourself at one stage, she says, so I imagine you're familiar with most of this.'

'Yes,' said Sterling. 'I know the score. I can tell you now that the charge is ridiculous, and I reckon that Andrews, the arresting officer, is running a personal vendetta against me. So I am contesting the charge very strongly.'

'OK,' said Evanston. 'Noted. Again, Becky thought this was the line you'd take. I've had a word with the police, and they've given me the broad background to the charge – that you found something up at the college you were connected with and as a result chased the boy who died down to Southwood Bay. What's in dispute is what happened after you both got there. Obviously the police haven't told me everything, but when they interview you we need to be prepared for some apparently compelling evidence. Andrews – is that his name? – seems very confident. He says you pushed the boy into the water. You're saying....'

'....That he tipped himself in. There was a witness. I asked Becky to track her down. Rosemary Richardson.'

'Yes, we're working on that. Becky will bring her down here if she can manage it.'

The two men talked until the custody officer brought two Styrofoam cups of scummy tea and some limp, cold toast.

'Just one more thing before kick-off, Mr Evanston. I don't expect your services come cheap, and you've already probably put a lot on the meter, coming down from London on a Saturday. I think we need a bit of a chat about your fees.'

The immaculately turned out solicitor patted Sterling's arm. 'No need to worry about that, Mr Sterling. This one's pro bono. You've got some good people batting for you, and I owe those people more than I'm ever going to be able to pay back.' He put his papers and notes back in his case, got up from the bed he'd been sitting on next to Sterling and looked at his Rolex. 'I'm off out for a bit of breakfast in the town. Looking at your toast, I'm sorry you can't join me. It's nine o'clock now. They're telling me that the interview will start at ten. I'll see you then.'

Twenty minutes after ten o'clock, Sterling and Evanston were facing Andrews and his new sidekick across the table of a drab, windowless interview room. The only discernible extra feature was a forlorn wisp of a long-abandoned spider's web in the top corner to Sterling's front and left. Behind the detectives was the one-way glass panel through which the rest of the investigating team would be studying Sterling – his body language, his replies to questions and his reactions.

Andrews pressed the record button of the tape recorder and went through the pre-interview rigmarole, in the process introducing Murphy's replacement, one Detective Sergeant Naismith, and John Evanston from the solicitors' firm Harper Burns.

'So, Mr Sterling, take us through the events of yesterday leading up to the young man John Fontana going into the sea.'

Sterling began, keeping his voice flat and neutral in his customary evidence-giving way. After half an hour of question and answer, Andrews leaned forward.

'It's all a bit far-fetched, isn't it, Mr Sterling? All this talk of conspiracies and shadow entities in a publicly-funded institution, rather than an isolated kidnapping and revenge by a disturbed and opportunistic individual. I think it's time to offer you a more plausible scenario about what actually happened on that jetty in Southwood Bay. He nodded at Naismith, who booted up a laptop next to the tape recorder and opened a file. An idea flashed into Sterling's consciousness – one of the things he'd been worrying at in his cell – the way Johnny Fontana's eyes, in his final moments, had flicked up and away from Sterling's face. Sterling knew then was what was coming. Naismith found what he was looking for, and turned the laptop screen at Sterling and his solicitor. There was footage, taken by a video camera or perhaps even a sophisticated mobile telephone, with the time and date in the bottom left hand corner. It was wobbly and occasionally blurred, as if the person filming had been struggling with distance and focus.

Sterling saw Johnny Fontana perched on the railing behind the turbulent sea, and himself in front of him and slightly to the left. The conversation looked as animated as he remembered. There was a roaring sound coming from the laptop. It had been a blustery day, and there were white horses rolling over the sea in the background. Johnny Fontana cupped his hand to his ear and Sterling moved forward. Fontana seemed to put out his hands in supplication, and Sterling stepped forward, momentarily blocking the view. Then there was a flash of outstretched arms and when Sterling had moved away, Johnny Fontana had gone. The clip ended suddenly in a blank screen.

Next to Sterling, the colour had blanched from Evanston's pink face. There could not have been a starker clash between Sterling's narrative and the visual evidence.

Andrews leaned further forward, his nose inches from Sterling's. The coffee and bacon he'd had for breakfast lingered on his breath. 'Let's cut out all the rubbish and all the lies, Mr Sterling. Here's how it happened. You find the young man and the young woman in a container in the basement of the college. Fair enough – it's pretty conclusive that Johnny Fontana tortured and killed the unfortunate young man. You rescue the girl – the secretary has confirmed that. Then you chase Johnny Fontana along the front. My goodness, you must have been angry, especially in view of how fond you are of the girl. Yes,' – in answer to Sterling's surprised look – 'we've been speaking to Mrs Williamson and various other people. So you corner Fontana at the jetty. Words are exchanged. Perhaps he goads you. Something happens. So, as per the video clip, you move in on him and push him into the sea. That's how it happened, isn't it? You can't deny the evidence, but of course there are mitigating circumstances. I'd be prepared to put in a word about them, if you sign a statement.'

'I'd like a private word with my client,' said Evanston.

Sterling ignored him. He sat back and folded his arms. The policewoman's turn of phrase on the jetty came to him as he stared back at Andrews. 'A pony to a pound that footage is anonymous.'

Andrews frowned, the smallest of tells.

'Yes,' said Sterling, 'anonymous and probably received within a couple of hours of what happened. How convenient – a passer-by with a phone taking in that particular scene. And note how abruptly the clip stopped. Nothing in there to show how Fontana flipped, by himself, over the side, and nothing to show how I threw him a lifebelt a couple of seconds later. This is a Mickey Mouse investigation. Sloppy. Too intent on nailing people who are being awkward, and not enough focus on the truth.' He yawned. 'You know what? I need a break.'

Andrews pressed the stop button. 'Interview suspended at 11:30 a.m. Saturday 18 October.' He looked at Evanston. 'Speak to your client, Mr Evanston. It can only get worse for him.'

'Hardly,' said the solicitor. 'What we need now is a quiet place without cameras and sound transmission.'

'This is a lot of nonsense,' said Sterling when he and his solicitor were relocated in a quiet room just next to the front desk.

'So I'm gathering.'

'I don't think they've even bothered to take a statement from Rosemary Richardson. That footage.... I was set up – again. Johnny Fontana must have planned it. He decided to top himself, but he was trying to take me down with him.'

'The Problem of Thor Bridge,' murmured Evanston.

'What?'

'Just an old case with some similar elements. You mentioned being set up – again – what does that mean?'

'When I first started investigating at the college, I went for a haircut that was filmed and then edited into a kind of porn video using other footage. I reckon the person responsible for that was filming the jetty from the promenade.'

'Interesting. Well, whoever it was did a pretty good job. When I saw it, I'm afraid my heart sank a bit. Let's hope that Becky....'

There was a sudden commotion at the front desk. Sterling caught a glimpse of Becky Strange with a larger woman. There was a small secret smile on Becky's face. The woman next to her spotted Sterling behind the Plexiglas. Her piercing voice, and what she said, were never more welcome. 'Mr Sterling, are they accusing you of murdering that boy? Utter nonsense. I saw everything with absolute clarity. He tipped himself into the water.' Rosemary Richardson turned to the bemused officer behind the glass. 'Officer, I made a statement at the scene about all this. Where is it?'

Andrews, who had appeared at the doorway of the small room where Sterling and Evanston had been having their conference, had the look of a football manager whose team has fallen for a sucker losing goal in the last second of extra time from a single opposition counter-attack.

'Don't prolong this, Superintendent,' said Evanston softly. 'My client is already considering an action for wrongful arrest and imprisonment.'

Sterling jerked up his head in an involuntary movement. Am I?

'My client,' continued Evanston with an unobtrusive hand on Sterling's sleeve, 'believes that the *anonymous* video footage you received was part of a conspiracy to entrap him, and that you'd be advised to pursue that line of investigation.'

On the pavement outside Dovethorpe Police Station an hour later, Sterling, newly liberated, John Evanston, Becky Strange and the star witness Rosemary Richardson shuffled awkwardly in the autumn sunshine.

'Let me buy you all lunch,' said Sterling. 'We can go back to Becky's. Excellent pies and CAMRA beers.'

Evanston looked at his watch. 'After all that excitement, I don't mind if I do. Shall I follow behind you, Becky?'

'Rosemary, have you got time?' said Sterling.

'I most certainly have,' said the older woman. 'Whatever happened to policing by consent, impartiality, respect for the public and all that stuff? They behaved like scum, those plods. That's why I agreed to come down here in person.'

Sterling looked at her, an elderly woman with a piercing, BBC-accented, cut-glass voice who lived in the best part of prim conservative Southwood and who he later learned had been a surgeon, including in war zones, before retirement. There seemed to be some disjunction in that little outburst. 'Tell you what,' he said, 'we'll discuss it in the pub.'

Chapter 27

Sunday 19 October and Monday 20 October - Fishing

'I can't tell you everything yet,' Sterling had said to John Evanston. 'There are still loose ends.' But he'd promised a full update when the time came. He owed that to a lot of people.

Now it was Sunday afternoon, and he was at home. He could still feel the effects of the night before.

'Hannah?' he said into the phone.

'Frank. What a nice surprise.'

'I'm calling to see how you're doing. Did your Mum tell you what happened to Johnny?'

'Yes. She told me everything she knew. Bastard. I could understand Johnny having a go at me, but poor Darren hadn't done anything.'

'Are you back home?'

'Yes, they let me go on Saturday evening. I've got enough drugs to start a chemist's, and they're wanting me to go to counselling.'

'Good idea,' lied Sterling. On the few occasions he'd been, after particularly traumatic experiences, he remembered being bored. Mind you, he still had nightmares every now and again. Counselling might have stopped that.

'Maybe,' said Hannah. It seemed as if she shared his views.

'I thought you might like to come fishing with me.'

'Fishing,' said Hannah. 'You want to take me fishing. Is that your idea of a date?'

'For clues,' said Sterling. 'It's not over yet.'

'Ah, that sort of fishing. All right, seeing as how the college has suspended me.'

'Yes, I knew about that. But it's half-term next week, isn't it? You could use that time. I think you have grounds for an appeal and you could even sue as well. You were kidnapped and held on college premises. The college clearly failed in its duty of care towards you, as the jargon goes. Actually, the college will probably withdraw the suspension if you make contact.'

'What about that thing with Darren?' said Hannah.

'Well, if it's that versus being kidnapped I think the kidnapping is more serious, don't you? And anyway, how old are you? 18? That's young and whatever you think you were manipulated – groomed even – and by college staff. You might think you know the ways of the world. I can tell you, there's a long way to go. This fishing trip, Hannah … What I'm interested in is Johnny Fontana's place. Do you know where it is?'

'"Course. Southwood. He never went far from the college.'

'Right. Well, why don't we meet at Southwood station on Monday morning, say, 10 o'clock? I'll come up from Sandley, and you'll be coming down from Whithampton.'

'See you then.'

'Hannah? You're sure you're going to be all right with this? You're well enough? Your mother will be OK with it?'

'I owe Darren. See you Monday,' said the girl.

Sterling was leaning on the wall by the station hall when the Whithampton train pulled in from the north. Hannah spotted him when she reached the top of the footbridge and gave a bold little wave. Apart from being a little paler than Sterling remembered, she seemed surprisingly unscathed.

She slipped her arm under his elbow as they went down the approach road, crossed at the zebra crossing and marched off down into the town. 'God,' she said. 'It's good to be out and about. Dungeons, hospital wards and our front room. I was going mad.'

'Well, girl, you've made an amazing recovery, considering what you've been through.'

She shrugged. 'You've just got to get on with it. What choice is there?'

They walked down the hill, past the villas, the cafés, the barbershops, the small park on the right, and then the pubs and the banks and the estate agents. The wind blew in from the sea, funnelling up the narrowing high street and making Hannah hunch up closer into Sterling's coat, both hands pressed against his sleeve. Their heads almost touched as they resisted and pressed on.

'We turn right here and go straight down past the offie and the deli. It's there, at the end of Buckingham Road.'

'You know your way, Hannah.'

She took her cheek from his coat and looked up at him. 'I was down here a lot, Frank. Johnny and me, well, we went out together for a while.'

'I knew there was something, but not....'

The girl shrugged. There was an old-fashioned ironmongery shop on the corner – J. Makepeace and Nephews, est. 1925. Each window was given over to a different display – from electrical appliances at one end to gardening equipment at the other, but the signs at the top – PYREX DE CORNING, RADIANT HEATERS, LOCKS AND TOOLS, and more – had long since ceased to have any connection to the goods in the shop front below. A galvanised steel bucket hung from over the open shop entrance, as if in place for a piece of slapstick. Sterling wondered if the shop assistants would be wearing brown work coats.

Then they were walking down Buckingham Road, parallel to the sea, and, with the wind's funnel effect cut off, it was immediately calm and relatively quiet. The road was squeezed between back premises on either side, and Sterling and Hannah passed a jumbled collection of rear fire escapes, hard standings and garages with shabby peeling paint. Halfway down was the back entrance of an undertaker. The final part tapered off even more narrowly, the road sandwiched between the high red-bricked sides of two houses and emerging in to Sandringham Square. It must have been convenient for Johnny Fontana, his home equidistant from the college to the south and the town to the north. But the square, full of detached four-storey Victorian villas like the ones bisecting Buckingham Road, or larger terraced blocks with frontages of red Kentish brick below, flint halfway up and topped with slate roofs, had a gloomy, oppressive air.

'This one,' said Hannah, threading her way between the cars in the central parking area and marching up the steps to a faded maroon front door. There was the usual plate of flat numbers and buzzer buttons to the right of the front door. 'JF', in scratchy hand, was scored in next to Flat 6. But it was Flat 1's button that Hannah pressed. A curtain twitched, and after that, with some alacrity, the door opened.

'Hannah, my dear, how lovely to see you. It's been much too long.' The voice was accompanied by fawning hands and a look that could only qualify as a leer from a short, thin man with over-large tortoiseshell glasses that he poked up his small nose with his forefinger when they slipped. He was perhaps somewhere between forty and fifty, but the paisley cardigan, baggy brown trousers and slippers hinted at an older mind-set. Under his shifty gaze Hannah was naked on the doorstep, while Sterling was entirely invisible on the pavement below.

'Hi, Stephen. My friend and I are here to get some of Johnny's things for him. He's not going to be around for a while.'

'I knew I hadn't seen him. Not since Friday.' The small man stood in the doorway and seemed disinclined to move.

'Yeah, he's gone away for a bit. Like I say, we need to get into his room. We won't be long. You can come up with us if you want.'

Stephen's eyes finally flicked down to acknowledge Sterling's presence. 'I haven't seen him before.'

'No, he's from college. One of Johnny's tutors.' Hannah was improvising and she was good. 'So....'

'I'm not sure we can allow unauthorised people in, my love. The owners wouldn't really approve of that. You're OK, of course. Johnny wouldn't mind you.' The bargaining was reaching a delicate phase.

Hannah stepped right up to the door, her face close to the little man's, only the edge of the door separating them. 'Ooh, Stephen,' she said, 'it's nice and warm behind that door, I can tell.' Then she slipped off her coat. Underneath was a black mini-skirt and a long-sleeved pale green top with her trademark low neckline. 'Don't let me get goosebumps,' she said softly.

Sterling shuffled his feet at the bottom of the steps. The man Stephen's face turned a bright puce. Wordlessly, he opened the door.

'Thank you so much, Stephen.' She gave him the lightest of kisses as she stepped past him in the dingy hall that smelled of chips and vinegar.

Sterling eased in and closed the door. 'We won't be long,' he said. 'We'll let you know when we're on our way out.' On the first landing, Hannah turned round with a small grin and mouthed 'perv' before starting on the second flight of stairs.

Everything grew down at heel on the ascent – the wallpaper, the dingy lampshades, the banisters – and on the top floor, the carpet was beyond saving – so thin and threadbare there might as well have been bare boards. There could be a formula for this, Sterling reflected – age of house times number of flat conversions times number of flights of stairs equals degree of shabbiness. Hannah went to the corner of the landing and extracted a key from a gap in the skirting board and let them in to Johnny Fontana's home. There was an immediate contrast with the dilapidation on the other side of the door. The bedsit was a large attic space with an air of lightness and order, and a fawn carpet in the living area of obvious quality. To the left of the door was a sofa and armchair arranged in front of a new looking flat screen television set up on a matching black stand in the corner. Behind the door, Sterling could see into a small kitchen alcove, where there was a sink, a kettle, cupboards, a small fridge and a large, sleek microwave.

As Hannah stood by the armchair, Sterling went over to the window and looked out. Straight ahead he could see right down the road he and Hannah had walked along to get to the house and into the centre of the town. To the right he could see over the pleasure gardens and the cliffside promenade along which he'd chased the boy on Friday. A herring gull hovered over the car park in the middle of the square as a young woman unloaded her SUV. Sterling could see but not hear her young daughter crying and squawking as she writhed against the restraints of her pink pushchair.

He rubbed his forefinger over the glossed windowsill. Not a smudge or speck of dust. Next to the window was an area screened off by a pale blue curtain, like a bed in a hospital ward when the consultant comes calling. Sure enough, behind the curtain was a smartly made bed with a bright blue duvet patterned with what looked like faint outlines of the seven continents. Behind the foot of the bed, in the far right corner, was a small bathroom. The bath, sink and mirror gleamed. Sterling went back to the small bookshelf next to the television. There were a couple of computer how-to books – *Spreadsheets for Dummies* and *Setting up a Website* – and a short guide on reading balance sheets. Next to them was a new edition of Machiavelli's

The Prince and Sir Alex Ferguson's autobiography. Sterling plucked out *The Prince*. It looked and smelt new, and there was a faint crack in the spine as he opened it for a random read. Johnny Fontana knew what he was interested in, but it didn't extend to reading about it.

Hannah watched him from the armchair. 'While we're here, Frank, do you fancy a cup of tea?'

'Sure,' he said. 'Old Stephen downstairs won't be kicking up a fuss?'

'He was used to me coming and going. He's a perv, no doubt about that, but he's harmless. Also, he's had a run-in or two with the police, so he doesn't have anything to do with them.' She disappeared into the kitchenette and Sterling could hear the kettle being filled, and cupboards and fridge door being opened. There was a crisp, zesty sort of smell to the flat, not just air spray and polish and fresh linen but the result of frequent thorough cleaning. He eased into the sofa and Hannah came and sat next to him with two mugs of tea.

'This is a nice place,' said Sterling. 'Cosy. And he kept it up well. Spent a bit of money. I'm trying to understand what happened in that box of his.'

Hannah took a sip of her tea. 'We were together about three months, sort of – about the longest three months of my life. He was vicious at the end.' She shuddered at the thought. 'And even early on I could tell he was a bit of a bully, the way he lorded it around the college and the blokes he ordered about. But there was another side to him when it was just him and me. He was a laugh. He was fun to be with. We used to go over into the town on little pub crawls. We did plenty of eating out. He looked after me and made me feel special.

I could tell there was something going on, but when you're with someone who's got a bit of standing it rubs off on you. Everybody treated me special when I was with Johnny.'

'Gangster's moll,' murmured Sterling.

'Yeah, exactly like that. I didn't know everything he was up to. I just thought it was a bit of drug dealing and that. Gradually it started going wrong. Look how clean this place is. It wasn't me doing that when I was here. He was obsessive. I'm sure that's why, you know, he couldn't get it up. He wanted everything perfect. He wouldn't touch me if we hadn't showered. Well, I can't be going on like that, so in the end I broke it off. Darren came along and it was much less complicated, and he had no trouble in the getting it up department. Then I discovered something else about Johnny Fontana. You couldn't just dump him – that's the first thing. The second thing was that he was unbelievably jealous.'

Sterling's mind drifted back to the far dark corner of The Box. 'Yeah,' he sighed. 'He certainly was. Anyway, so he didn't know about you and Darren doing the sex show?'

'No, not as far as I knew. Hissing Sid fixed that all up just with me. He could read us like a book – the good girls who just go to college and do their hairdressing, the ones who are a bit more adventurous....'

'.... And the ones like you, Hannah.'

She took another sip. 'Yeah, the ones like me.'

'You know that someone videoed you cutting my hair, don't you?'

'I knew something was going on, but not that.' Hannah's eyes were wide, and she was confirming what

Hissing Sid had said. 'I thought ... Well, I didn't know what to think, to be honest.'

'Then it was edited with you and Darren going at it to make it look as if it was you and me. I got a copy delivered to my office – a really crude blackmail attempt.'

Hannah shook her head. 'Honestly, Frank, I didn't know anything about that. Hissing Sid just told me where to cut your hair and to be nice to you. I admit I got a bit carried away. It was easy actually. You were fanciable.' She looked into her tea and then back up to Sterling's face. 'I was pleased when you asked me out to lunch, and then on another date.'

Sterling looked away.

'There wasn't going to be a date, was there? You just wanted information for your case.'

'So, what with your little honey trap, organised by Hissing Sid, and me offering to take you out just for what I could find out, we're about quits, wouldn't you think?'

'I s'pose.' Now Hannah was smiling as well. 'But I'd still be up for something.'

Sterling was glad of the conversation he'd had with Hannah's mother, the one about Hannah's ... addiction. 'We need to concentrate on the case. Tell me some more about Johnny. I was told that when the college came to suspend him, they discovered that he wasn't even enrolled on a course.'

'He did something – a BTEC in the business studies department, but maybe he finished that and just hung around. It's not hard to get student ID. That might have been one of his scams. That was the other thing about him. He told me he was 21, but that's just about all

I knew about him. He had this mystery about him – kind of the-boy-from-nowhere. He played on it. Only that woman up at the college, the one who got knocked off, knew anything, I reckon.'

'Do you think Johnny knocked her off?'

'No. Why would he? In the end, she was the only one he cared about. Sometimes, when we were together, I don't think he even cared much about me.'

Sterling eased back into the sofa and had a mouthful of tepid tea. 'I didn't mean to turn this into an interrogation. I was hoping to find something here about all the scams up at the college and Jane Casterton's murder – some evidence.'

'Like what?'

'I don't know... Papers, a laptop, a memory stick. Casterton was number one. Johnny was number two. She trusted him. Somewhere there are records.'

'He had a laptop. He had a fold-up table somewhere in here and he worked on that. But the laptop's not here and there's nothing else – not even a secret compartment or a loose floorboard. Not to my knowledge anyway, and at one stage I almost lived here. I tell you what, though ... Johnny had his own little workstation in college. No one else was allowed near it. He got a kick from knowing that everyone was too scared to say anything.'

'Will you come over to college with me so that I can have a look?'

'"Course. I haven't given up on you yet. The only snag about college is the ban.'

'You're with me so I'll make sure there's no trouble. You need to keep remembering that you're the victim. A predator and a manipulator recruits you and Darren....'

'Yeah, innocent little old me....'

'.... and you both end up in a dungeon under the principal's office, and he ends up dead. You might not exactly be innocent, but you are still a victim. In all this, you're part of the poor bloody infantry. Come on, let's find that laptop.'

The man Stephen's net curtain flicked as they went down the front steps of the house and Hannah gave a small wave. Then they were walking back to the college through the pleasure gardens and across the walkway between the cliffs, in the opposite direction from which Sterling had chased Johnny Fontana, and through the rear entrance of the college. There was no Z4 roadster outside Glen Lodge, and few other people or cars around during the holiday.

Hannah led Sterling to an open area in the middle of the Lavender building. They faced a long semi-circular information desk behind which there was a complement of administrative staff in front of a few computer screens. A man in a short-sleeved checked shirt, his turn for information duty, glanced up as the detective and his temporary sidekick entered and lost interest as they didn't seem likely to approach the counter. To their left and right were some interview-style rooms, the top half glassed. Hannah opened the one on the left nearest the door. A desk faced the window, with a blue office chair neatly pushed in underneath. Johnny Fontana had chosen well, or perhaps Jane Casterton had chosen well for him when she had set him up. Working at the desk, he would have had a panoramic view of most outside parts of the college, and, if staff, students and visitors had been walking up and down, would himself have been a visible presence.

On the way up, Sterling had been optimistic for a breakthrough. Now there was a snag, and a big one. Where according to Hannah there should have been a laptop, all there was on the desk was a clean, small, bare rectangle fringed on each side by a patina of dust.

Chapter 28

Monday 20 October - Snookered

'Snookered,' said Sterling, rocking and swivelling in Johnny Fontana's office chair. Hannah was sitting in the other chair, elbow on desk, hand propping up her chin. 'Who do you think would have taken it?'

'No idea,' said Hannah. 'To be honest, everyone I know who was mixed up with Johnny would have been too scared to come in here – unless he called them in.'

'Nothing in the drawers, either. What about back up?'

'I dunno. He wouldn't have used anything on the college's network. I don't reckon he'd have trusted the cloud.'

'So, a memory stick.'

'I guess. I doubt if he'd have carried it with him. He only carried keys and cash, and the laptop if he needed it.'

'And if he didn't hide it at home, would he have had someone else look after it?'

'No way,' said Hannah.

'Apart from here and the flat, did he hang out anywhere else – in college or in town?'

'Nope. I spent three months with him, and this was his little world.'

Sterling looked at the desk again – a functional grey block of plastic and metal with just two side drawers. He rooted through the untidy jumble of pens, paper clips and other office detritus once more, feeling carefully at the sides and back of each drawer, but it didn't look as if Johnny Fontana had ever even opened them. Rolling the chair away, he knelt down and put his head under the desk. He'd been wrong about the boy never using the drawers. The strip of shiny brown masking tape on the bottom of the desk top in the far right hand corner looked identical to the roll in the top drawer.

'Bingo,' said Sterling as he emerged from under the desk well, breathing quickly, with a memory stick wrapped in tape. 'Well done, Hannah. Your psychology was spot on.'

'I have my uses,' murmured the girl. 'Pity you don't make more of the whole range.'

Sterling pretended he hadn't heard. He unwrapped the stick from its brown cocoon. 'What a surprise,' he muttered.

'Meaning?'

'Meaning it's the same brand as all the others in circulation, like the one I got with the blackmail clip on it. Do you have a log-in password for the college's computers?'

'Somewhere,' said Hannah. She fished out her phone from her handbag and started scrolling.

'Learning Resource Centre,' said Sterling. 'Come on. There won't be any crush this time.'

'What?'

'I'll tell you on the way over.'

But the Learning Resource Centre in the Tuckett Building was where their luck ran out. It wasn't difficult finding an available machine, not during half-term. It wasn't difficult using Hannah's details to log into the system. The problem was Johnny Fontana. He might arrogantly have assumed that no one would dare to search for and find his memory stick, but he'd chosen the nine-character password to access it carefully. 'Johnnyfon' didn't work, nor 'Hannahwil', nor any combination of 'The Box' or 'Box of Joy'. Sterling unplugged it and slipped it in his pocket.

'What time's your next train, girl?'

Hannah looked at the clock above the librarian's desk. 'Fifteen minutes.'

'Mine too, roughly. There's nothing more to do here, but I reckon I know someone who might be able to get me into it. Let's get out of here.'

He hugged her on the station platform. 'Thanks for coming down. I wouldn't have got anywhere without you – not today, not before. I'll call you for that date when the case is over. You'll have an exclusive account.'

'It was fun, Frank. It could have been more fun, but....' She gave him a light kiss and slipped aboard as the doors of the train opened. 'See you soon.' She didn't look back.

Sterling stayed where he was for a moment, and then retraced his steps over the footbridge for the Ramston and Sandley platform. Midway across, he looked down with his forearms on the rail as the Whithampton and London train pulled away and off up the coast. He could see the Ramston and Sandley train approaching from the same direction in the white distance. He moved on and down to be on the platform when it rattled in.

The train was just edging past the ancient Roman fort when the calls came. Sterling knew that the old flint walls were just behind the rise, and the thatched roof of the visitors' centre just below the skyline. His father had taken him around all the ancient monuments in the area when he was a kid, but he'd never been fired by his father's enthusiasm. There was a secret railway around here, when the bay had been used as a port during the Second World War and a track led in a short spur from there to the mainline up the coast to London. On the other side the water meadows between the track and Sandley glittered in the sunshine, and the white windmill signalled that the town was only a minute or two away.

'Sterling,' he said.

'Frank, it's Adele. That girl you wanted me to track down – the goth – I think I've found her.'

In all the drama of the last few days, the girl had gone from his thoughts. He recovered quickly. 'Good news, Adele. I kind of expected it.'

'I'll e-mail you her photo. Then you can see for yourself. Her name, if I've got the right one, is Jody Bannister. Do you need me to do anything?'

The train was past the windmill and approaching Sandley station. Sterling moved to the door. 'Could you somehow call her in to college? Make an excuse that it's an interview or something. Don't scare her off.'

'OK. Where?'

An idea came to Sterling. 'Tell her Johnny's office. 10 o'clock tomorrow. She's not in trouble. There's just one or two things to sort out.'

'Johnny's office. I've never heard of that before. It sounds as though you've found something else out.'

'Maybe....'

'I'll confirm the arrangement when I e-mail her photo.'

'Thanks Adele. And Adele? Thanks for everything else you've done for me. I could get used to this support.'

'You've liberated me, Frank. Liberated lots of us by the sound of it.'

In the little station concourse, Sterling looked at the other 'missed call', vaguely recognising the number. He dialled back.

'Assistant Chief Constable Mamujee's telephone number,' said a cool female voice.

'This is Frank Sterling. Did he just try to phone me?' said Sterling.

'That was me – Deborah Sheringham, Mr Sterling. I'm ACC Mamujee's personal assistant.'

'So what's it about?'

'He'd like to make an appointment to meet you as soon as you can manage.'

Now he remembered the number – police headquarters. 'I'm not trailing up to Maidstone, Ms Sheringham. I've got too much on.'

'That's fine, Mr Sterling. ACC Mamujee is happy to come down to you. You have an office in Sandley, I believe.'

'What's it about?'

'He told me to say that he'd explain when you meet. What about tomorrow? Say two p.m.'

'I'll see him then.'

Sterling hotfooted it down Delfside and New Street into the High Street. The Cinque Ports Arms sign, a shield in a classic old French shape set in a black wooden frame, swung back and forth over the pub in the stiff breeze, the front halves of three lions passant on the left attached to the back halves of three galleons. But when he tried the door it was locked, and so were the gates to the yard. Now he remembered. On Mondays the pub was closed. Becky and Mike had a day of rest and made themselves scarce. There would be no chance of contact with a cryptographer today. In every case there were phases with two steps forward and one step back, or one step forward and two steps back. Today Sterling knew which it was. He ducked into Holy Ghost Alley. He'd walk up to his office, get Adele's e-mail and check if she'd got the right girl. Then he'd go home and cook. The long rumble in his stomach reminded him he'd had nothing to eat since breakfast.

Chapter 29

Tuesday 21 October - Dead Drop

The timid knock on the door drew Sterling away from the panorama in front of Johnny Fontana's office window. He swivelled the chair round and faced the door. 'Come in,' he called.

Adele had been right. This was the girl. Today, there were no holes in her tights and no globules of lardy flesh, but on the dark fabric a pattern of small death's heads, matched by a black t-shirt with a larger skull, underneath a short denim jacket. The outfit was completed by a short flared black skirt and shin-length Doc Martens. Her dark hair, with its purple streaks, framed a whiter face than Sterling remembered and a pale, slender neck. Mascara made the girl's eyes dark as coal, and her lips were purple. But no amount of make-up and goth fashion could mask the gentle naivety in the girl's expression.

'Thanks for coming in over half-term,' said Sterling, half rising and indicating the smaller chair. 'It's Jody, isn't it? I'm Frank Sterling. I'm sort of here instead of Johnny.'

'I've seen you around. About coming in – did I have a choice?' said the girl.

'I don't know. I didn't organise it.' Once again, Adele had probably showed ingenuity beyond her station.

'Am I in trouble?'

'I don't know,' Sterling said again. 'Are you?'

The girl looked at the floor.

'You know that Johnny Fontana's dead. And two members of staff here. And a student.'

'Yeah. It's all in *Earlsey Extra*. Plus all the students know.'

Sterling tried a switch. He might get more of a rapport. 'Thanks for rescuing me – up in the Learning Resource Centre.'

'What do you mean?'

'Those shelves in the library. They were squashing me.'

The girl's eyes widened. 'I don't know what you mean.'

'You told the librarian what was happening,' said Sterling. 'Why didn't you hang around? That would have been the obvious thing to do.'

'I panicked, all right?' said the girl. 'I just had to give you the message. I was going up to the LRC anyway. I didn't know you were going to get squashed.'

'Yes, that message – who gave it to you?' said Sterling. The girl looked at the floor again and twisted her hands together. The parting in her hair was as pale as her face. 'Come on. I believe you, but other people might not. Keeping quiet will make it worse.'

'Mr Havers,' she whispered.

'Right,' said Sterling. Another nail in Glen's coffin. The net was getting tighter. 'But that wasn't all you did, was it?'

Tears started to fall from the girl's eyes making parallel mascara-black twin streaks like prison bars down her white face. The one on the left made quicker progress. The girl sniffed.

Sterling found a tissue and pushed it over. 'I want information. I don't want you to get into trouble. I'm not sure you've done anything wrong.'

The girl sighed and composed herself, turning the lines into dirty smudges. 'I got a gig as a messenger. I knew Johnny when he was in my BTEC class. He said I could earn some steady money. He told me what to do. Said what would happen if I didn't keep my mouth shut.'

'Well, Johnny's gone now, so he's not going to bother you anymore. The others aren't dangerous. So now's the time to tell me what you did.'

'I was the postman....' – the girl giggled nervously – '.... postgirl around college. I'd get a text, collect something from somewhere and take it somewhere else. Two pounds per journey.'

Sterling considered what she's said. For a secret organisation it was better than e-mail and safer than ordinary internal mail. 'Just packages?'

'Anything really.'

'Did you know what was in the packages?'

'More than my life's worth,' said the girl. Then she smiled for the first time. 'But I had a feel sometimes, and once I saw Ms Casterton put a memory stick into an envelope. There were books too.'

'Books?'

'Books. I think she had books for different people. Johnny's was 822.JF because he got me to collect it for him. He said he couldn't be bothered with all the messing about. But I don't know any of the others because they must have come to the LRC themselves. The system was that Ms Casterton gave me the books and I had to put them on the right shelves in the library, using the Dewey Decimal Classification, which she showed me. Then I'd get anonymous texts when books were ready to take back to Ms C.'

'But supposing someone borrowed one of the books?' said Sterling.

Jody laughed. 'No one borrows books these days. Anyway, you should see them. Nobody would want anything so boring. Also, they weren't part of the LRC so they weren't security-tagged.'

Sterling thought of spies and what they did – this was a dead letter box with an extra twist, and seemed as good a system as any. 'I need the list of those book classifications.'

The girl took out a tattered, creased piece of paper and handed it over. Sterling unfolded it and scanned the list. If 822.JF was Johnny Fontana's book, could 613.MJ be Meg Jenkinson's, and 735.PM Pat Manton's? 'Would anyone on the list know the classification of another person's book?'

'No, only Johnny, Ms C and me knew those numbers. I didn't know who the books belonged to, and only Johnny and Ms C knew it was me doing the deliveries. I don't expect anyone knew anyone else's book number.'

Neat, thought Sterling. 'Come on,' he said. 'Let's go over to the LRC and see what books are on those shelves.'

Half-term bestowed on the college a calmness and tranquillilty that meant that the LRC was entirely empty when Sterling and the girl passed through the entrance.

Sterling looked over at the diagonally striped yellow and black safety tape, experiencing a lurch in his stomach and a sudden breathlessness. He remembered the soft grinding of the shelves and felt their pressure. But he still needed to get in amongst those shelves. He saw the tip of a shoe beyond the front counter and the door to the office-cum-staffroom. The person on duty was having a break. Sterling put his forefinger to his lips and motioned the girl to follow him. The only gap between the stacks was from 800 to 900 in the Dewey Decimal Classification.

'Don't let me get squashed,' he whispered. He ducked under the tape, crept between the stacks and cast around for 822.JF. And there it was – *The Early Industrialisation of Modern Belgium (1830-37)* by Jacques Feviers. It was surely misclassified in the Literature section, but perhaps Jody was right – it could stay there for months and not be noticed. He slipped the book into his pocket. He realised he was only half-lucky. The rest of the books were locked away in the other back-to-back stacks, compressed tightly together. At least no one else would be able to claim them.

He approached the counter. 'Anyone about?' he called out, and the librarian's head appeared from around the bottom half of the office door.

'You,' said the librarian. 'And your rescuer. I hope you've made a good recovery. I had to fill out an accident report you know, and the stacks are still not working.'

'I'm fine, thanks. When will they be repaired?'

'An engineer is coming out on Friday. They've never had anything like this before. They're trying to call it "human error". Tosh, in my opinion.'

'So, no borrowing from those stacks till Friday at the earliest....'

'Correct,' said the woman.

'Thanks,' said Sterling. If the *Early Industrialisation* book came up trumps, that would suit him very well.

In the corridor, the girl put a small white hand on Sterling's arm. 'Will I be all right?'

'How do you mean, Jody?'

'Johnny's dead. Ms Casterton's dead....'

'Yes,' he said. 'You will. None of the people linked to the list you gave me is dangerous. The dangerous two are gone. Johnny chose you because he thought you were discreet and reliable. You've done your work properly. No one else knows what you did. So yes, you're safe. But don't respond to any more texts, and steer clear of all this stuff. Keep quiet, like you've been doing all along. It's half-term now. By next Monday it should all be sorted out. Here's my card. Give me a ring if anything comes up.' He pointed to the Ladies and smiled. 'You might want to fix your face.'

Jody smiled back. 'The panda effect, is it?'

'You've got it,' said Sterling. 'Take care. I need to run for a train.'

Before he did, he put his head around the secretaries' door. Everyone except for Adele seemed to be out. She looked up from her screen.

'I saw her,' said Sterling.

'Good. Progress?'

'Maybe. I'll know later on. Right now I've got to get to an appointment back in Sandley with a policeman. What did you say to make her come in?'

'I told her a private detective needed to see her, that he was reasonable and kind if he was told the truth, difficult if not, and that he was a much better alternative than the police. And if she didn't turn up, not to doubt that he'd come looking.'

'It worked. Thanks.'

On the train back to Sandley from Southwood, with a change at Ramston, Sterling ignored all the landmarks. His nose was in *The Early Industrialisation of Modern Belgium*. It didn't give him any sudden passion for European economic history.

Assistant Chief Constable Mamujee, in his well-pressed police uniform and highly polished shoes, with immaculate grooming to match, was chatting with Angela Wilson at the reception desk of the library when Sterling arrived at his office, to the extent that Mamujee was half-sitting on the desk, his hands clasped in a relaxed pose. Angela was smiling and laughing.

Sterling approached. 'Mamujee?' he said.

The assistant chief constable stood up and put out a manicured hand. 'Mr Sterling,' he said. 'Thank you for the appointment.

Sterling ignored the hand. 'This way,' he said, 'if you've finished in the library.'

'Nice to talk to you,' said Mamujee to Angela. 'Thank you for reassuring me that I'd come to the right place. Goodbye.'

Sterling clumped up the stairs to his office, listening to make sure that the policeman was following, and settled himself behind his desk. He grunted and pointed to the client's chair. 'Right, Mr Mamujee, I'm very busy at the moment, so let's get straight to it.'

Mamujee smiled, a faint affair that barely altered the shape of his perfectly proportioned smooth face. His dark eyes looked almost gentle, but Sterling knew you didn't get to ACC without some steel. His family was somewhere from the subcontinent as well, and that wouldn't have helped, not as things currently stood in the force. 'I suppose you're right to be a little, shall we say, jaundiced, Mr Sterling. We've been reviewing things at Earlsey College of Technology, and at the same time your solicitor has been in touch.' He steepled his hands and crossed his legs. 'Things haven't been going quite as well as we hoped.'

'Is that right?' said Sterling. 'Well, every time I've come up against your lot, I've been insulted, interrogated, ignored, accused of lying, made to find my own way home long after the trains have stopped and then arrested for something I clearly didn't do. It's been sloppy, Mr Mamujee. Sloppy and hostile. One of your investigating officers seems to have a bee in his bonnet about me. God knows why.'

'That's rather come out of our review, Mr Sterling. I have to say, and I hope you can believe me, that I have some experience of prejudice myself, from a boyhood in Uganda and then over here with my family in Leicester. I am hoping that that will work in your favour.'

Sterling leaned back in his chair. This was unexpected. 'So if I instructed my solicitor to initiate proceedings for wrongful arrest, you'd be taking that seriously.'

'I most certainly would, Mr Sterling, and Mr Evanston has been persuasive in stating that he believes you have a good case. But I very strongly hope that it won't come to that. We were alerted to the problems by one of the other officers on the investigating team. He was very subtle and discreet – loyal too in his way, but he got the alarm bells ringing.'

The memory stick and Johnny Fontana's book were burning holes in Sterling's pockets. 'We don't seem to be getting straight to it after all,' he said. 'Where's all this going?'

Mamujee crossed his legs the other way. He was doing, Sterling calculated, what police officers found it difficult to do: admitting that mistakes had been made. 'We've made changes to the murder team. Superintendent Andrews has been reassigned to other duties – no criticism of him of course – just an acknowledgement of the burden of his workload and the fact that he needs a rest. I wonder if that would have any bearing on your discussions with your solicitor. That and a way of validating the contribution you've made to the case so far and involving you as we move forward.'

Sterling looked at his hands palms down on the desk. All that stupidity and awkwardness. All that mistrust. But why complain when you couldn't have got a better outcome? He looked up into Mamujee's handsome, clever face. 'I'll tell Mr Evanston to drop the matter. I'm happy to cooperate with your rejigged investigating team.'

'Excellent news, Mr Sterling. I'm very glad you see it that way. I've got the strong impression that your involvement will be vital in getting to the bottom of this complex matter and making sure justice is done.'

'Who's taken over from Andrews?' asked Sterling.

'Someone you already know pretty well, I think, supported by Detective Sergeant Murphy, so I think that will be helpful. Detective Chief Inspector Andy Nolan.'

Bloody hell, thought Sterling. It wasn't that Andy was taking over – Sterling knew that he had one of the sharpest minds in the force, so if the investigation was stalled there was probably no one better. It was that a year ago he'd still only been a sergeant. Now the promotions were coming thick and fast.

Mamujee and his team had been shrewd. They'd picked one of the only police officers with a chance of regaining Sterling's cooperation. He felt the memory stick in his pocket. But even Andy Nolan would have to wait for the next breakthrough.

Ten minutes later, everything smoothed over, Sterling looked down over the square. There was a delay before Mamujee emerged and called for his car, and after a few moments a sleek black sedan pulled smoothly up. Sterling watched the car ease away. Now he could get on.

Chapter 30

Tuesday 21 October - Codebreakers

Angela's footsteps echoed as she climbed the stairs, and it was her firm rap on the door. He'd heard them often enough. She came in and unfolded herself on the sofa. 'How to make friends and influence people,' she murmured.

'Well, I'd had it with them one way and another,' said Sterling. 'I really didn't appreciate getting arrested in my own local, and that wasn't the only thing.'

'That one was all right, though. In fact, he was charming. In fact, he took my card.'

Sterling frowned. 'Of course, it's none of my business, but....'

'Yes, Frank. It is none of your business.' Angela's voice softened. 'It won't make any difference ... you know ... to us – nothing would.'

'Phew,' said Sterling. 'Is anyone holding the fort downstairs, or have you got to get back?'

'Kerry's there. She knows where I am.'

'Have a look at this while I get the kettle on.' Sterling pushed *The Industrialisation of Modern Belgium* across his desk.

'What am I looking at, apart from a really dull looking book?'

'The numbers in one of the front pages to begin with. There's something in there. I've just got to find out what.'

He pulled the client's chair around next to his own, and set the two mugs of tea on the desk. They looked at one of the inside pages where an extra sheet had been pasted as if for recording borrowing return dates. Figures had been put in manually rather than with a date stamper, in a neat and precise hand. The book had been 'borrowed' on a regular basis and there were seven sets of them.

'This doesn't make sense,' said Angela. 'They look like dates, but there are too many digits using the usual dd/mm/yy approach. And why is each line of numbers highlighted? Blue, yellow, pink – it looks random. What about the rest of the book?'

Notepad and pen to hand, Sterling went forward through the pages again, as he had done cursorily on the train, page after dense page. He could find nothing in the first three chapters, but in the fourth, amongst the turgid text and close-packed tables he found individual letters and numbers highlighted in blue, nine in total. Written out, they too, like the lines of numbers at the front, made no sense. Other chapters had similar markings.

'Let's go back to the front,' said Angela.

'This is my thinking so far,' said Sterling. 'Each sequence of numbers ends in the two numbers for the current year. So it's possible that days and months are also amongst the sequences. If days are expressed in two digits, 01 for the first of the month, 16 for 16th and so on, that might make sense at the front end of each line. Concentrating on the first line – 0780514 – if 07 is the seventh day and 14 is the year, how will the month pan out? It can't be 80, so it has to be 05. In that line, 8 is a kind of surplus digit.'

'Try the next line, Frank. This is promising.'

'OK – 15100714. In this theory, 15 is the day, and 14 the year, but the month could be either 10 or 07.' He rubbed his eyes. Was this going to work? He went through the other lines. Using the same technique, there was no ambiguity.

On the pad, he wrote out the dates he'd extracted and next to each the surplus number. Although the lines were not in order, he'd identified dates for April, May, June, possibly July, August, September and possibly two for October. One of the October possibles could not also be July. He made the final adjustments.

'All these ducks are in a row.' He looked at the list of surplus numbers, the highest 15.

'Supposing these surplus numbers represent the chapters in the book,' said Angela.

'Exactly my thinking. Soooo … the April date is highlighted in yellow and the surplus number is five. Let's see.' Sterling turned to chapter 5 and looked for highlights. There were nine, and they were all yellow. Another two checks confirmed their hunch.

'Where does this get us?' said Angela. 'We've potentially just got seven sets of nine characters.'

'The last date's the key, in my opinion – just before I first clapped eyes on ECOT and Margaret Kingston. And this is why.' He got out the memory stick and brandished it in front of them. 'It's password protected….'

'.... and you think the code based on the October date will get you in.'

Sterling plugged the stick into his machine. 'We'll soon find out. Let's go to chapter 9 and get it – nine characters highlighted in blue.'

Angela swigged from her mug. Sterling wiped his sweat-prickled hands. Then he tapped in the potential password to access the memory stick and pressed 'Enter'.

'It works,' whispered Angela as the screen sprang into life.

Sterling realised he'd been holding his breath and breathed out noisily. He wouldn't be needing a cryptographer after all. And never mind making progress in little steps. This could be his own Great Leap Forward.

'It seemed quite straightforward,' said Angela. 'More quiz page than *Smiley's People*. Certainly not Enigma and Bletchley Park. In fact ... credit to us for working it out, but if you want my opinion, it's a bit contrived – childish even.'

'Yeah,' said Sterling. 'I only met the murdered woman, Jane Casterton, once, but I got that impression myself – she devised the code and everything else as a hobby, a bit of a lark. One of her henchmen said similar. She wasn't interested in money, just power and influence – because she was never in the running for the top job even before the current principal. Unfortunately for her, and others, it got dangerous and deadly.'

'Well, I suppose I'd better go and see how Kerry is getting on. You probably don't want me around for this next bit. And I'd better not ask where you got the memory stick.'

'You'll know eventually. It's just a bit murky right now.'

'It always is with you, Frank, one way or another. Maybe I'll ask my new pal when it's all over.'

'I doubt he'll ever know as much as me.'

When Angela had gone, Sterling started with the documents. There were two principal folders, one labelled 'Accounts' and the other 'Persuasion'. He double-clicked on 'Accounts' and came upon sub-folders – 'Recruitment', 'Factory', 'Distribution', 'Website', 'Research' and 'Club Night'. He tried 'Club Night' and a list of dated spreadsheet files appeared. The latest one coincided with his infiltration so he clicked it open. According to the heading, Meg Jenkinson was the manager. Sterling had never had a job involving budgets in the police, and his own business affairs were pitifully simple – about the only asset he had was the computer he was currently using. But the profit and loss statement on the screen in front of him was a model of simple clarity. Income came from a hefty £1,000 sub-scription from the 40 attendees, together with a similarly substantial £20,000 or so from the gaming tables. 'Services' – Sterling could guess from his conversation with Janeen what they might be – amounted to £12,000. There was further revenue from 'Catering, drinks and sundries'.

On the other hand, Meg Jenkinson had not stinted on expenses for equipment (further detailed as tables, cards etc.), laundry, staffing, catering and 'Miscellaneous Other Expenses'. The 'actors', presumably Hannah and Darren, had been paid £1,500 apiece. In the end, Sterling knew enough about accounts to look at the bottom line. For that one club night, according to the figures, income had exceeded expenditure by £23,000.

'Research' intrigued him. This was more straightforward. For 'services rendered', Joe Speltman, the marketing manager with dreams of promotion, received a hefty £1,500 per month for lists of 'targets' that ranged from three to five in any given period. Sterling noted his own name on the October entry, and the cryptic 'LA!' just below. Speltman cost Jane Casterton's enterprise £18,000 per year and provided no income. Still, it was presumably a valuable service by a skilled operator and worth the outlay.

Sterling moved on. In the 'Factory' folder he found a spreadsheet in the usual format for the dope growing, managed unequivocally, according to the heading, by Pat Manton. Again, income from sales comfortably outstripped expenditure. The union rep would be spitting if he knew. Sterling opened the 'Website' account and was not disappointed. At last Glen Havers was fingered as part of the rogue group. Again the numbers were impressive, principally advertising revenues exceeding set-up and other costs. There was a hyperlink to the site, www.peepingthomas.com.

The temperature in the office went up a degree or two as Sterling clicked on it, or perhaps it was his heartbeat quickening and the sudden spurt of adrenaline flooding into his system. There was little in the way of rubric on the home page, just a knowing welcome – mostly about the thrill of watching sex unseen – and then row on row of teasing pictures and racy titles, with gambling ads, pop-ups and links to other sites. Hannah and Darren inevitably starred in 'At the hairdressers – Harry gets more than a short back and sides!!' and there was Janeen

in 'Bedroom Frolics – Little Blonde Gets Carried Away!!'
At least names had been changed or not used at all.
Sterling wondered if Hannah or any of the other boys
and girls knew about their roles as porn stars beyond
'Club Night'.

Sterling gave his head a little shake. It was vicious, but
for the organisers the joy of it was that there was no tax
paid, no national insurance, no bills for heating and
electricity and none of the other burdens faced by
legitimately run organisations. Just by having a club
night once a month and managing the ongoing other
activities, people had been getting wealthy.

The other folder was 'Persuasion', split into
'Active', 'Passive' and 'External' sub-folders. 'Not
"Persuasion",' breathed Sterling, as he went down the
lists. "Blackmail".' He found files for Ellie Laski and
Adele Coppersmith in the 'Passive' category, and
amongst the 'Active' Hissing Sid and Meg Jenkinson. It
looked as though 'Club Night' members were in the
'External' folder. He ignored Ellie and Adele's files – it
seemed only right, and he was feeling grubby enough
already. Others, opened from each sub-folder, Speltman
had thoroughly researched and immaculately presented,
sometimes with pictures, video clips, hyperlinks or news
articles embedded as relevant. Sterling found his own file
in 'External'.

It was a clever web of scams and criminality, and it
had an elegant overall symmetry. As well as generating
its own profits, Club Night supplied web footage and
material for extortion and blackmail. No doubt drugs
from the factory were available there for purchase and
distribution. There were any number of other links
and overlaps.

It took another hour to go through the rest of the folders and files, and another few minutes to make copies – one onto the hard drive of his computer, one in the cloud, and one, fittingly he believed, on the only memory stick he possessed – the one containing his own blackmail file. By the end Sterling had virtually the whole picture – a shadow, parasitic organisation running brazenly in an apparently unremarkable southeast coast further education college – and until Margaret Kingston had engaged him, no one from outside any the wiser. Before he'd got his hands on Johnny Fontana's memory stick the evidence had been patchy. This was perfect.

He got up from his chair again and looked over the square. At just past 4:30 things were winding down. Freddy the grocer and his assistant were beginning to carry their unsold fruit and vegetables inside. Almost opposite his window Max Fortnum and his latest assistant, a young woman in a green satin dress, were sharing a joke near the window. An elderly man hobbled with his stick up to the cash till at the bank, and looked round furtively as he inserted his card. It occurred to Sterling that with suitable binoculars he could record PIN numbers being punched in from his window and then plan ways of filching the plastic. Often people's bulk would get in the way, but there were bound to be occasional opportunities. He could do it sitting in his chair, if things got really desperate.

He knew what he was procrastinating about. He dragged himself back from the comforting and the ordinary to the dark and corrupt. It was a question of sequence. He owed the police nothing, even Andy Nolan after all those years together. Anyway, Andy would be spending today briefing himself and getting up to date.

'Adele,' Sterling said into the phone. 'I've caught you. Is Margaret back in tomorrow? I need to speak to her.'

'She certainly is, Frank. You saved me a job. I'll be able to get home a little bit earlier. She told me to contact you. She wants an update.'

'Why am I not surprised?' said Sterling. 'What about 10 o'clock?

There was a pause. 'I've put it in her diary,' said Adele.

Chapter 31

Wednesday 22
October - Briefings

If anything, Margaret Kingston looked even tinier behind her desk than when Sterling had first met her over a fortnight ago. There was the same impression as before – a child playing at being a grown-up.

For him, the grind of coming back and forth from Sandley meant that all the freshness had leached from the case, and the college was no longer a place of mystery or even interest, despite all he had discovered. He barely remembered the feelings of unease he'd felt as he'd first came round the corner by the block of 1960s flats and seen the Tuckett Building in front of him. Looking at the small woman, it looked as though she was also grappling with ennui, even after a few days' rest.

They settled down on the sofa to the coffee that Adele brought through. It was quiet in the office and quiet outside as half term meandered on – just an ordinary morning – apart from...

The principal chinked her cup onto the saucer. 'Apparently there's a new investigating officer, though the police pretty much tell me nothing. A man by the name of Nolan. Mind you, I've said before that Andrews was useless – intent on his own hobbyhorses and not much else. I don't come out with much credit myself, to be honest. I should have stood up to Zoë Westhanger. We should have gone with the flow. Just let the police deal with it all. Not tried to interfere or influence events. Stopped the attempted PR and the manipulation. The suspensions – that poor boy and girl, the disciplinary against Pat Manton – more mistakes – dangerous, even disastrous. That's what we're doing now, going with the flow. Thank goodness it's half-term. Hopefully we can get back to some kind of normal on Monday. I've completely shut down the lower ground floor, and we'll dismantle the torture chamber when the police have finished. Security is going to be tight. Everyone will need their ID. As far as possible, we'll be keeping the press out. God, hindsight: it's a wonderful thing.'

'The new bloke,' said Sterling. 'Detective Chief Inspector Nolan.' The words sounded odd. 'I know him. I worked with him. He's good. Anyway, I'm kind of glad you're taking that line with the police, because I've found some more evidence on a memory stick. The snag is that I can't let you have it. It's as you say – completely a police matter now, and Andy Nolan has the nous to be able to sort it out. There'll be arrests, I reckon, and you'll be able to take the appropriate action after they happen. I'm telling you obviously to keep you informed and because you're my employer.'

Margaret Kingston leaned forward. Sterling felt a sudden atmosphere. Was it tension? Suspense? Maybe.

'This memory stick,' she said. 'Is my predecessor on it? Prestwick? Am I? Files, anything like that?'

'No and no,' said Sterling. 'If you had been, I would have warned you. That begs the question, of course....'

'.... That there are reasons we should be. Well, I don't think so, but Jane Casterton was enterprising.'

'Enterprising and discreet. I've found nothing to connect her directly to any of the illegal stuff going on in the college, but I know she was behind all of it.'

'What about the deaths? Meg Jenkinson, Jane Casterton and that boy, not the one in the torture chamber, the other one?'

Sterling realised that the principal did not know exactly what had happened to Johnny Fontana. 'Mrs Jenkinson's hanging is being treated as suspicious as far as I know. It might have been suicide; it might have been something else. I don't know how the police are getting on with Jane Casterton either. I expect DCI Nolan will contact me, and I'll ask him. As for Johnny Fontana, he tipped himself into the sea down at the jetty, so that was definitely suicide.'

'So as far as the police are concerned, there's still a long way to go.'

'To be honest, they might not ever get to the bottom of everything.'

'OK, Frank. Thanks for the update. I'll keep you on a little while longer, and then we'll call it a day, especially if Nolan is as good as you say he is.' Margaret Kingston tut-tutted and shook her head, but as Sterling left her office, he sensed another change of atmosphere. If his gut was right, it was relief.

Halfway on the trek to the station, his phone rang. 'Detective Chief Inspector Nolan,' Sterling said. 'I bow down before you.'

'That's congratulations, is it, Frank?'

'Sure, and it's happening much more quickly than even I imagined. We should celebrate.'

'Thanks. But we'll have to put the celebrations on hold till I've dealt with this ECOT thing. ACC Mamujee told me he'd got you up to speed. I'm based in Marchurch at the moment. Where are you right now?'

'Southwood. On the way to the railway station.'

'Excellent. Come over here and we can talk.'

'Whoa, Andy. You plods. I'm not at your beck and call, especially after the way Andrews messed me about. I'm off back to Sandley. If you want to talk, you can come over there.'

Nolan was flexible. That's why he was floating up towards the top. 'Right, wait at the station. I'll send a squad car to pick you up and take you back to your office. I'll meet you there.'

'Nothing less than I deserve. I'll see you in about 45 minutes.'

The tea was ready when Andy Nolan arrived. He and Sterling shook hands and settled down to talk. There had been some tension between them in the late stages of one case where Sterling had held some information back from his friend, but peace had long since broken out.

'This is cosy, Frank, and you're establishing a good reputation. In fact, you're making a go of it.'

'But you're the Detective Chief Inspector.'

'And my life is probably a whole lot more complicated. I can do the politics, but it doesn't mean I have to like it. Anyway, ECOT – I need you to brief me. I'm still working with Murphy, who between you and me managed to get the hierarchy to understand that we weren't getting anywhere under the ... previous regime, but there's a lot he doesn't know, especially recently.'

'OK, I'll tell you everything but it's only fair that you update me from your side. The college is still employing me, and I'll need to report back.'

'Your turn,' said Sterling, after half an hour of talk, question and answer. He handed over the memory stick. 'All the files and pictures and video clips are on there.'

'Hang on a second,' said Nolan, looking up from his notepad. 'I need a bit of recovery time. I've been around the block a few times, Frank, but I've never heard anything like this. Murphy has been pretty thorough, but clearly I didn't get the half of it.'

'They just weren't interested.'

'I expect I'll have to come back to you on various things.'

'Yes, and you'll have to think hard about the charges, Andy. It's complicated. You'll find kids doing dodgy things, but they're not the ones who should be punished. The whole set-up was rotten, and they were drawn into it. Hannah, Janeen, all those others, they don't need the book thrown at them.' Sterling held his friend the chief inspector's gaze.

'Noted, Frank. I'll do my best, I promise. I suppose in return for all that, you want an update from the police angle.'

'Of course,' said Sterling.

'Well, Andrews was concentrating on – fixated on, you could say – the four deaths: Casterton, Jenkinson, the boy in The Box and Fontana. In a way, why not? The bigger picture was a lot to take in. I don't think he was paying you much attention until Fontana because what you were implying – the bigger picture, as it were – was too … preposterous. The college management didn't help by withholding certain things to try and protect themselves. Something might come out of that. You really rubbed Andrews up the wrong way even before this ECOT business, from what I heard, so when he got that footage of you and the boy down at the jetty, he thought he'd won the lottery. You were lucky there was a witness.'

'I didn't rub him up the wrong way, Andy,' said Sterling. 'Any friction or bad blood was completely his problem. I was just doing my job. So, Jenkinson and Casterton.'

'Right. Jenkinson first. You can learn how to hang yourself from the internet, but forensics went over everything and it seemed too neat. The pathologist found bruising and what looked like finger marks on various parts of her. But there were a few clinchers. She was unconscious when she was strung up and there was a blow at the back of her head to explain that. And we found a set of fingerprints on one of the cups in the dishwasher that weren't Jenkinson's.'

'Fontana's,' said Sterling. 'He'd had coffee with Meg Jenkinson. When he killed her, he wiped everything down, but she'd cleared the cups and saucers away, and he'd forgotten about them.'

'Correct,' said Andy Nolan. 'And the fact that various areas had been carefully wiped down is suspicious in itself.'

'And of course you could always get me to testify about what Fontana said to me when he topped himself.'

His friend looked away.

'Oh,' said Sterling. 'Now I'm not on the job anymore, what I heard isn't reliable.'

'You know how it works, Frank. It's not just you either. Police witnesses these days are regularly disbelieved by juries. Anyway, we've got enough without that to prove that Fontana murdered her. Means, motive – to keep her quiet – and opportunity. Fontana was evil for someone so young.'

'And alarmingly competent,' said Sterling. 'We know about Darren. What about Casterton? When you've seen what's on that memory stick, you'll probably realise that her murder's the only part of the whole thing that's not been sorted.'

'Actually, no one in the college had a good word at all to say about that woman. She sounded terrible. But Andrews liked a couple of people for it. If we go back to MMO, the means was to hand – that great big golden tick – and loads of people had motive, but fewer had opportunity. Two of them did, though – the principal's secretary, Adele Coppersmith, and an art lecturer, Ellie Laski. It sounds as if they both had issues with the victim. The pathologist put Casterton's death at about 8 p.m. on the Tuesday evening. Coppersmith has the keys to the building, knows the alarm code and was working late. Laski had arranged to go in late so that she could fire the kilns for some pottery work. No evening classes take place in that bit, so that narrowed it down. The big snag about those two is that the pathologist reckons a man was responsible. It was a frenzied, savage, unpremeditated attack by a strong, determined person. We'll be questioning those two shortly and carrying on with the investigation.'

Sterling stuck out his lower lip. Margaret Kingston had told him it was reckoned that a man had done it, so that wasn't news. But neither Adele nor Ellie had mentioned last Tuesday evening, and people – women – were capable of anything. Even so, those two … it seemed far-fetched. Adele had been pretty handy with the table leg on Johnny Fontana in The Box, but far from 'frenzied'. He didn't mention that she was virtually a sidekick, or that Ellie, well, Ellie and he…. He didn't say anything. Andy Nolan had had a good enough crack of the whip to be going on with.

'You'll keep me posted if you find out anything more, won't you, Frank?' said Nolan as he got up from the client's chair and offered his hand.

'Cross my heart,' said Sterling. 'The one thing I want out of this is for Glen Havers, the technician bloke, to be nicked. A bonus would be for me to be there when it happened.'

'If this is the evidence you say it is' – he patted the memory stick in his pocket – 'we'll get him, and I don't see why I can't have you around.'

Sterling listened to his friend's footsteps down the stairs, and watched as he strode out splay footed in his scruffy shoes towards No Name Street and the Guildhall. A thought occurred to Sterling. Was 'No Name Street' an oxymoron? And in the random way of things, that triggered another – one that was much, much more important. A phrase uttered days ago came back to him almost word for word.

He picked up the phone and pressed the numbers he was coming to know well. 'Adele, is Margaret in the office for the rest of the day?' He listened. 'How about tomorrow? So she's in London at this conference all day? OK. This one might be a bit tricky for you but it's definitely necessary.' He finished the call and stared at the picture of the hop farm and oast house on the opposite wall. It was a hunch, but it was worth a shot.

Chapter 32

Thursday 23 October - Disclosure

'All those other things were fine, Frank,' said Adele. She stirred her coffee distractedly with a wooden stick. She and Sterling were sitting in the staff refectory in the Cara Building, close to the Earlsey College Hotel area. Now that half-term was drawing to a close, more people were around the college, including the administrative areas, so Sterling had suggested a quieter, more discreet venue than the secretaries' office for his request.

'It's a tricky one,' said Sterling, 'but I don't think we're going to finish this off without a search. I can do it really quickly, and carefully enough for her not to know that I've been rummaging. I'll be discreet. It will do no harm, and it could do some good. I'm sure I'm on to a winner. Look at it this way. Where did I put the memory stick with the blackmail shot on me? In the top drawer of my desk. Where's Ellie Laski's? In the beaten up drawer in her table in the pottery. That PR bloke who was jailed for indecent assaults a while back – where did he keep the letter condemning him from one of his victims? In the drawer of his desk. Where's yours?' Sterling slipped her a sly look and she blushed and fidgeted. 'I'm right, aren't I?

The top drawer of your desk up there in the Tuckett Building.'

'It just isn't right.'

'There's another reason....' Sterling leaned forward on the low seat, clasped his hands and looked round the refectory.

A chef in brilliant whites was fussing around the display of cakes behind the glass counter, adding some from a tray and then rearranging them. A group of lecturers were having an intense discussion at a table a few metres behind Adele. The youngest, a man with a dark goatee that failed to make him look older, was stabbing the table with his forefinger. The oldest, with a shiny pink face and an old linen jacket that almost matched it in colour and even texture, was leaning back with his arms folded and an expression that combined cynicism and amusement. Steam hissed from a drinks dispensing machine near the till, where a plump woman whose uniform indicated a position low down in the culinary pecking order slouched on a stool examining her nails.

'.... The police have you down as a suspect.'

'What?' Adele stopped stirring.

'You didn't tell me you were in the building the night Jane Casterton got done in,' said Sterling.

'You didn't ask. It wasn't relevant anyway, because I didn't do anything.'

'Look, I'm with you, Adele. I don't think you did anything either. That's why I want to do this small thing. It could crack everything right open.'

'Come on,' said the secretary abruptly. Sterling gulped down the last of his coffee as she stood up, all her usual diffidence replaced by urgency and purpose.

On their way up the slope, she spoke softly. 'I didn't go up to her office, Frank. She came down to mine – to hassle me, as usual – not directly, just by the usual horrible innuendo. Vile woman. I don't know whether you've found out – it wouldn't surprise me if you have as you've found out virtually everything else since you've been around – but in my previous, non-respectable life, I was a sex worker, at the, um, high end, as it were. There's another complicating factor, which is that I'm gay.'

'Really?' I didn't know actually – on either count. And Casterton....?'

'She didn't want sex, if that's what you're thinking. I can't imagine she was ever interested in that. She just loved the occasional bullying and goading, and the blackmail thing kept me quiet. But I did what I've not done before, and sent her packing. By that time, things were falling apart, and I felt a bit safer.'

Sterling shook his head. 'You didn't have to tell me. I've handed some evidence to the police, and there's a file with your name on it, but I didn't open it. I know the new investigating officer. He's a friend of mine and I trust him. He won't go after victims – just the law-breakers.

'What I used to do wasn't exactly legal, Frank.'

'Recent law-breakers. Whatever. You know what I mean.'

When they reached the pottery at the bottom of the main building, Adele stopped. Tears pricked her eyes. 'Let me just compose myself, Frank. I'm all right. It's relief, I think.'

'The police will question you, but you'll be alright.'

Outside the principal's office, Adele produced the key. 'Make it quick, Frank.'

Sterling slipped in to the large room and over to Margaret Kingston's desk, easing on his surgical gloves as he went. He would have been stymied if the drawers had been locked, but the principal had calculated that locking the door, and her status, would be enough. The top drawer on the right would be the one. He pulled it right open, and riffled through the contents. On this evidence, principals were like everyone else, he reflected. There was an untidy, disorganised mass of paper clips, pens, elastic bands, random bits of paper, Post-It pads, cards, boxes of staples, a hole-punch, treasury tags and ... a memory stick of the same brand as all the others. He made a quick and cursory search of the other drawers and found nothing similar. There was no point in pushing his luck. He closed the drawers, trying to make sure everything looked roughly as it was before, looked round the desk and the rest of the office, and moved quietly and swiftly back into the corridor.

Adele jerked her chin up and Sterling nodded. 'Who's in your office right now?' he said.

'A couple of people at the far end.'

'Can we have a discreet look at what's on this?' Sterling held up the small memory stick.

There was only one file when it was plugged in – entitled, 'Who's that girl?'

Adele clicked on it and a video clip began to load. Sterling looked over her Adele's shoulder at the unfolding scene. They spoke softly in a kind of commentary batted back and forth like a tennis rally, sometimes even seeming to speak just to themselves.

'Someone took this with an old video camera or something. The quality's not brilliant. It has a dated feel to it.'

'Isn't that a station? Victoria maybe?'

The camera panned the concourse. Then a number of young people began to drift into the picture, all in hoodies and American-style baseball hats. As well as the sounds of the station, the person filming was also breathing hoarsely. A small figure came into the centre of the group, back to the camera and by the shape of her legs, hips and backside, a slim, young girl in skinny black jeans. Her hood was up and her face obscured. On the back of her pink sweatshirt, 'Bad Girl' was emblazoned in a black that matched her jeans. The other youngsters, some white, some Asian but mostly black, began to gather round as she smacked her fist in her palm like a football coach at half time. On the edge of the clip, something blurry triggered a response in Sterling – more an impression than a memory.

Then someone motioned to something beyond the camera, and in an instant there was pandemonium as the group dashed off like a mob of meerkats. The camera operative's breathing grew more ragged as she or he tried to keep up. The clip ended at the top of some stairs down to the tube, the underground symbol wobbling as the picture faded. 'More soon!' had been superimposed onto the final frame.

'What did you make of that, Frank?'

'Enough,' said Sterling. He knew what he had to do next. He knew why he hadn't done it before. And he knew why he couldn't put it off any longer. 'I've got to get back to Sandley. When the police get back to you, tell them what happened. They've got nothing on you, and

DCI Nolan is reasonable enough. I'll have some more news before long, and that will help you. In fact, it will help everyone. I'll need to keep hold of this,' he said, as he put the memory stick away. 'See you soon.'

'Is Angela in?' said Sterling to Kerry, the library assistant at Sandley library.

'Not till just before closing, Mr Sterling. She's got a meeting in Maidstone.' The girl lowered her voice. 'Union stuff. All about savings and volunteers for the library service. She'll look after us, Angela.'

'Right, well, I'll come down at about five, but if I miss her, can you tell her to meet me in the pub for a drink and a stab at the crossword?'

Kerry knew the routine. 'Of course,' she said.

Later in the pub at six o'clock, Sterling was having the pint that Jack Cook had promised to buy him, the two of them sitting on bar stools as Mike Strange glided round behind the counter. Jack's large round face was florid and flushed, small streaks of sweat trickling down from his sideburns as he took pleasure at being back in the fold. Sterling had forgotten Cook's tendency towards pontification and noticed that the story of their rift in an earlier case was being subtly revised. Jack had been bamboozled into placing a tracker under the car he had lent to Sterling, thinking that it was for Sterling's safety. The promise of sexual favours in return for betrayal had been expunged from history. Sterling took a pull on his free pint and judged that more tweaks to the truth would follow to assuage his companion's guilt even further.

Angela raised her eyebrows when she saw the drinking companions aligned at the bar. Sterling got off his stool and pointed to the fire. 'I've got the crossword, Angie. Shall we go into the snug? Do you want your usual?'

'I'll get it, Frank,' said Jack Cook. 'And another for you?' His largesse was extending beyond Sterling to the investigator's circle.

Angela saw Sterling's little nod and gave Jack Cook a small smile. 'You know what it is, Jack.'

Sterling got out the paper and spread it out on the small table. 'We need a bit of quiet for a few minutes, Jack,' he said when the older man had brought over a tray.

'Sure, sure,' said the café owner.

'What's all that about?' said Angela softly.

'Bargains being bargains, I guess,' said Sterling. 'And a short spell of free drinks. I've been seeing something of Margaret Kingston again.'

'Yeah? Well, don't involve me, Frank.'

He put his hand over hers. 'I've got to, Angie. I should have before.'

The librarian looked towards the bar and round the rest of the pub. Jack Cook had engaged Mike Strange in a lengthy technical conversation about a mutually interesting aspect of cuisine. A young boy and girl were canoodling at the far end of the bar. There was a thud of darts over in the other bar, and the less regular click of pool balls clashing. Diners were beginning to drift into the restaurant area, even though it was early.

A look of something close to panic flared up and then faded in Angela's dark eyes. 'I've been ambushed,' she said.

'Yep,' said Sterling.

Angela took a gulp of her gin and tonic. Normally she made them last half an evening, but this one was almost gone.

'I'll freshen that up,' said Sterling, and she didn't protest.

When he returned, she dragged her eyes out of the long focus into something far back in her memory and turned her gaze directly to him. 'Back in the day, when you were a young policeman and I was a young student, you'd have been "boydem". If we'd been friends all those years ago, you'd have been "coz", and I'd have addressed you as "blud" or "bro". Instead of our evenings with the crossword in the pub, we might have "chilled" together, perhaps with a spliff. We might have lived in the same "endz".'

'You were in a gang,' said Sterling.

'I *ran* a gang, Frank.' Angela stopped speaking for a short moment, and a tear rolled down her face and dropped into her drink. 'My gang name was Ange. And Margaret Kingston was Little Ange.'

Sterling kept quiet and nursed his drink in both hands. He glanced up at the bar to check that Jack and the others were fully occupied and then hunched forward, seeking to obscure Angela from view as they sat with their heads together. 'And here's me thinking you were a goody two-shoes chorister in East Dulwich Elim Pentecostal Church,' he said.

She laughed and dabbed her eyes. 'Well, I did go to church. I come from a good West Indian family, as you know. But going to church where I was growing up didn't mean you couldn't be in a gang as well. Don't get me wrong. Not all black kids in London and the big cities are in gangs. And of course black kids, even from poor homes, can achieve academically – look at me and Margaret. Her Sociology degree was apparently one of the best in her year at LSE, and as you know, I didn't do too badly myself. The stats on it all might surprise you. But Margaret and I took a wrong turn. I wanted to avoid the bullying and be tough, and I wanted a bit more than pocket money and a paper round. Margaret did too. And the tougher and more enterprising you were, the less hassle you had.'

'And you were the toughest.'

'One of the toughest.'

'Tell me why Margaret was 'Little Ange'.'

Angela's eyes blurred. 'If you were in a gang, particularly a girl in a gang, a leader, it added to your heft and status if you found yourself a protégé, and if you were good, kids wanted to be your protégé. Margaret is a year younger than me. She wanted the role, and I was happy to give it to her, to train her up and act as her mentor, as it were. The thing was, a protégé had to prove herself.'

'Victoria,' said Sterling.

'Bloody hell, Frank,' said the local librarian who never swore. 'How did you find out about Victoria?'

'I came across some video footage which I think is of a younger Margaret Kingston. There's a blurred finger with a red-nailed finger on one of the early frames. It looked like yours, so I put two and two together.'

Angela nodded. 'Victoria,' she said. 'I've made myself not think of Victoria for all these years. If I go to London, I go to Charing Cross.' She shuddered and took another gulp. 'I was in the sixth form, doing my A levels. Yes, I was running a gang, but I was good at school, and the teachers supported me. It was April, just after Easter, in the first year of my A levels. Little Ange, who was also doing well at school, was on her GCSEs, but she wanted to get involved. At the time, our Clapham crew was involved in a feud with another crew in Peckham or Wandsworth or Battersea or somewhere. You know, it meant everything to us at the time. It consumed us, but I don't even remember where they were from. We were provoking each other – it was phone boxes in those days, not mobiles and Facebook and whatever now – and then we fixed on a venue to sort it out. I put Little Ange in charge as one of her initiation rituals, and told everyone I was going to observe.' She shook her head and rolled her eyes. 'I did too, with a video camera I borrowed from school – allegedly for a project.'

She shuddered again and put her fingers over her eyes. 'She could lead, that girl. My goodness she could lead. I thought I was the bee's knees, but she eclipsed me that day. She told everyone what to do on the concourse at Victoria. She *deployed* them for goodness' sake. Kids older, more experienced and allegedly tougher than her. And the ambush ... those kids from Peckham or wherever coming off the train – cocky, confident – didn't know what had hit them. All this taking place during the rush hour. But Frank, Little Ange didn't just lead. She led by example. She homed in on the biggest, toughest looking boy on that crew, followed him into the underground, leapt on his back, knocked him onto the ground, whipped him over and gave him such a pulverising. That girl, that day, was demented. She sat on his chest, clung like a limpet and with her fists beat his face to a bloody pulp. She got that edge, and she never let it go.

'I finished with my crew that day. The muggings, the dealing, the dope, the feuds you forgot the causes of, the endless looking over your shoulder when you weren't in your own 'hood, and yes, the casual sex – I left it all behind that day. My family doesn't have much, but it's decent, and it gave me a decent chance. And I realised that afternoon in Victoria, as I was recording all the mayhem from the balcony of Wetherspoons and then all over the concourse and underground, that I was in serious danger of throwing it all away. So I made my life college and home, the classroom and the bedroom where I studied, and worked harder than I'd ever done before in my life. I got the grades I needed, and it was off to UCL for me – still in London, still living in the same 'hood, but with access to a world and opportunities my parents and grandparents could only dream of, and a degree that gave me this.'

'Sandley, the library, volunteers, the pub … me….'

'Don't knock it, Frank, and don't underestimate yourself. I've been happier and safer here than I can ever remember in south London. It's a rich life, a good life.'

'Little Ange made some good choices as well.'

'Margaret did the same as me. She concentrated on her GCSEs and then her A levels. She knew she'd overstepped the mark that day, and she stepped well back. The kid she beat up ended up in hospital of course. He was still having operations on his jaw a year later. But no one, including Margaret, was ever caught or charged for that little battle in Victoria. We were lucky you could say. In those days, what, 17 odd years ago there wasn't nearly so much CCTV coverage. Her bloody 'Bad Girl' hoodie disappeared and was burnt, and all her other clothes. She led the fight, and she managed the aftermath, and nobody from our crew or any other crew dared to break the wall of silence. We talked afterwards, she and

I, but we weren't exactly friends anymore, and she was certainly no longer my protégé. It was as though we both had the same Damascene experience at exactly the same time. As I said, I went to UCL and she went to LSE.'

'Why didn't you tell me?' said Sterling.

'What, that I ran a gang? That I knew Margaret Kingston when she was a dangerous, not far from psychopathic wildcat from south London, and my protégé to boot? Tell you, an ex-plod?' Angela looked into the fire. 'Actually, I think you'd have taken all that into your stride. You're not one for judgements. It's more about me. I'd turned my back on all the shame and self-disgust and then Margaret fetched up virtually in the next-door community. I didn't want any reminders of that old life. I didn't want my new life, and my new friends, affected. I just wanted a clean break.'

'You're right about what I think,' said Sterling. 'I don't give a toss about what happened or what you did before. It's now that matters. Except ... how did that footage from the Wetherspoons balcony and the underground get out, Angie?'

'I don't know. It's like when they find an old Dutch master in someone's attic, or a tranche of long lost letters from a famous writer – only in my case much more dangerous and sordid. Anyway, afterwards, the camcorder disappeared from school and so did the videocassette, from my locker. I spent weeks worrying about it, but when nothing happened, I just forgot about it. When computers came in, someone must have transferred the footage onto a hard disk or something. It could easily have been one of my crew. Unlike Margaret and me, not everyone gave up on gangs. There was resentment and anger about us 'selling out'. I can think of one or two who might have kept it for leverage – well, did keep it. We got away with it at Victoria. Although no one in either crew said anything, not even the boy whose face was mashed in, there was speculation and media interest for years. A decade and a half later, it appears on the internet – 'Victoria Station fight – the truth at last?' I didn't get a mention, and nor did Margaret, directly, but that's when I decided to get out of London.'

'Well,' said Sterling, 'a dodgy researcher at ECOT found it and did manage to connect it with Margaret. He was clever, and it looked as though the footage was going to be released in chunks, each more incriminating than before.'

'Nightmare,' said Angela. She took a pull of her drink. 'What now, Frank?'

'Hang on. I've just got a text.' He didn't recognise the number but that wasn't a surprise. His address book was hardly full. He didn't recognise the sender either, apparently a desk sergeant at Marchurch police station.

'Mr Sterling,' it read, 'can you meet Detective Chief Inspector Nolan at your office in 10 minutes? He needs to see you urgently about breakthrough developments in the case you are working on. He's on his way now.'

'I've got to go. Andy Nolan's found something. I'll tell you all about it later, if you're still here and the pub's still open. And Angela, nothing's changed.' When he got to the door and looked back, she was approaching Jack Cook at the bar. He and I have made our peace, thought Sterling, so why shouldn't she go and talk to him? Why shouldn't she talk to Mamujee for that matter? Why shouldn't she talk to anyone?

Chapter 33

Thursday 23 October - Clash

Sterling strode down the High Street towards the quay, but just before the Masonic Lodge ducked into Holy Ghost Alley, the short cut through to St Peters Street. The blustery late October wind created a small mistral, strong and cold, which propelled him into the road next to the Old Town Gaol. Instead of Milk Alley, a sense, less powerful than a premonition and not even qualifying as intuition, guided him round the side of the decommissioned church along the pathway through the sward. The wind was less insistent here, but the night was dark and cloudy, and the council's policy of turning off street lamps, especially in the business quarter, removed any orange glow. Typically on a Thursday evening, the centre of Sandley was completely deserted. As he emerged from the corner of the church, he caught a movement on the corner of Milk Alley and Market Street outside Freddy Henderson's grocery. A tiny form was in the doorway, surveying up Milk Alley, down Market Street towards No Name Street and up towards Strand Street in a regular, methodical sweep. As Sterling emerged from the shadow of the church, recognition came to him.

'Margaret,' he called without thinking. 'Are you waiting for me?'

'Frank. Yes, hello.' The small woman, dressed in dark jeans and raincoat, stepped out from her surveillance point, a look of faint irritation on her face.

She's cross because she wanted to surprise me, not the other way around. There was something else too, Sterling suddenly realised. Andy Nolan never got underlings to make his calls, not unless he was changing as he climbed the greasy pole. 'You'd better come up to my office. I'm waiting for the investigating officer,' he said to maintain the charade. 'After you,' he was careful to say when he'd unlocked the door and got to the bottom of the narrow stairs. Keep your enemies close – and in this case, in front. 'So,' when they were settled in their chairs, 'what can I do for you this quiet Thursday evening?'

'I think you know, Frank. You've got something that belongs to me.'

'Really?'

'Something from the drawer in my desk at college. I should never have allocated Adele to support you.'

'You can't put the clock back now, Margaret.' Sterling looked across at the small woman on the other side of his desk. She was barely five feet tall, compared to his 5' 11", seven and half stones maximum compared to his twelve. She could handle herself – the clip on the memory stick showed that – but all those Saturday nights on the front at Marchurch and all the other Kent coastal towns at one time or another meant that he was no slouch himself.

The impulsiveness that he'd been warned about, time after painful time, got him talking. 'You know, I reckon I'd worked everything out in this whole rotten business.

I did everything you planned for me to do. I shook everything up. I found out about the blackmail, the drugs, the Club Night, all of it. When Zoë Westhanger re-engaged me you must have been pleased that I concentrated on finding Hannah and that poor boy. All that stuff with Meg Jenkinson, Johnny Fontana, the torture chamber under your office and finding Hannah and Darren was OK because it took me away from who did Jane Casterton in. That was the one thing that didn't add up. But I think I've worked that out too.'

'I'm all ears,' said the principal. A smile played over her face, but Sterling took more account of the way she sat on her chair, her hands gripping the armrests.

'It was a phrase you used when I first reported back to you – it must have been the Monday morning after I'd got into the Club Night on the Saturday. I couldn't dredge it up, and then it came to me when I was thinking about something else. You must have had that experience.'

Margaret Kingston sat very still in her chair. The old building creaked and rumbled, and the trees around the churchyard swayed and soughed in the stiff wind.

'You said something like, "she didn't...." and "God, worse than I was led to expect." Who was the "she"? And it certainly wasn't me who'd led you to expect anything at that point. I was just reporting back. Someone else was in the picture. I don't imagine I've got the details right, but this is what I think probably happened. You had a meeting with Jane Casterton sometime before I came to see you – maybe even before the Club Night on Saturday, maybe on the Sunday. My guess is that you already knew something about what was going on and there was some kind of truce. Maybe Casterton agreed to stop the activities if you didn't go after her.

'Putting the fox in the henhouse is how I thought of it at the time. You'd let her get involved in the disciplinary activities so that she wouldn't be tainted – that was the deal. In return, she agreed that some of her 'employees' would be jettisoned – Hissing Sid, Meg Jenkinson, Johnny Fontana and so on. It would have been difficult for her to let Fontana go, but you were probably driving a hard bargain. Then between Monday and Tuesday evening something else happened. She went back on her side of it. Perhaps by then Joe Speltman – who turns out to have been her researcher – had found the evidence to blackmail you and you got the dreaded memory stick blackmail treatment. You went up to see her in her office. She provoked you some more, and then you buried that golden tick in her skull. You must have been mad with rage.

'And I remembered another thing – how satisfied you looked when the police reckoned Casterton had been done in by a man. Of course, the Victoria footage showed what you can do and that clinched it. I can assure you that the evidence is safe with me.' Then he went too far. 'And of course … *Little Ange*… there's no statuette here….'

Afterwards Sterling wondered what he had been expecting. Was it congratulations – along the lines of how clever he'd been to work it all out; that the details were broadly correct but he'd got a couple of things wrong? Was it a confession – admitting that it was such a burden off her chest? Was it the just desserts defence – Jane Casterton was a terrible, evil woman;

she was destroying the college and she got what was coming to her? Or the self-preservation argument – 'All I'd worked for was in jeopardy; all that effort; she would have destroyed me'. Or did he expect all those things in a rambling, teary justification?

What he was too complacent to predict was what he got. Margaret Kingston casually drew her left knee up to her chest and lodged her heel against the edge of her chair. Leaning forward she used her leg as a catapult to propel herself over the desk. Her whole body cannoned into Sterling's shocked face and tipped his high backed chair against the sash window. His head hit the bottom pane, which cracked on impact. He could feel the tiny woman's hands gripping his throat. The chair tipped back to vertical but then her whole body was pinning his and her knees were digging into his stomach. All control and pretence gone, she was snarling and squeezing with a strength far beyond anything remotely predictable for a woman her size. Sterling's extra weight and strength meant nothing against the element of surprise and the fact that his legs were useless in his seated position. He writhed and pawed with his hands at her face but she was implacable. Even as he felt himself drifting away, one of his attacker's hands left his throat and seemed to scrabble in the pocket of her coat. Through blurred eyes he saw the glinting blade of a kitchen knife.

He made one last desperate heaving effort.... But it was no good. With the hand at his throat and the knife upraised, Sterling awaited his short dark journey to oblivion. He was still waiting a second later. Behind him was a rattle and then a huge loud splintering crash as another body hurtled into the room and tumbled over, followed by another. Momentarily distracted, Margaret Kingston's frenzied eyes turned behind her. A hand as dark as hers grabbed her wrist, and a fist punched her full in the face. Sterling's chair finally tipped completely over sideways, sending him, with his assailant on top of him, sprawling across the rough floor. The knife went skittering off into a corner.

Sterling and Jack Cook, lying in different parts of the office, watched in astonishment as Angela picked up her former protégé by the collar of her raincoat and the waistband of her jeans and hurled her against the window. Weakened by Sterling's head and bedded in a wooden frame that was already rotting, the pane completely gave way, and there was a rending crash as Margaret Kingston, accompanied by splinters and shards of glass, went tumbling and flailing into the street below.

Angela, hands on knees, was panting. Sterling dragged himself to his feet by grabbing at his chair and then the desk, in a painful progression. Jack stumbled to his feet. 'Strewth,' he muttered. 'Is it like this every day in your line of work, Frankie-boy? If so, you're welcome to it.' He poked his head out of the shattered window. 'She's not moving down there.'

The three of them – private investigator, librarian and chef – clattered down the stairs and into the street. There were signs of other activity in the vicinity – lights coming on, doors opening, people appearing. Freddie Henderson, the greengrocer, emerged from Milk Alley. Sterling knelt on one knee by Margaret Kingston. Her body looked even tinier than usual under the pale streetlight and her head was at a very wrong angle. Shards of glass glittered in the dimness, and blood was beginning to pool in different parts of the pavement. He put his fingers to her neck and then her wrist but there was no pulse.

'She's dead.' Then Sterling saw Henderson. 'Freddie, there's obviously been an accident. Can you call for the police and ambulance?'

The greengrocer took in the bloody scene. The pebble-thick lenses in his glasses made him look more than ever like a large insect, but he took himself to a quiet corner and reached for his phone.

Sterling, Angela and Jack shuffled awkwardly round the body, shooing back new arrivals from the neighbourhood as they arrived.

'Your door upstairs is rubbish, Frank,' said the chef. 'When you get it fixed get a proper one. Oak. Something heavy like that.'

'Well, you went a bit overboard there, mate,' said Sterling. He had only just realised that the principal had put the catch on the Yale lock. 'I was just about to use the adjuster lever to flip the back of the chair, throw her off balance, whip the knife away and tie her up.'

'Yeah, yeah,' said Jack.

Sterling turned to Angela. It occurred to him to mention that she had just disposed of the woman who was going to pay his bill. Then he saw her face. 'Are you all right?'

'Not really. I just meant to get her off you. She wasn't meant to go through the window.'

He put his arm round her shoulders. 'I was actually a goner there, Ange, if you and Jack hadn't turned up. She would have finished me off just like Jane Casterton. How did you know she'd be around?'

'I've known her a long time. She was in my crew, remember. I recognised one of the tricks we used so often – the urgent message from a plausible caller. You want to scam a dealer, or rob a supplier, or even set up an ambush on another crew, that's what you do. You scuttled off and I thought something was up. I spoke to Jack, and over we came, on the off chance. Fortunately I know most of the creaks on your stairs, and' – she looked at the big man leaning on the library door – 'Jack is surprisingly quiet and nimble on his feet. We listened outside the door, and then broke in when everything kicked off.'

'Well, I'm glad you did.' Sterling motioned to the chef. 'Jack, over here for a second.' Then he addressed both of them. 'Before the police arrive and all hell breaks loose, we're going to be taken away, probably down to Dovethorpe, and questioned separately. With luck, Andy Nolan will be notified, and he'll take the lead. Even with him, though, I reckon we'll be cautioned and charged – maybe with manslaughter. Don't say anything till you've got a solicitor present. You haven't got a right to a phone call, but the police have to make one on your behalf. I'll try and get you the bloke who got me out last time – his name is John Evanston. The key thing is to tell the truth. If we all do that, then our stories are completely straight and we should be OK.' Sterling looked hard at Jack Cook. 'The truth means no embellishments, Jack – right?'

'Got it.'

When Jack had wandered off back towards the action, like a groupie to the stage door, Sterling turned to Angela. 'One last thing,' he whispered. 'For you and me, not the whole truth. The Victoria footage, when it comes out – you weren't holding the camcorder. You weren't even there. That little ... adjustment ... will do no harm.'

As Angela nodded, they could hear sirens from the edge of town, and then Market Street was awash with the flashing blue that turned the glass around Margaret Kingston into sapphires.

Printed in May 2022
by Rotomail Italia S.p.A., Vignate (MI) - Italy